Don't Fu#k With My Heart 2

Linnea

2

**Lock Down Publications
Presents
Don't Fu#k With My Heart 2
Love Don't Live Here Anymore
A Novel by *Linnea***

Lock Down Publications
P.O. Box 1482
Pine Lake, Ga 30072-1482

Copyright 2015 by Linnea Don't Fu#k With My Heart 2

First Edition June 2015
Printed in the United States of America

This is a work of fiction. Names, characters, places, and incidents either are products of the author's imagination or are used fictitiously. Any similarity to actual events or locales or persons, living or dead, is entirely coincidental.

Lock Down Publications
Email: authoresslinnea@gmail.com
Facebook: Authoress Linnea Ldp
Like our page on Facebook: Lock Down Publications @
www.facebook.com/lockdownpublications.ldp
Cover design and layout by: **Dynasty Cover Me**
Book interior design by: **Shawn Walker**
Edited by: **Tumika Cain**

DEDICATION

This series remains dedicated to Ray. Some days are definitely harder than others, but know you live on in me and Mal's hearts forever.

ACKNOWLEDGEMENTS

First I have to give praise to GOD who strengthens me to press forward in the journey of life.

To my babies, Kieran, Kearsten and Kamryn. You make me proud of you every day.

To my Momma, Daddy and Joe. Thank you for the continued support.

To my sister, Glynn. New York isn't ready for you.

Melissa, Here is your book, cousin. Thank you for always being 100.

To the rest of the Green, Sorapuru and Carriere clan. To name everyone would take an entire page. I love all y'all with everything in me. Thank you for always having my back.

To all my other people. I thank you for each contribution you have made. The words of encouragement, laughs and good times I will always cherish.

To my boy, Nay. Thanks for the conversations and laughs. You'll make it to the top of the industry soon. Just keep pushing forward. One day I'm going to get you to N.O. for your very own po-boy.

To my Peachy, JPeach. Two things no one can ever say about you is that you don't keep it real, although you act quiet at times and that your pen is not fire. I can't wait to see what's next after Peaches and Blaze. I stand by the fact that it's never my friend's fault.... LOL

To Ashley, You have the determination to succeed in anything you do and don't ever let anyone tell you different. No matter what, never allow the feelings or actions of others alter who you are.

To Nikki Tee, Let's continue to represent the N.O. in a way they didn't think could be done.

To Stiletto, You're a great person and I wish all your heart's desires come to fruition.

To my editor, Tumika Cain. Thanks for all the hours of advice. I appreciate the time you took to make my novel even greater.

To the remainder of Lock Down Publications and our extended family: Sharon Bell, Jane Panella, Kim Leblanc, Latisha Lewinson. Thanks for the support that each of you give.

All the fans, supporters and fellow authors that I have met along the way words can't express how appreciative I am for the reviews, inboxes, post or sharing of my work. You guys are awesome and I could never have added this chapter to my life story without you.

Prologue

"Krissett, look at me, ma. It wasn't what you think." I wiggled from under him and scrambled to my feet with him on my heels. Reaching the gun, Stone tried to subdue me again, but was limited because of his hand. It was bleeding profusely.

"I warned you not to fuck with my heart, Stone." My love had become pure rage. The tears had stopped flowing and I saw him clearly enough to take the direct shot to his heart. He still had enough strength to put up a fight, though.

"You don't want to do this. This isn't you," he petitioned as the struggle for the gun ensued.

I grabbed enough of the gun to get to the trigger, but Stone wriggled with the clip, trying to free it from the gun. We battled, knocking against the chair and sofa. I wasn't giving up until he was dead.

Our bodies spun like a top, sharing equal control of the weapon high in the air. Gaining another slight edge, I brought it down to neck's length where the battle continued.

"Calm down, ma, before one of us gets hurt." He locked eyes with me.

"Fuck you!" I spat furiously. We slipped on the papers spread across the floor, bumping into the desk. Pinning him to the desk, I pulled the trigger, but he quickly turned it downward. The gun fired.

Boom! Boom! It sounded off as we both fell to the floor.

Stone landed directly next to me, still breathing. My adrenaline was at an all time high. I had no fucking bullets to waste. I scrambled on hands and knees in a race with Stone for the gun that had landed under the desk. We reached it at the same time, wrestling around the floor.

"I'm that bitch!" Takiesha came up suddenly, knocking Stone in the head with the crowbar meant for me.

"Look what you made me do!" I barely ducked her second attempt as Stone mumbled something in a momentary stupor. "Don't worry, baby, I'm about to deal with this bitch." She dragged me back across the floor by my hair.

Stars appeared as Takiesha banged my head into the door. I shook my head to regain my composure, blood trickling down the side of my face. She clawed her nails into my face, damn near ripping my eye from the socket. My legs bicycled briskly to keep her as far back as possible until I could gain an advantage. Using my hands, I shielded my face while she shredded flesh from my arms.

"Ahhh!" Finally, I landed a kick to her slashed ankle and she buckled to the ground.

"You a dead bitch!" I exerted force to her ankle.

Stone had shaken off her lick. He lifted her up off the ground, locking her outside of the door. While Stone was occupied, I crawled around with one eye, rigorously feeling around for the gun. The shine of the metal piece on the butt reflected off the light under the sofa, catching my attention. Takiesha pounded like a maniac, demanding to be let back in. Stone raced over on foot, grabbed the barrel of the gun as I turned over, ready to fire the shot.

Boom!

A final shot exploded close to my ear. Blood seeped onto the floor from the wound. I felt emotionless and void as I watched it fill the floor, my skin feeling cold and wet.

Chapter 1

Blinking my eyes rapidly to gain control of my hazy vision, I guided my drooping head to full attention and assessed the scene. My brain pulsated from the deafening toll of cathedral bells resonating in my ears as sensation returned to my frame. Lying in massive piles of piercing glass, my legs stung from the sharp pieces embedded in them.

Searching the empty room was difficult, because chunks of drop ceiling tile lay on top of piles of papers that littered the floor. Shards of glass splattered with blood and dust were strewn about. Holes from the hammer head sat dead in the center of the computer and surveillance monitors from where I had hit it. The cracks that held the encasing glass in place wouldn't provide video footage for evidence of what transpired. Turned completely upside down, the wheels of the computer chair faced the ceiling. I had been a category five hurricane, demolishing everything in my path.

Never had I felt a more intense rage than finding Takiesha's head bobbing on his dick so fucking hard I thought the Olympics committee might consider her for a gold in the dick sucking competition.

I should have known the motherfucker wouldn't change. Being my normal foolish self, I had believed he was going to stop fucking with her after the coming home party. Once a cheater, always a fucking cheater. A nigga who could have his woman and another bitch he was fucking under the same roof wouldn't magically repent and want to do right.

Refusing to run away from the party like a broken female, I walked briskly down the pathway and turned on my car with the automatic start.

"Ask that nigga where he was last night, Krissett, since he doing all this damn frontin' like he is not fucking with me. I'm the bitch that kept you on top during your bid. Cutting shit up, stashing money until you came home and you play me for a trick." Takiesha hollered behind me and Stone as he followed me to my car, trying to explain.

This was the breaking straw. Living paycheck to paycheck, I had used every dime, including my student loan money, to be a good woman to Stone's so called reformed ass. All that to find out he had a hoe sitting on top of money for him the entire time. What the fuck?!

"Bitch, if you don't shut the fuck up, the first time I punched the fuck out your ass is going to seem like an old school love lick." Stone turned to face Takiesha. The promise of whipping her ass confirmed she was telling the truth.

Takiesha halted in her steps, calling out everything else she had done from the middle of the walkway.

"Hold up, Krissett." Stone realized he wouldn't catch me before I reached the car, so he jogged to catch up. He spun me around to face him.

I remained silent as he held me in a bear hug, defending his actions with all kind of bullshit that ranged from it was for us to he had to keep fucking with her so that she wouldn't give him up. There was no justification in my mind. When he finally released his grip, I got in my car and pulled off without one word.

Having his sister, Ja'Riane, corroborate that Takiesha was lying about his whereabouts and the stash, I took his simple ass back. According to his cell phone records, there had been no contact between them and none of his moves had been suspicious before tonight.

Sickened by the images, the contents of my stomach rose up, spilling to the floor beside me. Feelings of anger returned to me. The stinging in my legs had given way to numbness. Finding my last wind, I crawled over to the bathroom door, briefly stopping every so many moves, willing my hands and knees forward.

You can do this, I gave myself a mental pep talk. Gripping the handle tightly, I drug it upward, almost falling back to the ground.

"This stupid bitch!" I shrieked. The floor was slippery from Takiesha's leaking ankle leaving behind a huge trail of blood.

"Umm." I turned my head around at hearing Stone's groan. He sat with his back against the wooden desk, blood coming from what appeared to be a gunshot wound.

"Stone! Baby, please get up." Takiesha bawled, furiously banging on the glass and turning the door knob.

"Shut up, you dumb bitch!" I screamed, gaining my balance. I proceeded slowly toward him, wanting to savor every moment of the agony he appeared to be in. Squatting down in front of him, I looked him squarely in his eyes.

There was no greater truth in the existence of a thin line between love and hate. In the blink of an eye, all the love I had in my heart for my husband transformed into an immense loathing for his very being. This time there was no redemption or forgiveness.

"I know I fucked up, but I swear I never wanted to hurt you, Ma," Stone pleaded, wincing in pain.

"You're a motherfucking liar!" I hollered, smacking him across the face. The imprint of my ring was branded into his cheek. "Was it a fuck up because I caught you?" I didn't even give him time to answer, my rage wouldn't let me. "I trusted you, you low down son of bitch. Now, you'll pay for fucking over my heart," I spat with purely wicked intentions in mind.

Using my finger as a spear, I dug into his thigh, twisting it like a power drill.

"*Fuck!*" He barked.

"How does that feel?" I raged.

Blood seeped from the wound, warming my skin. Rubbing my thumb and index fingers together, spine tingling pleasure streamed through my body. I yearned for him to experience at least a shred of the anguish he'd caused.

"Krissett, please. I know you don't mean this shit you doing right now," he breathed heavily from the trauma I inflicted.

"You really think so?" I grilled through squinted eyes, smearing my bloody hand in his face.

"Come on, Ma. Stop this before it goes too far." He tried to reason with me.

I would show his ass just how much I meant everything that I was doing to him. Scanning the room, there was nothing in plain view that would accomplish it.

There has to be something.

"Never that, hubby," I replied cynically. "The sky's the limit for us. Only the grave will undo this bond."

Grabbing a large remnant of the cracked computer screen, I drove it through his other leg, impaling him to the floor. He looked to the sky, trapping his yelp on the inside.

"Do you see what you made me do?" I showed him the cut.

"You gotta call someone to come see about me." The blood from his legs stained his pants.

"See how down that ho is for you," I motioned to the door. Takiesha had disappeared, probably to call the police and paramedics.

Retrieving the first-aid kit from the bathroom, nothing at first glance in the mirror required any serious medical attention. There were a few red spots in my eyes from burst blood vessels as a result of Takiesha's clawing. What I thought of as her pulling my eye out the socket turned out to be a deep scratch underneath. Less than an inch closer would have probably blinded me. I dabbed a small amount of alcohol on my injuries and gathered my hair into a ponytail to leave. The images of what led me to this point appeared in the reflection.

"Suck that motherfucker dry." Stone's eyes glistened with enjoyment. He was enjoying every second of the head game.

"Like this daddy?" Takiesha came up for a quick break to make sure she was pleasuring him in the manner he wanted. She allowed a long trail of spit to trickle onto his dick.

"Yeah, just like that." Stone guided her head back down.

I shut my eyes tightly to dismiss the replay.

You're letting this nigga off far too easy after fucking over you. Make him suffer to the max.

The voice inside of me ignited an insatiable desire to make him suffer in another way. Fuck whether this nigga walked out the room in a body bag. Why should I care? Had he given a lovely fuck about me when he was moaning in gratification? An added bonus would be the helpless cries of his bitch, Takiesha, as she watched from outside the window.

My mind had masterminded a torturous plan. I was going to break every bone I could with the hammer before crushing the back of his skull. To begin I would start with each of his fingers. After tonight there was not a motherfucker in the universe that would fuck with my heart before having second thoughts.

"I'll tell you what," I was saying to my husband emerging from the bathroom, but my words caught in my throat when I saw Takiesha in the room holding my gun. Apparently, she had located something to pick the lock, judging by the screwdriver that lay at the door seal.

"I'll see you in hell, bitch!" She fired two shots and dropped the gun to the ground.

I collapsed to the floor, panicking at the immediate and excruciating pain that radiated the length of my body. Rapidly scanning my body for the source, I saw that blood leaked from wounds in my right side and shoulder. Tears flowed as my hands trembled uncontrollably at the sight of blood rushing effortlessly from my wounds.

"What the fuck?" Stone barked as Takiesha rushed over to his aid.

"The bitch was going to kill you!" She sharply replied as she limped to roll the computer chair over to him.

Takiesha's fair complexion appeared flushed as she grunted to help Stone into the chair. Only 5'2," one hundred thirty pounds, her small frame was no match for Stone's bulky build. Working out in the gym for the last few weeks to tone up for our honeymoon in Jamaica, Stone had picked up even more muscle. His arms now resembled inflated balloons. She unintentionally choked him, trying to get him seated.

"Go get some towels out of the bathroom in the other building," he commanded, situating himself.

"You've got to be kidding me. You going to try and save a ho life that tried to end yours?" she shrieked.

"If you don't do what the fuck I'm saying," Stone warned harshly. Takiesha obeyed, dragging her ankle behind her. "I'm not done with you yet, bitch." She hocked spit onto me, kicking me with all her might in my right side.

"Fuck you." I mouthed, my voice hoarse.

"Bitch, have you lost your mind? What the fuck did I say?" He growled at Takiesha for not following his directive.

"Krissett, hold on," he called out to me while using the desk and walls to maneuver the chair over to me. The lingerie I had worn to surprise Stone on his overnight job stuck to me, marinated in my own crimson blood.

My eyes fought to stay open. All the times my life had been spared when I'd tried to take it, I couldn't believe my end would come behind a nigga and his side bitch. Two short weeks of marital bliss wasn't worth my life.

"You surprised this happened? You've always been so fucking stupid. Niggas have been playing your naïve ass since the beginning of time. Right, baby?" Mariah's face appeared in the darkness. It was the last hoe's face I wanted to see on my death bed. The weight on my eyelids kept them sealed.

"No doubt." My son's father, Quameer, replied. The mindless fuck went along with anything she said. He was the reason older people said you had to be careful who you had children by. A follower all his life, the only reason this tag along bastard sought custody of my baby was because Mariah had put him up to it.

"Hollow, what you think?" She requested the opinion of my first love.

"You know what it was. I wanted the pussy and the young bitch popped up pregnant. My other baby momma handled that situation for me though." There was not a hint of remorse in his voice. To think there was a possibility he was glad that his children's mother, Nija, had killed my baby.

Mariah continued to call out the names of those I had previous relationships with and all the gullible things I had done for love. Rodney, the one night stand I had tried to turn into something. He used me for thousands in shopping sprees before he moved and changed his cell phone number. Dwight, the fuck buddy who brought me to his corporate apartment for nights of the best sex ever. A few outings together and sharing my life plans after sex had me fooled into thinking we were going somewhere. It crushed me to discover his girlfriend and new baby at an unknown mutual acquaintance's graduation party. The list ran longer than the ten fingers she used to count them off.

My insides blazed with anger at the truth of my stupidity over the years. When people said keep your friends close but your enemies closer, they were speaking about motherfuckers like this. Mariah went after my son's father, Quameer, and my baby that had ended her ever be considered a sister of mine, even stepsister. Hollow treated my innocence like garbage, handing me bloody sheets to discard on the curb after taking my virginity. Quameer had given me the greatest gift, Na'Siah, followed by the most pain when he abandoned us, without any explanation, a few months after he was born. Add Stone's cheating, Deborah's hate, Takiesha's disrespect, Janasia's treachery made for quite a catalogue.

The fire on my insides exploded into a furnace cooled by a sudden icy chill that ran through my veins straight to my heart. Warm and fuzzy feelings for those in my immediate circle were barricaded into a small chamber escaping the hateful and vengeful frame of mind conquering me. Despite my initial thought, Stone's life could not compensate for the entire group. You reap what you sow therefore one by one those who crossed my path would pay. Some would die on sight, others would suffer before I ended their existence.

First and foremost, I had to survive and return to the land of the living.

Linnea

Chapter 2

Beep. Beep.

The faint sound of machines grew louder. I could feel each of my hands being squeezed tightly, beckoning me back to life. Opening my eyes, the bright, white light above the hospital bed stung from my extended period in darkness.

Those closest to me surrounded the bed. My grandmother, Hattie Mae's, head rested on my shoulder, praying. Her tears dampened the hospital gown I had been changed into. My brother, Quincy, and best friend, Meishelle, massaged her shoulders.

"Amen." Everyone raised their heads.

Instantly, their facial expressions went from solemn to ecstatic. My momma immediately summoned Quincy to get the doctor. She kissed me all over my face, each time thanking GOD for allowing me to awaken. Quincy obviously had grabbed the first doctor he saw. The physician was in my room in an instant, straightening his coat. He briefly reviewed my chart before speaking.

"Well, Mrs. Robertson, you gave us a slight scare for a minute. Can I speak in front of your family?" The short, stubby, white man scribbled notes on a chart. The mention of Stone's last name sent my blood boiling.

"Baptiste, please, doctor." The moment I got my ass out the hospital my intention was to head to the courthouse. Hopefully the city was behind in issuing the marriage license like they were for any other damn process.

Giving him my approval, he explained I had been out of surgery for a few hours. They were able to retrieve the bullet from my right side without any internal damage. The one in my right shoulder had knicked several ligaments. His recommendation was a sling to minimize movement of my arm and physical therapy for six weeks. If unsuccessful, there was the possibility that it would require surgical repair. The moment the doctor disappeared, my momma's smile faded.

"Krissett, what the hell really happened? And where is Stone?" She demanded answers.

"Not right now," Hattie Mae intervened. "The child just woke up. We have time to discuss it. Let's go get her something to eat," she suggested, trying to ease the mounting tension in the room.

"What do you want, baby?"

I was so glad that the doctor mentioned I was not on special diet.

"Cheeseburger po-boy from Red Rooster." It was a snowball stand in Uptown New Orleans that made the best fresh, ground beef hamburgers in the city. I didn't know how long it had been since I had last eaten, but I was starving.

"Ok, come on everyone." Hattie Mae nudged my momma and Meishelle out of the room.

"I'mma chill here with Krissett." Quincy spoke up. "Ya'll go ahead and bring me back a hot sausage."

"Alright, babe." Meishelle returned to give him a kiss before leaving. His ass barely let the door click closed before he transformed into my father.

"Now what the fuck happened that had this nigga blowing up my phone in the middle of the night, but not telling me shit? And why ain't he here right now?" He gave me an uncompromising look that told me he wanted answers right then. Telling him that I'd talk to him about it later wouldn't fly.

Helped by the remote to raise the bed, I winced from the pain and stiffness that had set in. The doctor said now that I was awake they would be removing the IV and begin an oral medication regimen. I would be checking with the nurse on that very soon.

An orderly thankfully interrupted, peeking his head into the room to take me for a follow up MRI the doctor requested.

"I'll be right here waiting when you come back." Quincy eyed me sternly as I was wheeled out the room. I sure hoped everyone would be back by then.

To my dismay, Quincy was still alone when I arrived back to the room. He had called my momma to pick me up a few more things so that I would have no excuse not to explain what happened.

Spilling the details, Quincy startled me when he rolled the bed. Apparently the orderly had failed to secure the latches on the wheels. I made a mental note to ask the nurse about the locks and medicine when she came to take my vitals.

"Sis, I warned your ass about this nigga months ago. If nothing else, you have to hear me when I'm trying to put you on game." He scolded me the minute I finished talking.

"Yeah, well that nigga will get his. I ain't done," I said confidently. Takiesha and Stone were battling for first place at the top of my hit list. Her attempt to end my life had made her just as high of a priority. The bitch should have been wise to make sure my ass actually coded when she shot me.

"Man, fuck that. I got this nigga. Bitch ass nigga called to tell us you got shot and hung up the phone quick as fuck. No wonder his pussy ass didn't want to explain shit. I'mma punish his ass for that, if for no other reason," he pledged vengeance on my behalf.

"Don't worry about it, Quincy. I got this," I assured him.

"What the fuck did I say?" With the tempers they had, if Quincy and Stone got in a beef, someone was bound to be six feet under.

"You're my brother, not my daddy. Let me handle this my own way. I need you to keep your hands clean. Promise me, Quincy." I demanded of him.

Before the words could leave his mouth, a silver cane came through the door with Stone attached to it. His ass was a fucking omen of bad situations.

"Nigga, you have the balls to show up here after you tried to fuck over my little sis?" Quincy roared, moving faster than he ever had in life. He snuck the shit out of Stone like Money Mayweather.

"Quincy, come on. Now ain't the time for this!" I screamed. Anyone was welcomed to beat the shit out of Stone, but I had just finished telling Quincy I wanted him to stay clear of any trouble.

Stone's cane clanged against the shiny linoleum, his body slid a few feet across the floor. Quincy stepped back, daring Stone to challenge him. Stone examined Quincy, dumbfounded that he would try him. One thing that had attracted me to Stone was his fearless spirit. Even if his ass was dead wrong, no man would put his hands on him and get away with it. Brushing the side of his mouth, fire shot from his eyes when he noticed that blood had been drawn.

21

"Man, you must be out your motherfucking mind." Stone sneered, bouncing off the floor as if his legs weren't injured.

The imaginary bell sounded and they came out of their respective corners. Stone came back with a one-two combo, landing one on the left side of Quincy's face.

Thwack!

Thwack!

They delivered blows, unsparingly, to any unguarded part of each other's bodies. Jolts to the face sounded powerful enough to snap necks. Blood particles flew through the air, some ending up on my bed. Quincy threw a jab at Stone's stomach that he blocked. Before he could regroup, Quincy landed an uppercut that sent him dusting the floor again.

"You gotta come harder than that, nigga." Stone charged at Quincy like a bull. He grabbed him around the waist, driving him into the media center that held the TV. His back thundered against the wood and Quincy let out a grunt of pain. The TV went crashing to the floor, the screen damaged beyond repair.

The nurse came into the room screaming, "Call security!" In their own world, they ignored her comments and kept at it.

Stone got an edge and pummeled the side of Quincy's body. Hunching over to try and block the blows, Quincy was beginning to wear down.

"You right, bitch ass motherfucker. I don't hear your punk ass talking shit now!" Quincy came back with a number of jabs to Stone's side. The nurse should have called for ice, because neither one of them would probably be able to see after that shit.

Stone landed in the visitor's chair at my bedside and I watched with pleasure as Quincy tore his ass up, momentarily. Then Stone grabbed Quincy around the collar, choking him, which gave him a brief break from the ass whipping he was receiving. He pounced up, knocked the chair into my IV, ripping the needle out of my arm.

"Aaaaahhhhhh!" I screamed in pain at the needle being torn from my flesh.

Quincy got back on top, leaning Stone over my bed, choking the life from his body. Stone struggled, eyes widened, as he clearly felt his wind being cut short. I smiled an evil smirk of happiness.

"This is how a foul nigga dies. You see death calling you?" Quincy spat.

Security came in, struggling to subdue Quincy while restraining Stone on the other side.

"I got something for niggas like you," Stone threatened. With a bloody nose and a busted lip, he formed his fingers into a gun and aimed it at the side of his head.

"I ain't finished with your ho ass, nigga," Quincy snarled at Stone, spitting blood from his mouth to the floor. He had a small cut above his eye that would probably cause it to swell. He slammed one of the smaller guards against the wall. The officer restraining Stone called for assistance on his radio. It took two additional guards to restrain the monster in Quincy that had been unleashed.

"What is going on here?" My momma shrieked, opening the door to Quincy being escorted from the room.

Hattie Mae and Meishelle promptly about faced following behind security, who had cuffed Quincy as the last resort in containing him. My mother barely made it to the room with the tray of food before exiting the room.

After security released Quincy from their hold and I ate my food, everyone decided to leave. The tension was at an all time high and the doctor assured them I was in stable condition. The nurse came in to put my IV back in and gave me another dose of meds. Waiting on the drugs to kick in, it was time for *Love and Hip Hop Atlanta.*

One of the pills felt stuck in my throat, so I called the nurse for a juice. Lying back, I thought about the difference 24 hours could make in a person's life.

"Thanks. My mouth…" I halted mid-sentence, the door cracked open slowly. This motherfucker had the audacity to come back. He had to have some fucked up understanding and a death wish.

"I didn't get to check on you earlier as I intended to." He held out a dozen roses with a teddy bear and balloons. His knuckles looked purple through his caramel complexion. Unfortunately, outside of a busted lip and facial swelling, it looked as if he would live.

"Stone, take those cheap ass trinkets and go on your fucking way." I brushed off his comments with a wave my hand and refocused my eyes

23

on the TV. I laughed hysterically at his sincere act. That fool needed to be nominated for an Oscar.

"Man, a nigga tryin' to apologize, but you just ain't lettin' it happen. There was a reason for that shit." Stone defended himself.

In my mind, there was no logic he could provide for it. "There's no need, my love. What's done is done at this point," I replied contemptuously, flipping through the channels in search of something interesting to watch.

"Oh, and by the way, don't make the mistake of being at my house when I get there," I added. Stone's name was on the paperwork for the new Lakeview's house, but not on the one we had been living in.

"What?" His face furrowed in confusion. "You and your brother taking me for some ho ass nigga, but ain't no bitch in me. I ain't going no fuckin' where. I'm still me." He issued an idle threat.

"If that was a threat, sweetie, please know I give less than two fucks about it. All I can tell you is not to be at my house when I get there." I replied calmly.

Fear tactics were played out. Actions speak louder than words, so fuck all the back and forth. The shit he had done in the past had no bearing on who I was in the present. It was a new day and a new me. He didn't want any of me.

The nurse knocked on the door before entering. This was a new nurse on duty, so she didn't recognize him.

"Here you are, Mrs. Robertson." She placed the juice on my tray.

"Thank you. Please have Mr. Robertson follow you out. He is not allowed back in."

"Yes, ma'am. Sir, you will have to leave or I'll be forced to call security." The nurse summoned Stone out of the room.

"Yeah, alright." He balled his face up. "I'll see you when you get home," he stated defiantly, leaving with the nurse.

"Uh huh," I mumbled as the door closed.

Chapter 3

Because I wanted Krissett so bad, I manipulated the truth. I had to in order to satisfy the other women in my life. Not a side chick, but the one who raised me, my grandma.

Raised in the Magnolia, my moms was only thirteen when she had me and dropped my sister two years later. Still a child herself, she was nothing but a baby with babies. Grams did our overnight feedings, changed the dirty diapers, and made sure we had clean clothes, while my mom picked back up being a kid. By the time we could walk, our week with grams started with Second Line Sundays and ended with card game Friday and Saturdays in the Calliope Projects.

When moms got her GED, she kited, leaving us in the wind. I had to be about seven watching TV in my room that sat across from the stairway.

"Stone, you been helped me all this time, what's the problem now?" She said with attitude, standing in our living room with packed bags.

"These are your fucking kids. They didn't pop out my pussy is the problem." Grams sat on sofa smoking a cigarette.

"Man, drop them off at the nearest hospital or firehouse then, because I'm out." She picked up her bags without another word. The screen door slammed shut and that was the last time I saw her for at least ten years.

Grams never abandoned us though. I shed a few tears for a couple of nights after she left. At the end of the day, moms had occasionally stepped up when she was in the mood and the times were good.

The kids at school were brutal as a motherfucker. Grams was always too busy doing something to be able to attend the mother's day luncheons or promotions exercises. However, there was no staying home. School was too much like a babysitting service for her to do what she wanted. While the other moms would give their kids hugs for the personalized holiday cards or to congratulate them on moving to the next grade, I sat foolishly looking around. At the conclusion, the kids would tease the shit out of me that no one ever showed up. Resentment set in for the fact that my mom had left me to deal with this bullshit.

A couple of times the lights and water got cut off, the projects would threaten to evict us, but things always got paid when we saw a stranger on his way out in the morning. The summer before my tenth grade year she introduced me to the school of hard knocks.

"It's time you learned about being a man. The Bible says a man who don't work don't eat." She hypocritically used church principles for her gain.

"What you mean?" I knew I couldn't get a job yet.

"Follow me." She cut her daytime soap operas off and brought me to the corner.

"Damon, this is Gregory." She introduced me to the larger than life dude on the block. Damon had the newest Jordans, fresh Polo tees, and kept a fresh cut. All the shit the kids with parents at school had.

"What's good lil man." He dapped me off. "Y'all give me one second alright?" He excused himself for a minute when he saw a chick coming up the street toward him. She was walking in a group mixed with males and females to the corner store. The kids saw him and scattered like roaches as he approached, but she was paying no mind laughing with one of the dudes. She turned around as the boy ran off, but it was too late. Damon landed a blow to her face that made me wince. She fell onto the ground in a daze.

"I told your fucking ass to stay away from other boys. You taking me for joke."

"No, I didn't. My momma sent me to the corner store for bread and they was coming down my block." She cried wiping her busted nose.

"I'll be right back." He called out to grams. She nodded that she understood. Damon pulled the girl by her hair, screaming and kicking, back to her house. Seeing some shit like that for the first time was fucking crazy.

He returned a few minutes calm and collected, apologizing to grams for the mishap. I know Grams saw the small blood stains splattered on the light green polo but waved it off as nothing, compassionless to the fact he had just beat the hell out of a female. The chick was young enough to be her daughter.

"One thing you will learn in these streets is fear equals submission. Next to money, it makes the world go round. Man, woman or child

26

sometimes you have to beat them into obedience, especially if you love them," he schooled me.

We talked and he arranged for me to do a little work for him, eventually taking me under his wings like a big brother. Over the years, I saw how people submitted to him because of fear. He would beat people to within inches of their lives and they would all be right back like nothing ever happened. Ole girl especially. That bitch would beg for forgiveness, still nursing black eyes and bruises. Damon met his match two years later. He underestimated the fear he could instill in one nigga's heart and payback was a bitch. The dude surprised him one night, him and ole girl, with a bullet to the dome.

By then, I was next in line and took my place with no questions. My name, Stone, came from the streets, because they viewed me as cold and heartless. Following in Damon's footsteps, the methods I used to produce submission were pure torture. Niggas would come up missing teeth, fingers, toes or whatever else I felt they could survive without. Live to make them regret it was my get down for the most part. Every now and then I would put my mom's face on their body and they didn't live to tell about it. Chicks came, of course, but I never had to beat any of their asses. They didn't mean that much and my money was long enough to satisfy them. Fuck 'em, leave 'em and protect myself against them was my motto. My name wouldn't be on the wall as no motherfucker's baby daddy.

"This is my brother, Stone." My sister introduced me to her friend, Takiesha.

"What's up?" I was watching Belly. That shit was classic to me.

"Nothing." Takiesha's smile was a mile long. I could see she had pushed my sister up to introducing her. I wasn't feeling her, but in the lifestyle I was living, you used what came to get where you needed. Women on the workforce gave an advantage, because the people never suspected them.

"Money or food which one?" I could tell she wanted something the way my sister took a seat on the sofa and stared at me.

"Both but food first." My sister greedily responded. "I'm in the mood for Copeland's."

"Alright, come on." I had turned her into a spoiled brat.

I ended up smashing Takiesha's ass that night and the bitch fell face first for me. She was on the payroll, running a few drops for me, but it was nothing in my mind. I still brought the hos around all the same while she pouted. It's a hard knock life.

The money was flowing, grams was keeping her hair done, nails on point, and supporting her habit with money to spare. At the end of the day she had ultimately taken care of me and been my reason for getting put on this life so she deserved the best.

The day I met Krissett though that shit changed. For the first time in a minute a chick handled me like I wasn't shit. Denying me was something I had never known, so to come from a cashier was mad crazy. Man the chase on her was real. I mean ole girl wasn't trying to hear nothing I had to say. It was kind of cute. Eliciting the help of grams, I convinced her to do a supper, but only for where Krissett was working. I went through the whole nine, printing flyers and everything. Krissett liked grams, so I knew she wouldn't refuse her offer.

Just as I planned, she went for it, not getting me any closer really. She let me give her a ride home one day, because she was in a bind, but that ended it for a hot minute. Finally, a few months later, she at least agreed to my friend and from there I made my way in. Fine as shit, Krissett had much going. She told me she had some issues, but none held her back. She did for her little man and had a focus that most women lacked, or at least the bitches coming my way. Them hos wanted me to fund their lives fully, whereas Krissett believed in working for hers.

We got close and she became my girl, eventually introducing me to her son. Na'Siah gained a spot in my heart instantly. I swear when I heard lil' man call me daddy nobody couldn't tell me he wasn't mine. When his ho ass paw pulled that move and took him from Krissett for a trick, I could have murked him on the spot. Despite what that bitch nigga thought, he wasn't going to Na'Siah permanently. I had hired the best family attorney to get him back where he belonged, with me and Krissett.

Although I knew Krissett was the one, I wasn't ready to give up all the pussy just yet. She caught me down bad more than once, but as a nigga predicted, those bitches went south when I did my bid. Every Sunday she showed up, smile on her face until she found out about Keedy. She forgave me and came back under the stipulation I would give the streets up when I came home. Breaking the news to grams, she stopped talking to me for a minute. I should have known when she allowed my coming home party to be held at her house she had an ulterior motive. The yard was filled with family and people from the streets to try and convince me that the game was my life. When I didn't give in, grams started the silent treatment again.

Four months later, she suffered a mini heart attack. The thought of something happening and she wasn't speaking to me was too much for a nigga's heart to bear. Honoring her wish, I returned to my street hustle and hid it from Krissett. Most of my former street connects dealt in large quantities so I used Takeisha's stupid ass to run product for me in small amounts until my weight came up. That delusional trick still held on to a hope for me and her. I damn sure wasn't about to fuck her for loyalty, but I went for her mouth game a couple of times at the job on nights when Krissett wouldn't come.

Old folks said what's done in the dark coming to light and it proved true when a nigga got caught with his pants down. I couldn't trip on Krissett's initial reaction, because I was down bad like a motherfucker. Even Quincy's performance I excused to an extent. I couldn't fault him for being mad because I had a sister but ain't no nigga alive was going to put his hands on me and I bow down. That shit just now at the hospital though. Krissett was on some other shit talking about not to come to her house. She said it with that look I used to have on the street, not giving a shit about anything.

She had to understand a nigga's plight straight up. I loved my wife with everything in me. The new house coming up, planning for a family, and all the other shit costed money. I went along with that legit shit for a minute but I felt less of a man than to keep letting Krissett's money primarily carry us. I was doing what the fuck needed to be done.

Driving home I could hear Damon's voice, "Fear equals submission," so I guess I gotta go about this another route. All I know is she isn't leaving me unless it's in a body bag.

Chapter 4

"Here is everything you will need for now, Ms. Baptiste." I was relieved to see the nurse enter with my pain pill prescriptions, orders and aftercare instructions after being robbed of rest for an entire seven days.

Going over the script she called in, the doctor had honored my request for the Soma since I was used to taking it with my Lithium. They had kept me longer than I expected for my inability to have a bowel movement. I told them it was the damn pain pills and lack of fruit, but they insisted I couldn't go home before I was able to perform one.

The doctor had made his rounds earlier and praised me for my improvement thus far. My progress note from the physical therapist indicated that my arm was doing far better than they anticipated. The pain made late at night and early mornings hell. I would cry from the simultaneous throbbing in my side and arm. The pain pills gave me little relief, my tolerance for them had grown from taking Hattie Mae's over time. Using the physical hurt to push me harder mentally, I strategized on ways to wreak havoc when I left this bitch.

My momma insisted on coming to get me, but I wasn't ready to be interrogated and then hear her lecture. She would do her usual spill about what a man should be, where I had gone wrong in this relationship, and analyze all my past relationships. Most definitely one of my biggest supporters, she would also flip the script in a second becoming one of my biggest critic. Contrary to Hattie Mae's tender delivery method, hers was harsh and direct.

Although he was unable to re-enter the hospital, Quincy agreed to come and wait for the hospital staff to wheel me down. Even with cloudy skies, the temperature for the last week of September made it impossible to decipher the difference between summer and early fall.

Once inside the car, I popped a pain pill for whatever aid it would give and went directly into business mode. After giving Quincy directions on what errands had to be handled, I pulled out my phone. Since I would be out of work for at least eight weeks, the first item on the agenda was my joint account with Stone. I was a little upset to see he had already taken his usual five hundred dollars out that he budgeted for two weeks. Although the small change wouldn't get him far, I wanted that bitch to be absolutely broke. Phoning Capital One to report the card on my joint account stolen, I requested all six thousand dollars be transferred from the joint into my individual savings account. The representative seemed leery about performing the transaction until I threatened to call the FDIC if my damn money came up missing.

Next, I logged into my rainy day fund, another joint one, but this one was shared with Quincy. He held the debit card as a precautionary measure. With an average cycle between mania and depressive stages lasting anywhere from one to three months, the irrational spending during a mania period could cause serious financial hardships. My depressive stages, where I wanted to be locked in the house in total darkness had to last about twice as long to make up for the money I blew through. Shit like that could fuck up everything I was planning. It made it of the utmost importance that I take my medications as prescribed and keep all psychiatrist appointments for successful execution of my plans.

Blinking twice at the available balance, I just knew my eyes had to be playing tricks on me. Where the hell had one hundred thousand come from? I selected the full site option to review the deposit slips, the handwriting was a perfect match.

"Quincy?" I called his name, still in a daze.

"What's up?" He kept up his eyes on the road.

"What's the deal with this extra hundred grand in my account?"

"What you mean?" He wore a baffled expression.

"Don't even play them type of games with me. The slips are in your damn handwriting. Now isn't the time to test me." I cut him with my eyes, holding the phone out for him to see, although he couldn't look at that moment.

Far from an ordinary bitch on the street, he had ample opportunity to notify me of what he was doing. Thick as thieves since children, we were too close for the secretive bullshit between us. Checking the dates on the deposit slips, we had met sporadically for our brother-sister catch up dinners since the deposits had begun. Not one time did this motherfucker throw a courtesy my way and say he was funneling money into my account. He was strictly on there for emergency purposes. Outside of my funds entering and exiting the account, there was to be no others at least not without my permission.

He groaned, wiping his hand over his face as he pulled into the lot of Capital One. The way the scary ass phone representative handled my earlier call had pissed me all the way off. I was about to close and empty my account except the joint account with my soon to be ex-husband. They claimed to need his consent to do so.

"Let's talk about it at the house." He got out the car to open my door.

"Yeah, ok." By his expression, I was about to have extra bullshit on my already full plate.

The next stop was Regions to lock my money into a one year certificate of deposit. I loved money making money.

My impeccable knowledge of investments was thanks to my stepfather, Craig, and his broker, James. As kids, Craig required me and Quincy to save five dollars of our allowance every month, matching it dollar for dollar at the bank. When were old enough to withdraw it, he and James helped us invest a small portion of the money into the stock market. Then every quarter James arranged meetings to report our progress and teach us different strategies of how to continue to manage our money in the current market. It was all about having equity and assets.

When I was done handling my bank business, I stopped at FedEx to fax over my paperwork that would temporarily relinquish my job duties as Call Center Manager at Entergy to someone else. In the driveway of my house, I located a locksmith to install a new set of deadbolt today. Quincy went ahead of me, bringing my bags into my room. Throwing my keys onto the table in the foyer, my mood of vindication deflated as I turned the corner.

A week ago, Stone and I had been preparing to move into our new home. Searching the room, brown boxes and clear thirty gallon sized plastic containers lined the hallway walls, packed for the moving company. The empty bookcase caught my attention and a flash of Stone playfully tickling my sides while I was taking my book collection off of a top shelf came to mind. He had purchased many of the autographed books for me during a surprise trip to the Harlem Book Fair. I got a chance to personally meet some of my favorite authors like Wahida Clark, Nene Capri, and K'Wan, getting signed copies of their paperbacks.

Son of a bitch! Fighting the memories, I kicked over a stack of brown boxes filled with kitchen appliances. The contents in the boxes spilled to the floor. Fuck wallowing in sorrow about a cheating, lying nigga. That bitch didn't deserve me from day one. I just wish it hadn't taken me so long to realize that.

In the midst, my cell phone vibrated in my hand. The locksmith called to inform me he would not be able to make it as expected this evening. Immediately, I headed back out the front door for some air to gather my thoughts. My chest heaved up and down, gasping to gain control of my emotions.

"What the fuck you doing out here?" Quincy stood in the doorway, peeking out at me.

"I want to go stay with momma." I rocked on the porch swing.

"You can't let this shit get you down. What does Hattie Mae tell us?" He came outside taking a seat next to me.

"Love those who love you back." I recited her saying. Hearing the words put everything in perspective.

"All day. Now you ready to discuss the good news." He sarcastically smirked helping me up of the swing. Inside, he flopped on the sofa and inhaled deep.

"To the grave." He held out his pinky for a promise. I smiled that as grown adults we still practiced pinky swearing like we did as kids.

"Pinky promise." We locked our fingers in agreement of the treaty.

"Remember the robbery suspects the feds been searching for? The ones that robbed an Uptown bank a few months back?"

I thought about the morning after Stone asked me for the threesome. I had turned on the TV as I got dressed and Crime Stoppers was airing on the news, offering a reward for information on suspects in an Uptown bank robbery. The news could be so depressing. Since I was using the TV just to have some noise in the house, I didn't pay the story much attention. "Yeah." My stomach bubbled.

"Well, that suspect would be me," he confessed.

"What the fuck?" My face frowned in disappointment. Quincy had done some shit, but nothing that damn crazy.

Quincy said the armored truck men were dudes that had worked for him back in the day when he was managing the chop shop. They came at him with the idea of doing a heist about a year ago. They had an advantage because no one would suspect them of planning a heist. In my mind, though, they would have been the damn first.

Recruiting his best friend, Jeremiah, as the getaway driver, they did a mock run or two before setting a definite date. Splitting the money four ways, each person walked away with two hundred grand a piece.

"Quincy, I got your back in anything, but you gotta tell me the deal. You know my court date for Na'Siah is coming up. It's been two years and I'm ready for my baby to come home. I can't afford any more complications."

"Sis, I would never put you out there like that head first. I got this shit," he assured me.

All of a sudden the question he asked me a while back about borrowing money when I got paid made sense. He didn't need the money, just wanted to find out my payday to align the deposits with it. The overtime he worked was to make the deposits look as kosher as possible, however my salary could've easily substantiated them.

Quincy damn sure wasn't one of those dumb criminals we saw on TV. With his money management knowledge and intelligence, I just wished he chose legal ways to make come ups and not one that involved losing him for years at a time, if he were caught. He had graduated in the top ten of his high school class before briefly trying college out of state. Maintaining a 3.9 GPA his freshmen year, he grew home sick and allowed the fast money of the streets to beckon him back quickly. He resumed his job as a manager until he was ready and needed a verifiable source of income. Welding school seemed to be the shortest school time with decent income, so he enrolled.

"Is there anything else I should know about?" I offered him the option to confess whatever else needed to come out. I hated for a bitch on the street to bring me information that should have come from the source, especially if the source was in my close circle.

"Remember, you asked me for it." He went to the mini bar for a drink.

"Uh huh," I mumbled, rolling my eyes in light of the recent disclosure about the money. If it hadn't been for Stone's infidelity, no telling when Quincy would have come clean with me.

"That shit Janasia threw out at my wedding about us fucking wasn't a lie." He took the shot of Jack to the head.

"Wait! What the fuck is wrong with you, dude?" I almost leaped up and slapped the shit out of Quincy. He was turning into one of these everyday niggas I had been fucking with. Robbery, deceit, lies. I questioned how much I could really trust him now. He was a hypocrite for hitting Stone yesterday when he was doing the same thing with Meishelle.

"Hear me out, Krissett." He requested the opportunity to defend himself.

"Quincy, it really doesn't matter to me. You know what this plagued ho did to me. I promise you will not justify your actions, but go ahead. Get it off your chest."

Hoping my feelings would change, he proceeded with his explanation. Apparently, Jeremiah dropped him off at his car a few blocks away. He had parked on a cul-de-sac where our cousin who worked for NOPD told him no street cameras were located.

Throwing the duffel bag into the car, he was changing clothes when Janasia walked up. Of all the streets in New Orleans, he had parked on hers. He tried to brush her off, but the trick wouldn't take the hint. She nosily peeked into the trunk, grabbing the duffle bag to get Quincy's full attention. He tussled with her to get it back, snatching it from her grip, but not before the zipper came slightly open, revealing the big face Benjamins.

Obtaining his number by way of Meishelle's mother and Janasia's sister, Ms. Williams, after the story broke Quincy got a call from her that they needed to talk. Agreeing to meet her, she informed him that she knew what he had done and her silence would come with a price. He denied it until she revealed the pictures she had taken of him in her phone.

She had pulled up from work as he was hopping out of the car with Jeremiah. Sensing something was up when she saw the duffel bag, she snapped a few pictures for collateral. He tried to bribe her with a settlement, but the bitch made good money. Therefore, for at least the last eight months he had been dicking her down to keep her quiet.

"Is this the only bitch in New Orleans?" I asked facetiously, shaking my head at the trick. That ho was getting passed around more than the collection tray in Sunday church. She had OCD when it came to fucking other people's men.

Quameer was a prime example. A one-time friend, Janasia and Meishelle were the first to show up at the hospital when I had Na'Siah. Janasia made sure her godson had the top of the line swing, bouncer, car seat and stroller, which Quameer reimbursed her for in dick down payments. Quameer displayed the ultimate southern hospitality by passing venereal diseases she gave him to me. Apparently with pussy to die for, Quameer dressed for work one morning and never returned.

"You know if that bitch didn't have me by the balls I wouldn't fuck with her whatsoever. She calls all hours of the night trying to bust my shit with Meishelle wide open, holding this shit over my head." He wore a worried look.

Quincy was strong-willed, unlike Quameer, and could not be tamed with pussy. His woman needed the three I's: integrity, intelligence, and independence, none of which Janasia possessed. However, that wouldn't stop her from trying to break up his marriage. Careless in her method or means, breaking up Quincy and Meishelle's marriage was no dirt off her back if she came out with the greater prize, Quincy.

"We will think of something." I reassured Quincy.

Meishelle could never find out about that shit. It would crush my girl and after everything she had done for me, it wasn't an option. It was my turn to protect her. I smirked at the thought that the next couple of months would be very interesting. Janasia would get hers, too.

Chapter 5

Quincy and I continued our conversation over dinner, brainstorming on ways to infuse his money into the market. He would stick to his regular routine of depositing money into my account and open an additional portfolio in my name. Using Quincy's house as a cover, I decided to check into a suite at the Hyatt Downtown to get peace and quiet. Quincy agreed to meet the locksmith the following day at the house for me. There was no point in having spontaneous confrontations with Stone until I come up with my next move. Being in the heart of the city, I would be walking distance from the court to complete any paperwork to annul the marriage and the hospital for physical therapy.

After checking in, I pulled out my laptop to research how to annul my marriage. According to the criteria online, Stone and I didn't qualify to have the nuptials negated. I wasn't intoxicated, under-aged or mentally challenged, at least by the state's criteria, when we were joined in holy matrimony.

Our only option seemed to be divorce. In Louisiana, we had to be separated at least six months if there were no children together and a year if we had kids before we could qualify. Thank goodness I was sterile and wasn't able to conceive anymore, so I had six months to legally make his ass suffer in various forms.

Finished for the night, I showered and took my meds. It had been a long day.

The week went by pretty fast, but productive. I had checked on a few methods on torture and was ready to make some purchases. Earlier in the week, my doctor gave the clearance on my surgical incision. The stitches had dissolved and everything was healing fine. I had almost forgot about having the procedure. The hospital had not taken care of business, so my physical therapy had been temporarily put on hold until the insurance company received the necessary paperwork to issue an authorization. For the most part, I had stopped wearing the sling because the pain had been minimal since there was no therapy agitating the injury.

Fed up that the locksmith cancelled two more days in a row, I found another more reliable company to handle my needs. From what Quincy reported, Stone hadn't been to the house. Stone was far too persistent to give up that easily, so I knew it wasn't over.

Quincy picked me up at checkout on Friday and brought me back to the doctor's office. Sling around my neck for appearance, I picked up a new pain med script and progress notes to fax them to the insurance company myself. He promised to get it right over, but it had taken his staff an additional three days and it still hadn't been done. The only reason I kept behind them about it was so he would keep dispensing pills. At my request, he increased the dosage. The ones from the hospital had become like eating skittles. After dropping off the script, I went to house to pack for Hattie Mae's. She was going to help me with Na'Siah over the weekend.

I got a glimpse of myself in the full length door mirror bending over to get a pair of my tennis. I had gained a few pounds in my stomach. My legs and thighs had gotten fuller. It confirmed what my clothes were saying. My coke bottle shape had expanded in almost every aspect and I loved it. Everything on me, my hazel eyes, cocoa butter colored skin, round face and long hair was perfect. There was no one I should have ever wanted to be but me.

As we were walking down the driveway to leave, a black, tinted out, older model Impala blocked us in. I had been in enough trouble to recognize a police detective's cars on sight.

"Man, what the fuck?" Quincy pushed me behind him.

"I knew it was coming. You know the debit card pin right?" I stepped back in front.

"Yeah, I got it." He then repeated it to me.

"Krissett Robertson?" Two plain clothes officers got out and approached us. The male officer called out to me with the female officer on his tail.

"Yeah?" I already knew what he wanted.

"You're under arrest for two counts of attempted murder." He pulled at my right arm with the damn sling on it.

"Man, I know motherfucking well you see she can't do all that with her arm in the fucking sling." Quincy barked.

He brought my left hand up to allow my arm to remain in the sling and cuffed them in the front of me.

"I got you, Krissett." Quincy called out as the officer read me my Miranda rights and led me to the car for a ride.

With the holding cells full, I was escorted to the deplorable conditions of the four by four, windowless ten-man cell in general population. Holding my arm at heart's length, I silently cursed the guard out that said my sling wouldn't be allowed, even under doctor's orders. Thanks to officer friendly tugging on it like he was crazy, it was aching. Fifteen women, other than myself, occupied a space clearly not meant to accommodate seven people. Six already inhabited bunks that adorned the stone, dingy, graffiti-covered walls. By the countless written names of those who had already been there, the jail had been around since the beginning of creation.

A camera hung in each corner of the cell to monitor our activity, but the hanging red and yellow wire tips gave a warning signal that if one inmate had beef with another, they were on their own.

Calling Quincy to let him know that the magistrate wouldn't be setting anymore bonds for the night, the tier rep came around with something they claimed was food. I wore a scowl on my face as I examined the dry tuna fish on soggy bread. The wetness was a mystery because mayonnaise and mustard came solely by way of the commissary.

Finding a corner spot on the sweaty, damp, grey concrete floor close to a kitchen-sized fan that was supposed to help the sweltering heat, I checked out the remainder of food. I tucked the fruit away for later, if the flies encircling the toilet didn't get to it first.

"You gonna eat that?" A chick asked me over my shoulder.

"Nah, I'm good." I reached behind me and handed her the sandwich. The fan rotated in my direction, blowing her putrid stench up my nostrils. Curiously, I turned around. I had to see what kind of woman would be ok with smelling that way.

"Actually, I'll hold onto it just in case breakfast ain't shit." Taking in her appearance, I brought the sandwich back to my body.

She undeniably wanted to buck, but the mug on my face counseled her better. Instead, she rolled her eyes and wobbled off, clearly strung out on something. I drove daggers through her back as she returned to the bunk she occupied a few feet from me.

Even though the bitch didn't even recognize me after all those years, I never forgot the face of the woman that kicked my firstborn out of my belly. The ho that stood before me was none other than Nija, Hollow's baby momma. He was the very first man I gave myself to, robbing me of my innocence in every aspect. Skid marked arms adorned the skeleton framed woman dressed in booty cheek shorts and a tube top that her breasts peeked from under. Her burgundy tracks were matted to the crown of her head. She was far beyond professional help.

Fresh out the hospital, instead of carrying Ketoyia in the pink Minnie Mouse car seat, the nurse handed me her remains in a polished pine box. Over twenty four weeks when I delivered her, the law required she be buried or cremated. The idea of burning her like she had never existed wasn't something I could bear.

My momma hired a funeral director who arranged for the cemetery to open the mausoleum where my grandfather was to be buried. I insisted on having it done the same day so her little spirit could rest among family. Hattie Mae said my grandfather would take good care of her until we met again. Quincy and Craig placed her coffin on the lifter as Hattie Mae's minister said a few words. Since it was an informal ceremony, the funeral director opened the coffin outside for our final goodbyes. My momma had picked a white lace trimmed ruffled dress, fitting for my angel.

The tears that fell from my eyes trickled down Ketoyia's cheek as I placed a kiss on her forehead. My heart shattered into pieces that would never interlock the same again. Everyone helped me to the car and we headed home. Tomorrow, I had to attend the school board hearing on whether I would be expelled. The inconsiderate bastards gave me no opportunity to grieve before summoning me to appear before them. Although the eye witness' statements said that I had been jumped, they considered me as involved in the fight and subject to possible disciplinary action.

Finding the room where the hearing would be, I left my momma and headed to the bathroom. The secretary said once we entered the room we had to remain inside. She offered to come along, because I had been so sick on the way there, but I declined. Hopefully, if they saw one of us here we could get this over with faster.

I stared in the mirror at my reflection. Honestly I couldn't give a fuck if they ever let me back in school. Teased about my looks and shunned for becoming a mother so young, I didn't want to return anyway. Maybe GOD would answer that prayer for me.

"Well, look who we have here." Nija came into the bathroom accompanied by two of the other girls.

They surrounded me like it was about to be round two.

"Can't hold your own, huh? Five bitches to kick me down because you alone are nothing." I asked Nija.

Weak and outnumbered there wasn't shit I was able to do, but fuck if I was going to let it show. One day I would get her ass alone one on one though. I would see how bad her ass was with no help. Bitches that couldn't handle their own needed help.

"Actually, I did what I needed to all by myself." She pointed at my stomach. That one powerful kick to my belly that day caused Ketoyia's death. "You know my old man thanked me when I got out. Said he loved me more for taking care of you."

"Now that was some fucked up shit to say. Come on, bitch." One of the other girls spoke up, pulling her towards the door.

"Don't worry. The younger the pussy, the faster it heals." She giggled as the door closed.

I remembered it all like it happened yesterday. My lips trembled as I wanted nothing more than to beat that bitch's head into the concrete floors and steel bars of the cell. I went into the corner and rocked myself, trying my best to calm the inner beast. *Be smart about this,* the voice within me tried to reason.

With the charges I was facing, the chances of getting Na'Siah back was slimming by the moment. Being caught up in another charge wouldn't be in my best interest. Keywords, being caught.

I lay with my back against the wall, formulating a plan to deal with that bitch after lights out. Glancing around, the perfect idea came to mind. This thot had just replaced Stone's spot as number one on my list. Hattie Mae always said to seize the moment.

While the prison favored her with a shower, I moved my pallet in between the two bunks before hers. I quickly ripped two strips of the sheet and settled back down onto my side until lights out. Patience had never been my greatest virtue, but it would prove to be in this situation.

Click!

The half broken lights in the hallway was all that illuminated the jail. Putting my thirst for revenge to the forefront, I calmed my rising nerves. Turning over to my right side, my eyes roamed the cell for anyone who might have been awake. Although I didn't see anyone, I allowed a few more minutes to be absolutely sure.

Light beads of sweat formed on my forehead from the torturous lag. Figuring I had allowed enough time, I did one more spot check for any movement before slithering my body across the floor. Kneeling in front the bed, I maneuvered the sheet through the opening at the edge. A malevolent smile adorned my face while looping it around her neck as she lightly snored on her stomach, her head facing the wall and resting on her arms.

Getting into position on the floor, I began twisting the sheet around each of my fists, allowing her to scarcely move her head into the position I wanted. Feeling the constriction, she sleepily brushed her head along her arms in an attempt to shake off whatever it was. Little did she know, it was death knocking at her door. The second her head landed in the center of her arms, I propped my foot against the bed and slid back wrapping the sheet tighter into my fists.

Let's play a game of tug of war, bitch!

Her eyes popped open in alarm trying to see what was happening. Wedged between her bunk and the next, I yanked with all the force inside of me. Now was this trick's opportunity to hold her own when she had no one around as she claimed she could. I envisioned her throwing the first blow to the beating she gave me all those years ago.

In a face-down headlock position, she desperately wriggled and squirmed to for air. My fists burning from the friction of the sheets she appeared to obtain an advantage. I knew that it would take about thirty pounds of pressure to begin fracturing the bones in her neck. I scooted back toward the bed, increasing the pressure on her trachea. Her legs wind-milled fiercely against the limp mattress as she tried to free herself, but made little noise.

"You know who I am, bitch?" I whispered, tilting my head so she could get a glimpse of me. Her lips moved like fish gills grabbing air. "You took my baby from me."

Her expression changed from fright to sorrow as her eyes revealed that she remembered who I was. People don't usually kick pregnant girls in the belly every day. A rush of exhilaration overtook me as I watched her gasps for breathe become more intense. Retaliation felt so fucking fulfilling as I watched red spots take over the whites of her eyes where vessels ruptured from compression.

"Let Lucifier know I sent your ass."

Her fight continued to slow as her soul succumbed to its fate. Violet jerks and convulsions along with the slobber dribbling out her mouth indicated the final stage, oxygen deprivation to the brain indicated that the end was almost near. A few seconds later a lonely red tear fell from her eye as blood followed from her nose and I knew she was done.

I wondered if the tear could have been out of remorse, but it was too late for regrets. Releasing my grip, her head fell limply to the side. Taking the second strip of sheet, I knotted it to the bed in front of her face in an attempt to make it look like a suicide. I stared into her lifeless eyes a minute until the stench of the urine and bowels she passed overtook me.

A few inches available, I wrapped the strip of sheet I'd used to asphyxiate her around my neck into a makeshift sling and relocated to have the perfect view of her body. Stretching out on my pallet the pain pills I was on a natural high at the excitement of my first kill. It was hard not to shout to the heavens thank you for finally allowing me the opportunity to be alone with Nija. The scripture an eye for an eye had never held more meaning than in this moment. Not only had I served justice for Ketoyia, but for her children and society. She was nothing but an evil leech, sucking life and resources. One less motherfucker my tax dollars had to be wasted on.

Days when my classmates went in extra hard with the insults I would cut school and head over to talk to her. For the first year, I placed a rose for each month she would have made into the flower holder. I would pour my heart out to her about the boys who groped me thinking I was easy, the girls' locker room taunts out of jealously at the attention of the

45

boys and the teasing that was being done before I became pregnant. My momma had been to the school a million times, but it seemed to make it worse. They would gang up, swearing up and down that I was lying. Every evening I said good-bye I left her with the promise of handling Nija.

Feeling like I had just managed to doze off, my eyes popped open when the guard walked down the hall, calling for us to line up for Court.

"Oh *shit*!" Nija's bunkmate hollered, jumping down from the top. The other women hurried over to see what was going on. I stood up, covering my mouth, pretending shock at the discovery.

Hearing the pandemonium, the guard entered the cell and saw the lifeless body. "Call the medic!" She hollered at the other guard.

We were put against the steel bars for a lockdown until the coroner arrived to pronounce Nija dead and collect her body. The deputy eyed the sling on my arm suspiciously, as if trying to put a case together. Pulling me out for questioning, I explained making the sling with the bed sheet as a last resort since I couldn't bring the one medically ordered into the jail. She gazed at me skeptically, but her ass was no medical professional to judge me.

We barely made the evening magistrate by the time they concluded their investigation of the inmates and of the cell. My bond was set at fifty thousand for each count that I faced. In addition, he issued a restraining order for absolutely no contact with Stone or Takiesha.

After returning to the cell, I called Quincy to tell him how much I needed. He said he would be down to the bondsman momentarily, having withdrawn a lump sum of money earlier. Now it was time to play the waiting game.

The guard called my name in what had to be the morning round up since lights out had come and gone again. I pushed up off the floor, wincing in true pain from my arm.

Getting dressed and collecting my items took damn near another eight hours based on the clock, so it was afternoon when I got out. The doors buzzed and the pack of inmates rushed out, some dapping each other off for getting out. I shook my head at them because we each held a sheet of paper with a court date early next year. Some of their asses would be returning for a very long time.

I was expecting Quincy to be there, but I guess dude missed the memo that the judge had issued a restraining order for no contact between us, because Stone's ass sat booted up in the lobby. The charges and bond information easily accessible online at the Orleans Parish Sheriff's website, there was no mystery how he found out where I was. What I wanted to know was where the money had come from to post my bond. Having withdrawn everything from our joint checking account, I frowned in confusion as he rose and approached me.

Quincy didn't answer his phone, leaving me with no choice but to call Yellow Cab for a ride home. Good thing I had kept my damn house keys, because I would have been assed out. The dispatcher estimated my wait to be about five minutes.

"You really locked me out my own shit, huh?" He posted up like a statue in front of me, rudely disturbing me as I made transportation arrangements to get the hell from around Central Lockup.

"I don't know what you are talking about." Not allowing myself to be picked for information, he could've been talking about the house or the bank account.

"Don't play me for stupid. I turned the key to get into my house and it don't fucking work." He gritted his teeth to maintain a hushed voice, stepping into my face.

"Get the fuck out of my face with that shit. I told your ass don't come to my house." I continued to walk. That nigga had shit confused, stepping to me about something I had been managing the mortgage on. I'd be damned if I didn't unpack that motherfucker and stay there just off the principle.

"You fucking with me in the wrong way." He grabbed my right arm through the sling and squeezed, bringing instant pain. Tears welled in my eyes, but I wouldn't dare shed one.

"No, you fucking with *me* in the wrong way. Keep it up. I suggest you bring your ass by your bitch, Takiesha, and leave me the fuck alone." We entered into a stare down.

"Krissett, you don't want me as an enemy." He warned.

"That's funny, because I already consider you mine." I proceeded through the door of Lockup.

Stone ensued, hollering my name. I kept my eyes straight ahead, muttering that he would find out soon enough about messing with the reincarnated Krissett. Then I hopped into the waiting cab and never looked back.

Giving the driver my address, I reclined my head back. My phone vibrated on my hip. Checking the caller ID, I saw that it was Stone's ass. That's when I caught a glimpse of Stone's truck through my peripheral vision. He was veering from the left lane over to us in the middle lane.

When he was almost close enough to ram us, the frantic cab driver jerked the car into the next lane, almost striking the car already in that lane. He jumped at the boisterous sound of the older lady's Lexus horn warning him of the impending crash with his car.

Keeping my expression void of any emotion, my heart rate lightly accelerated as I looked over to see Stone laugh in anticipation of the collision. Last night, his apology included cheap trinkets, today he was in full temper tantrum mode because I hadn't given in to the bullshit. To him terror equaled submission. However to me, a grown man employing scare tactics was desperate, especially when it was due to the consequences of his own actions. Granted I had only heard about some of the punishments he dissed in his street days, but I supposed he believed he would get the same reactions niggas from his former street days had when he raised his voice.

That was a negative. If he was going to do something, I wasn't going to show his ass any fear.

Suddenly, he yanked his truck back into his lane and the lady in the other car sped up, avoiding the near accident. With no driver now next to us, Stone veered again, coming within an inch of ramming into the side of the cab.

"What is going on, Miss?" The driver of the cab snatched the wheel of the cab over into the right lane, recognizing we were being intentionally targeted.

"He's an asshole trying to scare us, Sir." That motherfucker was ridiculous.

Stone kept approaching until we were on the shoulder. The passenger side scraped the guard rail and the driver's eyes grew big like he saw the grim reaper.

Gathering he wouldn't get a reaction from me, he blew a kiss. His smile faded when he saw me blow one back and wave bye as he sped off. I chuckled in disbelief at the incident that had just occurred. Stone had not been a first for many things, but definitely had introduced me to an innovative method of showing someone you loved them.

"Do I need to call someone?" I offered assistance to the driver.

He sat, taking puffs of his asthma inhaler. He shook his head no and reclined it onto the seat to rest for a moment before his breathing was finally under control.

"Do you have a pen and paper?" I scribbled down Stone's license plate number and insurance information, although I would be cancelling it as of the next day. His stupid ass wasn't about to have my insurance premium skyrocket.

When the driver was better, he put on his emergency light and maneuvered back into traffic.

I couldn't wait to get out of the cab and home into my bed. My mind was fixated on finding out where that damn bail money came from. I knew for a fact there had to be a stash somewhere and I was going to find it. By right as his wife, half of it was mine.

I knew I would be MIA for a few days while nursing the throbbing that had begun in my arm again. But when I got up, I was definitely going to work on him. Getting another gun for his unstable ass was my first mission. Then I was going to find the treasure.

Linnea

Chapter 6

Chasing my prescribed dose of Lithium and an extra Soma with a shot of crown, the prescribed dosage of pain pills wasn't working. Taking Hattie Mae's for months had my tolerance for them at an all-time high, so more were required for the desired effect.

I sent a quick text to Quincy, instructing him to distribute a copy of his key to my mom, Meishelle, and Hattie Mae. If they wanted to check on me, they would have to come inside and wake me up.

In the middle of typing the message, a text popped in from Cionna. Stone and I were ignorant of where to begin, so he asked his lesbian cousin for assistance in locating a woman that might be interested in a threesome. She happened to have a fuck buddy, Cionna, who was game for things of that nature. Cionna took her up on the offer and his cousin forwarded a picture to the phone. After a dinner date, I was comfortable with moving forward. Due to a family emergency we had never been able to hook up before the wedding.

Cionna said she wanted to check on how the newlywed life was going and let us know that she was back for now, since her mother was doing pretty good.

Shit if I know how the hell it feels, I thought as I read her text.

Lady in the streets, freak in the sheets had been my motto. Figuring he could have easily just cheated behind my back I decided to reward his honesty about wanting to sex another woman and open up my bed to Cionna. At the least it would keep our sex life interesting and I never had to wonder who he was doing, because it was done in front of me. The idea of a woman's touch was inconceivable to me, but for my husband I would do anything. Eventually, I came around, having wet dreams of me and Cionna, her lips sloppily eating over my pussy. The night of pleasure would be epic.

Yet all the while I'm giving him credit for keeping it one hundred, the low down bastard was fucking Takiesha behind my back. Any woman who claimed to have a faithful man was delusional as a motherfucker. Pussy had no face or no name attached, so a nigga could fuck and leave without any information.

Had Stone's bitch ass been in front of me I would have sliced his dick open to the white meat and with the help of a Facebook video I had recently seen, stitched it into pussy.

I ignored the message since we wouldn't need her services for anything.

Shielding my eyes with a mask, I nestled under the covers for the night. In the middle of transitioning into a deep sleep, the vibrating of the phone scared the shit out of me. I reached behind my head to retrieve the phone on the mantle and answered it without looking at the caller ID.

"Hello," I answered groggily. Turning on my side, the clock on the nightstand said one a.m.

"This dumb bitch really thought this nigga loved her. I tried to warn her dumb ass of who the Queen B was." I recognized Takiesha's voice immediately. She was apparently holding a conversation with another female. It was clear they wanted me to hear, because I could tell that I was on speaker.

"I told her the best bitch would win and she's sitting here in my living room." Stone's grandmother, Deborah laughed like a hyena.

"Now, she done put him out and he is where he has always been, over at my house. Letting him sell her lies about working."

"Girl, bye. In case both of you dumb hoes forgot, I'm the wife and entitled to everything. Takiesha, bitch you been on your knees for years and entitled to nothing. Get the fuck off my line with this dumb shit." I hit the end button, done with the petty shit over the phone.

Calling at least twenty times in the next five minutes, I turned my iPhone on do not disturb.

Petty bitches with nothing to do.

I flung the pillow, my bottles of perfume crashing against my marble top dresser. If I could reach out and touch these tricks, I would slit their fucking throats to the white meat. I had to be a serious threat to be on two bitches minds this time of morning. I popped three more Somas, but aggravation wouldn't allow my body to respond.

Sex had been my tension reliever. If Stone were there, he would have gotten the best dick ride of his life to ease my frustration. I had yet to replace my damn toys that had gotten misplaced during my incident with

Stone. A detective had probably scooped them up, with their trifling asses.

The balancing scale of my mind swayed at the idea of sleeping with Stone. My pussy stayed loyal to whatever dick she was involved with, but that nigga was so undeserving of my sweet treat it would have been an atrocity to sex him.

Frustrated, I threw the covers back with enough force that the sheets snapped. Maybe the alcohol cabinet held something that could take me out of my misery. By the moonlight, I took shots of Patron, but that only exacerbated the high of the medicine and the constant pulsation of my pussy muscles. Even the gentle touch of my own damn hand couldn't soothe the humidity.

With no men available in my life, I was going crazy. I needed some relief and felt as if I was going to die if I didn't get it. When my core went from pulsating to pained, I became desperate. It was then that I decided to do something I never desired to do before. But at that moment, the desire and the pain that accompanied it was forcing me into a place I had never been before. I needed relief and I didn't care who I got it from.

And there was only one alternative.

Cionna.

I held my phone, contemplating if I should make the call. This wasn't me. Hell, nothing I had been doing or feeling for the last few days had been me. So why stop now? I wasn't. I was going to go for it.

There was a chance that Cionna wouldn't be interested in sleeping with me alone. I felt that sleeping with another woman, especially while I was married wasn't cheating, but she may have felt differently. I hoped she didn't.

The plight of a desperate woman with a thump between my legs grew increasingly stronger than my own heartbeat. I needed extinguishing, immediately. Nothing beat a failure but a try, so I shrugged my shoulders. It was time to indulge the curiosity that killed the cat.

Krisett 2:43 a.m.: You up?

Cionna 2:45 a.m.: Hey! Yes, I am. Got an overnight job, so I don't sleep when I'm off. How have you guys been?

She included a happy face emoji. I hoped that was a sign of good faith that she was willing to accept my proposition.

Krisett 2:46 a.m.: We doing. You in the mood to come out?

It was time to get to the point. Every minute that passed was being wasted.

Cionna 2:48 a.m.: I could. Is everything ok?

Krisett 2:49 a.m.: Yep. I could just use a listening ear.

And a warm mouth.

But I kept the last part to myself.

***

More than the hot chocolate with the fried sweet treat made my mouth water in the early morning heat sitting next to Cionna. She had offered to come over to my house, but there was no need for her to know where I stayed for a one night stand.

Contrary to doctor's order, this was a night I would drive myself. We had decided to meet at Café Du Monde in the French Quarters for girl talk. Unbeknownst to her, the twenty-four hour beignet spot was minutes from the Four Points Sheraton on Bourbon Street, where I had made reservations for us.

She had put on a few pounds, but still looked good. Her newly dyed, jet black hair accentuated the roundness of her chubby red face. Wearing fitted black spandex jeans and an unbuttoned polo shirt that revealed the crack of her breasts, made me squeeze my legs tighter.

We had grabbed seats in the back corner where we could look out onto the mostly vacant street. Every now and then a batch of straggling tourists came in to get their order of the popular French donuts.

"So, what's going on with the arm?" Cionna bit into her beignet, licking the confectionary sugar remnants from her lips.

"Girl, I tripped down on my side and dislocated my shoulder," I made a lie up about the sling.

"That's too bad." The light reflecting off the remnant juices left on her lips made the thumping return with a vengeance. The taste of blood slipped onto my tongue as my teeth sunk into the corner of my mouth.

"So, how is your mom?" I asked, changing the subject to make small talk.

The conversation went on for a few minutes with talks about getting her on at my job, her mom's health, and a few other local topics.

"So, didn't you say you wanted to talk?" She giggled.

"Yeah, I did. But not with my mouth." I ran my hand up her inner thigh to put actions to my words. My patience had worn down. All that damn talking was not my intention for meeting up with her.

"You sure about that?" The corners of Cionna's lips curled into a sultry grin.

"Without a doubt." I asked the waiter for a bag to take the remaining beignets.

Wasting no more time, we headed to the hotel, playfully running from the street sweeping truck that lightly sprayed us as it passed down an empty Bourbon Street. Once we made it to the hotel, we quickly completed the check-in and headed to the elevator that would take us upstairs.

My sex was pounding like crazy.

The moment the elevator doors closed, our hands began barbarically exploring each other's parts. The sensuality of her fingers tracing my skin sent tingling chills up my spine. My eyes rolled to the mirrored ceiling where I gazed down upon the woman ravenously taking my body. The once innocent woman I was glared back at me pleading one last time for me to rethink what I was about to do. Cionna's fingers found access under my tube top dress teasingly caressing the inner walls of my pussy. My spigot turned on, lubricating her hand with my icing, drowning out any reservations I had.

Fuck it! I gotta live my life.

Chapter 7

My alarm sounded at six a.m. I noticed another sixty calls from a blocked ID. It could be no one but Takiesha and that old ho, Deborah. Normally, I had mad respect for my elders but she was the exception. She had done so much hateful shit to me since Stone decided to retire from the dope game it was ridiculous. The most recent was insulting me on my wedding day. Now her ass was tag teaming me with Takiesha. Something had to give with these bitches.

I forcefully shoved Cionna's head off of me, aggravated that she had made her way back under me for the third time. I had inched up each time as a gesture that it wasn't that type of party, but she seemed to have missed the hint, finding her way back, repeatedly. This was nothing more than a good fucking and an amazing stress reliever. Getting dressed, I tapped her to let her know she could complete the check out with the TV remote when she was ready.

"Ok. I'll call you later." She caught me of guard with a kiss on the lips and went back to sleep.

At home, I plopped down on the living room sofa and texted Meishelle to come over and help me unpack. Then I grabbed my laptop to kill time until the evening.

Checking the Orleans Parish Sheriff's Office website, I saw that Takiesha was facing charges of voluntary manslaughter for shooting me. I was sure the District Attorney would be calling soon and very interested in her playing on my phone.

Within a few hours I closed the laptop, feeling accomplished. I had found a product called Trap Call that would unmask the blocked calls and provide me with the telephone number of the caller that was playing on my phone. In addition, I had placed an order for supplies that would hopefully aid in my first planned act against Stone.

Cionna 11:05 a.m.: Hey I checked out and everything. Talk to you later sweetie.

Cionna put a heart behind the message.

Closing out my messaging app without a response, I swallowed my regimen of meds and packed me and Na'Siah's things for the weekend. My mom would be by shortly to pick me up for my evening therapy.

Quincy had agreed to come get me on his lunch break to bring me by Hattie Mae's. She had insisted that I come stay by her so she could help me with him.

Messed up arm and all, I wouldn't cancel my time to have him. Quameer and Mariah would use the one instance I couldn't get him as ammunition to keep me from getting him.

Instead of the forty-five minutes the physical therapist told me, the session ended up being an hour and a half. It was too early to pick up Na'Siah and Quincy now had to make up the extra time he had taken. My mom was showing a house, leaving no one available to pick Na'Siah up from school. I huffed at the thought of having to call Quameer to bring him by Hattie Mae's after school, but I had no other option.

"Hello, Quameer. How are you today?" I attempted to be polite since I was asking a favor of him. Technically, I owed him shit.

"Yeah, Krissett?" He ignored my pleasantries.

"I was wondering if you were able to bring Na'Siah to me by Hattie Mae's today."

"Nigga, been asked to get at you to talk, but it's cool. My gas is limited so unless you paying, I got nothing for you."

His lazy, nonworking ass motherfucker struck my nerve. Mariah was a fucking fool allowing this bum bastard to lay up on her. Bitch couldn't even keep gas in a car. I never understood any human that was comfortable with laying up on someone, especially someone who always claimed to be a man.

"Quameer, I am more than willing to give you some gas money for your trouble."

"What about my time?"

"Time? Who the fuck pays you to lay on your ass? I'm not that dumb bitch." Fuck the formalities. "Yes or no?" He gave a final ultimatum.

"I'll tell you what, all I got for you is a hot twenty with your name on it. Take it or leave it."

"Yeah, alright then." He disconnected the call without a definitive answer.

He called about four saying he was outside with Na'Siah. Mariah normally didn't get off until five, but her ass was front and center in the passenger seat, peering intensely at our interaction.

My baby ran over to me, asking what happened. Quameer stood there, nosily awaiting my answer. I refused his offer to bring Na'Siah's bag inside, holding out my arm for the bag. He wasn't a bellhop earning tips. The twenty I had balled up in my hand was my maximum contribution to their household. If Mariah couldn't afford three mouths, then she could return my son and drop Quameer's dead weight.

I saw Mariah out of the corner of my eye with her face pressed against the glass. She was Kool Aid red, hot enough to melt the glass. Seeing her agitation, I stepped into the driver seat with an opportunity to ram the gas.

"Actually, can you bring the bag inside for me? It's a little heavy on my arm." I lowered my arm, feigning as if the bag was hefty.

"I can get it, Mommy," Na'Siah volunteered.

"No. Let your daddy get it for us."

Quameer followed us inside and sat the bag down. Hattie Mae came out of the kitchen and held conversation while I sat on the bed playing Bejeweled on my phone, pretending to get the money. A few minutes later, I chuckled as Mariah's hand rested on the horn. She always wanted to play secure, but she was far from it when it came to me and Quameer. Any hope for us being a family ended years ago when he decided to ever cross the door seal of the apartment we shared together again for Janasia.

Walking into the living room, I inconspicuously passed the money to Quameer. "My bad. Working with this one arm is no good," I apologized.

"It's cool. Thanks and take care of yourself. Let me know if you need me to bring lil' man to school on Monday." He seemed genuinely concerned suddenly. "See you later, lil' man." He nodded to Na'Siah, closing the door.

"Bye, Daddy," he screamed with a mouthful of cookies.

I grinned at the ensuing argument I knew was going down in the car at that moment. Rule number one was to never let another bitch see what makes you tick.

We helped Hattie Mae prepare dinner. Loaded mashed potatoes, meatloaf with gravy, string beans and chocolate cake. Na'Siah and I aided by scooping the left over cake batter with our fingers and licking it off. The sugar rush carried him long after dinner while we played his Xbox.

My aching arm took over and I took a few more of the pills before laying down to rest. Grabbing my phone, I saw that Cionna texted me two additional times. I finally responded to let her know I got the first one and that I was okay. She and I needed to have a talk to set boundaries about what this was going to be.

***

"Good morning, Mommy!" He jumped onto the bed at Hattie Mae's. I had no idea when he had gotten up. "What do you want for breakfast? Me and Sugar Momma are going to make it for you." Sugar Momma was the name Hattie Mae had wanted to be called when he was born.

"Hmm, let me think," I paused. "How about a kiss to begin with and then you can fix me whatever you want," I proposed.

He leaned in, giving me a kiss on the check. "Mmmmuah," he hummed on my cheek, putting a little extra love on it.

"Hmh." I sighed. "Doesn't get any better than that."

"It's a surprise." He got off of the bed and ran into the kitchen calling out to Hattie Mae.

They came back a short time later with a peanut butter and jelly sandwich accompanied by apple slices and orange juice. I took a bite of the sandwich and motioned for him to come and get another kiss.

Even by Hattie Mae's, Na'Siah had endless energy bottled up to wear both of us out. I found myself popping pain pills and an extra Soma every four hours and then sleeping in between.

My phone went off while I laid down waiting for Meishelle to come get all of us for dinner. We had to get out and do something, because Na'Siah locked behind these four walls wasn't working.

Text: 5:07 p.m.: What's up ma? I know you have seen me texting you. I need to come over and collect my stuff when I can.

I wish the fuck I would.

Stone had to be out of his got damn mind. A few days prior he was trying to run me off the damn interstate and now he thought he could get his clothes. I shook my head, powering off my phone. Anyone important would know how to reach me.

"Krissett! Come here for a sec." Hattie Mae called me from the living room about an hour later.

"Yeah," I whined. The drugs had rendered me immobile for the time being.

"You know I don't play with you like that. Bring your behind in here."

"Ughhh," I grumbled, knowing that I had better obey.

I hoped it wasn't Stone because he *would* do some off the wall shit and pop up. Even if she had known the details of what happened, she would have summoned me because of her forgiving spirit.

I dragged myself into the front room to see what she wanted, wiping the sleep out of my eyes. Na'Siah sat next to Hollow, their hands frantically maneuvering the game controller.

"Long time no hear from. How are you?" Hollow took his eyes off the set to look at me for a minute.

"I'm good." I kept it brief.

"Thank you for the food and just being there for us." Hollow had apparently stopped by for food.

"Boy, please, it was like reconnecting with long lost family the day I saw you in the casino." Hattie Mae rose from her chair and headed to the kitchen.

Only Hattie Mae had been so forgiving of his past mistakes. Since the day she saw him at the casino, Hollow started checking on Hattie Mae weekly, delivering her coveted Popeyes chicken that she was not supposed to be eating. When she felt that she bothered us too much, she would have Hollow take her to doctor's appointments. I did my best to avoid coming over when he was there. Unfortunately for me, he showed up today of all days.

"Your lil' man is getting big."

"Yeah. That's what they do."

"Hollow, come tell me what pieces of chicken y'all eat and Krissett, you come help me get these plates prepared for him." Hattie Mae called out. I knew we had fried way more chicken than we could eat for lunch.

61

Hollow disconnected his controller and joined us. Hattie Mae had set about ten plates out on the table, packing them with enough food to feed the multitudes. Hollow told her any pieces of chicken she gave them was fine.

"How are those babies holding up? I don't know what kind of person would do such a hateful thing." Hattie Mae handed me the knife to cut the cornbread, informing me of what happened to Nija.

So what? I already knew that! I thought, feigning interest in what she was saying.

"They took it pretty hard. At the end of the day, regardless of her lifestyle, she was their mother. She told her sister that she was on her way to the Greyhound bus station, because a bed had opened up in Baton Rouge. Police thought she was hoing standing outside the bus station since she had a record. The other sister was ordering her ticket online." Hollow remained in the doorway.

Yeah, yeah, yeah with the bullshit. Someone else more deserving could use the bed now.

"Lord have mercy Jesus! Now those babies don't have a mother." She handed him the plates of food in plastic bags.

The display of emotion was making me nauseous. Hell, we were even. I didn't have a daughter and now they had no mother. No telling what those kids had witnessed her do. Based on the way she was dressed, she was clearly tricking, probably in front of them. Why people mourned worthless individuals such as herself was beyond me. I had to get from around them.

"Stay up, Krissett. Hattie Mae has my number if you need anything." Hollow said as I squeezed by him.

"I won't." I strolled off. He had to be out his damn mind. Desperate and on my death bed, he would be the last person I called.

***

"Home sweet home." I sighed Monday evening as I looked at the red and white for sale sign staked on the front lawn.

Over the weekend I had decided to continue through with selling the house. A fresh start with a new mindset was what I needed. There was a nice condo under development Uptown that would be ready within the next six months. I had discussed it with Hattie Mae and with no questions asked she was happy to have me stay with her until then.

Because Stone had left me at least thirty messages threatening to catch me on the streets, I decided to arm myself.

"Man, what the fuck is wrong with the motherfucking bank account? Call me now!" He blared into the phone on one of those messages.

I guess he finally went to get his payroll and realized I had closed the account. A fake ID and Jeremiah, pretending to be Stone did the trick. I saved the message in case I needed the laugh for another day.

Quincy and I stopped by the gun store for me to pick up double protection. A .22 for my purse and a .38 for the house. For an extra two hundred and fifty and my telephone number in promise of a good time, I seduced the older gentleman into letting me bypass the state required wait on all gun purchases. As for the good time, I had no intention of making good on it.

Now that I was ready for war, the only thing Stone would catch on the streets would be a bullet in his ass fucking around with me. The way my mind was set up now, I was taking no bullshit and no prisoners.

When I arrived home, the package waiting for me on the porch was an unexpected surprise. Opening the box, I saw that both of my products, industrial strength paint remover and boric acid, were there. The instructions let me know that the products were easy to use, so all I had left to do was coordinate a date. While Stone now knew about the bank account, there were tons of surprises in store for him that he knew nothing about.

After dealing with my package, I hit Meishelle up to make a girl date at the nail shop and go over my plan. She was my ride or die, so I know she would have no problem helping me with what I had in store for Stone and Deborah. Today was a good day.

Chapter 8

"You already know you don't have to ask. Just tell me the time and place," Meishelle said as she drove us to the nail shop.

That's why I wouldn't hesitate to lay my life on the line for my girl. Before knowing everything, Meishelle wanted to get at Stone almost as bad as I did.

"Whenever works best for you. I don't have a job to go to. I know I need at least a week or two to see where the nigga is laying his head and to learn his schedule. When we do it though, it definitely has to be late at night or in the wee hours of the morning."

"Sounds like we have a date, hun, but you really need to tell me what happened that night." She had been adamantly pushing for what transpired. Knowing it was unfair for her to enter the situation blind, I filled her in on all the details.

"Fuck just getting at him. What you going to do about these bitches, Takiesha and Deborah?" Meishelle's hood side came out full force.

"I have some ideas, but nothing definite yet for them. You know I'll keep you posted." Ideas had definitely crossed my mind, but nothing that had been worked out to completion.

Meishelle threw out an idea for a girl's vacation. It was something I could definitely use in my life. My first thought was my favorite and most frequent place, the "A," but she was thinking more of Hawaii or Vegas. I texted my cousin Schtanya to see if she wanted to join and break the tie on where we would go. I had chosen the beautiful island of Hawaii and Meishelle chose the high roller Vegas life. Schtanya replied back a few hours later confirming her attendance and voting for Vegas.

High roller life here we come! I began searching airlines and hotels on my phone.

I popped three Somas for the muscles aches at the end of my long day before settling down on the sofa with a wine glass, a bottle of wine, and *The Best Man Holiday*. While I was relaxing, I reached for the cordless phone to do my research on Stone's employment and patterns. After making sure my number would not be revealed on anyone's caller ID, I dialed the number for Stone's job and listened to the ring.

"Hello, Crown Company Warehouse. How can I help you?" I immediately recognized the gentleman's voice as not being Stone's.

"Yes, may I speak with Gregory Robertson, please?" I sweetly requested.

"I'm sorry, ma'am, but he no longer works here."

"Thank you. Have a good night," I courteously ended the call.

Interesting.

Maybe they fired him after the foolishness that went down. Tomorrow, I would have to make a call to his day job and see if he was working there, although I doubted it. I had been the one that held his ass grounded and out of the dope game. If Deborah had anything to do with it, she would have his ass back out there.

Cionna: 7:25 p.m.: *Hey boo! Doing my daily check on you before work.*

Cionna was getting out of hand with those messages every day. If I ignored one, she sent four more. It was time we had a talk to set our expectations on being friends with benefits.

Krisett 7:27 p.m.: *Hi. I'm good. Thanks for asking. What are you doing tomorrow? Maybe we can have lunch.*

Cionna 7:29 p.m.: *No plans. Let's do it. Give me a time, place and I'm there.*

Krisett 7:30 p.m.: *Acme Oyster House at 1 p.m.*

Cionna 7:31 p.m.: *See you then. *Kisses**

Reviewing the Hertz website, they had nothing until the weekend after next. I wanted everything else out of the house in case the agent needed to schedule a showing. The already cramped walls were even worse now that I had decided to move in with Hattie Mae. Quincy offered to move the stuff after work during the week, but that seemed so inconsiderate. A tour would just have to wait, possibly extending the amount of time the house was in my possession.

Irritated at the thought, I got a second wind to clean and get rid of shit. The reserved storage unit was large enough for four to five rooms of furniture, which required major condensing. Doubling and tripling garbage bags, I wildly tossed mostly new things with price tags that would never be worn or were too small for myself and Na'Siah. Stone and I had discussed having customized walk-in closets built so our clothes could be in one room, but that was a dream of the past. Looking at the discarded lawn bags lined along the walls, they would have made for a good garage sale, but even for the extra money I wasn't organizing anything. Finishing up, there was one last closet that needed handling.

My heart galloped, standing, staring at the door that led to my room. For the last few days I had dodged it like a bill collector. After sleeping in the guest room and wearing the extra clothes I kept in the closet, it was time to face the inevitable.

Stepping inside, the smell of perfume from the bottle that I had tipped over the night of Takiesha and Deborah's juvenile charades had dried on the dresser. Inhaling, I opened the closet door and eyed Stone's side, lined with name brand apparel. The Versace shades I'd bought him last Christmas sat on the top shelf. Something in me snapped.

"I bought this motherfucker for you!" I screamed, yanking the Polo shirt off the hanger. Breaking the sunglasses and watches, I ferociously tore the clothes from their hangers and slung them onto the floor.

"I stood by your side, you bitch." I pitched the Clive Christian cologne against the wall. The bottle shattered, spilling onto the heaps of shirts, shoes, jeans and pants. Dribbles of blood fell staining the beige carpet, a sign my blood pressure had risen to the sky during my reign of terror. Picking up one of the yellow shirts, I caught a glimpse of a hefty, fireproof safe concealed under my suit bags. Walking over, the small crack in the door revealed a few grams of stashed coke.

Son of a bitch!

Obviously he had decided to return to the life that taught him who really had his back. Normally, I would have flew off the hinges on Stone for bringing this shit up in my house, but given the circumstances I could use it to my advantage.

Judging by the weight, he was working his way back into the ranks of big timers quite nicely. Unknowingly, coming up short on a hustle could get his ass murked. Confident that everything was there, he would head out without counting. It was a stretch, but maybe good fortune would be on my side.

I took a few pictures of the contents for later use, flushed a gram down the toilet out of spite, kept two for myself that could come in handy later and packed the remaining belongings into duffle bags. Sitting them in the garage, I secured the new lock that I had installed which could only be accessed from inside the house.

Utilizing the empty clear containers I had purchased for packing, I loaded his clothes into them and hauled them out to the lawn. Making three trips, mounds of garb lay sprawled about the backyard that now required attention. Retrieving the mower out of the garage, it was time to tend to grass. Tugging the crank cord, the purr of the engine made my heart race with excitement as the blades reduced the fabric to pieces.

By the end of the night I had six bags of donations to distribute between the organizations, eight bags of the tattered remnants I had gathered for Stone to piece together and a fucked up house that now had to be cleaned for showing. However, destroying Stone's shit would be worth every minute it took to restore it. I figured if I dropped off two bags of contributions every day that I went to therapy would have them gone by week's end. With my high diminishing, I threw my head back with another three pills and watched TV until the alarm sounded the next morning.

"Girl, what is this? I don't have room for that mess in my car," my momma grumbled while I dragged the bags down the driveway.

"Good morning to you, mother. Stuff that I need to drop off at the Goodwill or Salvation Army on my way to therapy." Good thing I had tripled the garbage bags, the first one shredding against the pavement.

"Come on here with that mess, Krissett. I have appointments." She lugged them into the trunk of the car.

Pitching the bags into the bin, she dropped me off early for therapy. Grabbing some breakfast from the hospital cafeteria, I decided to make the telephone call to Stone's first job. My assumption based on the previous night's evidence was spot on, his ass had to be back on the street.

Walking over to the therapy department until my name was called, I busied myself reading *A Dangerous Love* by JPeach. *Love Knows No Boundaries* had given me everything a few months ago on my trip and I needed to get back into something that would keep my mind off the madness.

Time passed by quickly reading about Blaze and Peaches. Pissed that I reached the end, I felt the author needed to come her butt on with the next part. Good thing the therapist called my name before I could get onto Facebook and inbox her.

Since Cionna was still my little secret, I called a cab company to bring me to our meeting, but hearing it would be an hour wait, I decided to hit Cionna up instead to meet at the Walgreens near the hospital and then head over to the restaurant. She seemed elated to see me as we talked at the table. When our food arrived, it was time we discussed the reason for this lunch.

"I want us to come to an understanding on what we are and what we are expecting. Personally, I'm looking for an occasional stress relief, but not for an everlasting relationship." For me, being brutally honest was the best.

"Most definitely. I feel you. I'm not looking for anything serious, but I do want to continue the sex. Our bodies were in sync the other night." She agreed.

"Being honest, I'm slightly concerned by the number of calls. I appreciate you checking on me, but if I don't respond, give me a moment instead of texting me repeatedly." It was borderline stalker behavior to me.

"Ok. I can do that. It's out of love, however, I can see how it might come across wrong." Her mouth said. We would see if the actions aligned with her words.

Interested in home ownership, she had a few questions about owning property, city taxes and the overall process. Educating her on it all, I cautioned her about the agent that she chose. One out for the money would care nothing about the sale. Once your name was on that dotted line, the house was yours for better or worse. I knew that first hand.

Schtanya reached out about our trip to Vegas, momentarily stopping my dialogue with Cionna. Her contact at the airline had come through with great ticket prices for us. I had finalized the hotel reservations and in four weeks we were off for a wild time.

Stone's message popped up on the screen interrupting my response to Schtanya. Any other time my phone rarely went off unless I sparked conversation.

Stone 1:25pm: This is my last time nicely asking for my shit.

It didn't matter how he asked, the answer would be the same. He could have the shards of clothes, besides that there was nothing left. The final decision has been made on the most expensive things that just didn't seem right to chop them up. The Cole Haan shoes, Diesel jeans, Ralph Lauren Polos, authentic throwback jerseys and jewelry, including the seven hundred fifty dollar Swarovski watch I had recently purchased was generously donated to the Veterans. I was sure they could benefit from the items and I was more than ecstatic to be the bearer of bad news to Stone that I would receive a huge tax credit for my generosity at his expense.

Krisett 1:26 p.m.: What shit? You have nothing at my house.

Stone 1:27 p.m.: Keep fucking with me like I'm some ho ass nigga. Where the fuck is my clothes and shit?

"Is everything ok?" Cionna questioned my balled up facial expression.

"Yeah, I'm good." I simulated a smile. The last thing I was about to give her any insight to was my marital status. We were having lunch because she already didn't know how to act.

Krisett 1:28 p.m.: Correction: You mean my shit? Your little ass money ain't paid for a motherfucking thing.

He would recognize on today what I had done versus them hos he was playing with.

Stone 1:30 p.m.: Man, I'm not about to go back and forth with you. When can I come?

I laughed my ass off as I typed the reply. He would get the answer in a few, but it wouldn't be anything he was ready for.

Stone 1:45 p.m.: Hello

Krisett 1:50 p.m.: Yes Stone. You can go between your local V.A. donation centers to obtain what's available back.

Stone 1:52 p.m.: I know you better stop fucking playing with me.

Krisett 1:54 p.m.: Trash day is tomorrow if you want what's left.

Stone 2:15 p.m.: Krissett!

The fun had ended and now my responses would. Putting down the phone, I returned to wrapping up my meal.

"Dessert on me?" Cionna questioned.

"Sure." I picked up the menu to look over the selections.

"Nah. That ain't what I had in mind." She licked her lips lustfully.

"Excuse me." I motioned the waiter over for the check, ready to give her some of my ice cream.

Linnea

Chapter 9

Hattie Mae had me never wanting to leave the nest again. She made sure I had three home cooked meals a day, did my laundry, and kept my room clean. If I went to make up my bed in the morning she would get upset.

We sat next to each other at the table, reminiscing with the old family photo albums reserved solely for me and Quincy. She had captured every moment under the sun. The infamous naked bath pictures, first steps, the professional pictures with the number in the background for how old you were at the time, and of course the yearly school pictures.

"Those were the times. Now y'all are all grown up, married, and have kids." Hattie Mae brushed over one of me and Quincy's first day of school pictures. It had to be my kindergarten year and maybe Quincy's third or fourth grade. His rabbit size teeth could be seen coming through the gums.

"You're not taking your medicine." I examined the swelling in her fingers.

"And I'll tell you again that I am grown." Hattie Mae yanked her hands from me, turning the page.

"And so are we, but we still need you all the same. Please take your meds, Hattie Mae," I begged, resting my head on her shoulder like a little girl. She sucked her teeth, brushing off my plea. The small pressure pill seemed to be a huge ordeal for her.

"No, you don't. You are doing great, but until you are ready to face your past and embrace the future you're welcome to stay right here," she hinted.

Following our stroll down memory lane, I sat Indian style on the floor thinking about the infinite wisdom Hattie Mae had laid on me. Reaching for my cell phone to call the list of divorce attorneys, I realized it was in my room. After retrieving it, I saw that I had a voicemail from the real estate agent regarding the home we had been in the process of purchasing.

Apparently, Stone had called her and increased the offer on the home last week. According to her, he claimed we were very anxious to move in and willing to do whatever it took to close on the house. Unfortunately, his phone had been going to voicemail so she was calling to see when we were available.

There was no telling what else this mentally deficient bastard was up to. I immediately returned the call to inform her that I had no idea what Mr. Roberson's intentions were. I then explained to her that I was filing for divorce and had no intention, whatsoever, of going any further with the purchase of the home. She sounded extremely confused at the two different versions of plans she was getting, so I referred her back to Stone's voicemail. Maybe he was speaking about Takiesha as his wife to be.

Going back to my original purpose for getting the phone out, I learned divorce attorneys were more damn expensive than criminal. Something would have to give to manage all this shit.

Next to shopping, hoarding money was my next favorite thing to do. The idea of tapping into my rainy day for three different legal defenses, house note and other expenses made me nervous. In addition, Schtanya's connection had come through, but the ticket had to be paid for right then. According to my calculations, I would have roughly ten stacks remaining after everything. I needed a damn plan and quick.

Looking up, the TV was tuned in to *Snapped* on the Oxygen channel. The episode about a woman that killed her husband because of infidelity was quite fitting. During Kris Kringle her coworker presented her with a gorgeous gift box filled with pictures of the husband cheating with several women on the job. Forgiving him, she agreed to work on it, but the immature women on the job wouldn't leave well enough alone. They ridiculed her daily until nothing but malice for her husband remained. She ended up hiring someone to kill him and disguise it as a home invasion.

Motherfuckers will drive you to do it. I would have killed the bitches, too. Cost that woman her fucking life.

Hattie Mae called out, asking me to take a walk to the store for some sugar. I clicked off the TV and headed out.

Walking down the block, some jackass pulled up in a Dodge Ram on 22's.

"Can I get at you for a minute, ma?" He leaned his weight on the arm rest.

First off, no man was getting at me, and secondly, with the way I looked at the moment, no man should want to. I wore fitted, faded black cotton capris, a white tank top and flip flops. My head was pulled back into a sloppy ponytail with an exercise band to tame my edges.

"No, I'm good. Thanks though." I refused to look his way, wanting to get where I was going and back home.

"You passing up on a good thing?" He tried to sell himself.

"And I'm ok with that."

"Stuck up bitch." I heard him say as he pulled away from the curb and sat in the cross waiting for an oncoming car to make a u-turn.

That motherfucker had to be out of his fucking mind to disrespect me, especially one I didn't know. We were about ten feet from the store in front of an abandoned double. Picking up a loose chunk of brick from the steps, I hummed it, smashing the back windshield in, concealing myself behind the cars that passed on the street.

"I'll buy you a drink if you didn't see anything," I bribed the older, skinny gentlemen standing in front the store.

"Saw what?" He smiled, earning a bottle of his choice.

Getting back home, the aroma of collard greens, baked macaroni, fried chicken and cornbread welcomed me. It was my favorite meal. Quameer called to ask if I could keep Na'Siah so he and Mariah could go to the New Edition concert. A couple of days ago he didn't have gas money, but they could afford a damn concert. Their priorities were clearly wrong.

Quameer arrived about five o'clock with Na'Siah and he hung around long enough to get a plate. Hattie Mae kept the sectioned Styrofoam plates for him. After Quameer rushed off to get ready for the concert, we sat at the dinner table and Na'Siah shared his day with us.

Our conversation was interrupted by the doorbell ringing. Hattie Mae stopped me from getting up from the table.

I heard her thank the person at the door before it shut. Her eyes twinkled like a new star in the sky when she returned with Hollow and flowers. For the fifth time in two weeks he had shown up at some point in the evening. I wondered if he knew how long ago he had worn out his welcome. Hattie Mae invited him to take a seat while she retreated into the kitchen.

Hollow held his hand out for Na'Siah to dap him off. Na'Siah brought his hand way back, bringing it down as hard as he could. He greeted me with a hug around my neck, kissing me on my nape. I wiggled under his touch. He took a seat directly across from me.

"So, how is everything going, Hollow?" Hattie Mae emerged with plates prepared to feed multitudes in two plastic grocery bags. She sat one in front of him to eat with us.

"You don't have to do this," Hollow replied.

"Boy, hush and eat that food. Those plates should take care of you tonight and I'll have something different for you tomorrow, ok?"

"Yes, ma'am." He took a bite of chicken.

Hattie Mae again asked about the kids. Hollow was getting them individual therapy and noticing improvement daily. They were slightly malnourished from her selling the food stamps.

The oldest boy, Jai'Shon, had started following directly in her footsteps, getting high and drinking daily. Xavier, his baby boy, had been placed in an alternative school for the constant fighting. Alainnah, their daughter, was having nightmares every night about her momma beating the hell out of her in fits of rage. From the sound of it, they should be thanking me for ridding the world of her dead weight. I chuckled on the inside at the pun.

Excusing ourselves from the table, Na'Siah asked Hollow if he would race him. I quickly reminded him about his homework, hoping Hollow would leave, but that failed miserably. Hollow and Hattie Mae sat in the living room talking while I bathed Na'Siah and helped with his homework.

"Can we play now?" Na'Siah huffed, placing the pencil down. One would swear he had just worked a full time job writing his name ten times.

Nodding yes, he wiggled his way out of the chair, racing to the living room. Using Na'Siah as leverage, Hollow suggested that I play the winner for the championship. I seethed on the inside, accepting on the strength of my baby who liked the idea. Playing the best of three, we both let Na'Siah win. He ran into the kitchen, thrilled to let Hattie Mae know he had beat both of us.

"So what's the real deal with you?" Hollow asked as I got up to leave the room.

"What?" I looked at him confused by why he would think I would talk to him.

"It's the second time I've come through and you've been here, combined with your arm being in that sling. Something's up. I can see that."

"Hollow, we ain't on the level."

"I feel you." I left him standing in the hallway rubbing his chin.

Sitting in the room on my laptop, I started writing like my psychiatrist suggested. I had begun a daily journal of my feelings and I poured my soul onto the paper for hours. My shit could be an autobiography.

Hattie Mae had enlightened me as always, but Hollow reinforced my hate for men today. Niggas would be on some crazy shit thinking that when they wanted, all their fuck ups should be forgiven and erased. Women were meant to be a compliment to man, not a damn convenience.

Hungry for a piece of cold chicken and a bottled water, I went into the kitchen. Hattie Mae startled me, still up in her recliner. The TV was on QVC showing the next item up for sale. Her eyes may have been closed, but she would dial that number in a heartbeat.

"I want you to really think about what I am about to say. The one thing I want you to always remember is to forgive. Hollow, Stone, and Quameer have made mistakes, but they each love you in their own way. There is no person who is perfect and if you can't forgive mistakes you will find yourself alone and empty. You can't force a particular type of relationship with who you want. Let love blossom into what it is supposed to be." Hattie Mae started rocking.

"Hattie Mae..." I went to respond.

She held up her hand to silence me. "Uh uh. Give it heartfelt consideration, that's all I want."

"That's way easier said than done," I mumbled, going back to the room.

The heart wanted who it wanted and it was difficult to reject the emotions that it caused. I tossed and turned on her words that night with little sleep. Hattie Mae had attempted to infuse some of her wisdom into me, but it didn't make any sense. If Quameer, Stone or Hollow had not wanted me I would have had to accept it and move on. However, they allowed me to remain for selfish gain: money in the case of Quameer and Stone and pussy in the case of Hollow which made their transgressions inexcusable. Settling on the best defense to avoid rejection was not to develop emotional attachments to anyone, sleep came without further thought.

"Krissett!" Hattie Mae came out of the room terrified, wrapping her robe around her waist.

Delirious, I jumped up out of the bed, scattering for clothes, unable to find any in a haste.

The damn banging on the door sounded like the ATF about to bulldoze it. I peeped out the window to see what the fuck was being rammed into it. Stone's idiotic ass was pounding on it, garbage bags at his feet.

"Stupid bitch," I mumbled, heading to the door. "I got it. It's just Stone." I ushered Hattie Mae back to her room as she crossed into the hallway.

I allowed him to bang harder while I went to the kitchen and grabbed the butcher knife. Clearly this nigga had lost his motherfucking mind showing up at my grandmother's house startling the fuck out of her. He could have ran me off the interstate, costing me my life a few weeks ago, never said he was sorry, but could come here about materialistic shit that he could easily afford to replace with dope money. He was going to learn today. Fucking with me, he would draw back a nub. Swinging the door open, it crashed against the wall putting a hole in it.

"Bitch, are you out of your motherfucking mind bringing your ass around here?" I bucked, swiping the knife within inches of his hand.

Stone leaped back while I continued swinging. One slash landed on his forearm where the tattoo of my name was. He bobbed and weaved my wrath, walking backwards until he was at the edge of the stairs.

Hattie Mae came behind me, capturing my wrists. She briefly wrestled with me for the knife, but my grip was so strong she could not fully free it. I wasn't crazed enough to swing at her. This knife strictly had Stone's name on it.

"Girl, get inside with no clothes on." Enraged, she shoved me backwards by the arms toward the door. Caught in my feelings I had come outside in a skimpy pair of boy shorts and satin night top, ass shaking everywhere.

"Stone, whatever happened didn't happen here. You need to leave," she commanded him to the stairs.

"You would want to thank my grandma for saving your ability to walk away from here!" I paced the floor inside the screen door gesturing with the knife in my hand. Hattie Mae had blocked the screen door so that I couldn't get back outside.

"If you don't go sit your tail on that sofa." Hattie Mae glared at me sternly from the other side of the door. I defiantly remained in the door. Her chest heaved up and down, full of anger waiting for Stone to collect his belongings.

"I got you, Krissett. Hear you loud and clear." Stone mean mugged me before snatching up the bags of tattered apparel on the porch.

"Yeah promise because I definitely got something coming real soon *for you*." I put emphasis on the last two words.

All I needed was for Hattie Mae to move a few feet to the left. It would have given me a clear path to stab his stupid ass in the back. I needed to draw blood to settle down.

"What you got, huh? What the fuck you really going to do me? My reach is way longer than you." Stone threw his arms in the air with the garbage bags.

"You'll see this ole' bitch add nigga way sooner than you think! You started it and I promise on everything I love, I will see it to the finish!" I screamed as he tossed the bags in his truck bed and peeled off.

I stormed off to my room to call Meishelle. Apparently my catch back thus far had not been drastic enough, but when I came back from Vegas I was going to make Stone a believer about fucking with me.

Chapter 10

"Vegas, baaabbeee!" I stuck my head out of the window and screamed into the wind.

Since neither I nor Meishelle knew the next time we would get a vacation, we spared no expense for the trip to Vegas. Gambling, drinking and partying were at the top of the agenda. Taking my phone off of airplane mode, I saw that Schtanya had texted me that she would be waiting for us at *The Great American Bagel* since her flight arrived an hour earlier.

Cionna 11:30 a.m.: Hey was calling to check in. You got time for me?

Cionna had been calling daily for sex since the day we had lunch. I was wondering if maybe somewhere along the way I sent her conflicting messages. In my book, cut buddies usually fucked on occasion, but not every day. At the moment, my sex drive was on an all-time high so most times I gave in for a quickie.

"Hey, cuz!" I excitedly waved my good hand in the air like a lunatic. It was about to go down on that trip.

"Hey!" Schtanya covered her mouth full of food.

We walked over and she stood up, hugging my left side. "I'm so sorry it didn't work. I was so ready for you to be happy," she spoke into my ear.

"It's cool. If I can't find happiness alone, I can't find it with a man."

Vegas was all about me. Bouncing from relationship to relationship I had discovered myself through others. Always wanting to be under my man, I tagged along everywhere he went. When a new one came along that didn't have the same interest as the previous one, my interests quickly changed and adapted to fit theirs. Eventually, simple things like picking a movie was a chore. I would stare at the movie theatre app not sure whether to select an action, horror, drama or romance movie. It would frustrate me to the point that I wouldn't go see anything. Hell might freeze over before I ever embarked on another relationship journey, but at least I would be an individual before and after.

We joined her while she finished her breakfast and then hailed a cab to our destination. Paying for the previous night's stay allowed us to check in at four o'clock in the evening. Tall ivory pillars welcomed us to the countless towers and smaller buildings that seemed to consume the entire block welcomed us to the world famous Caesar's Palace.

Excitement fizzled through my veins as we rode past the brightest green palm trees and shrubbery beheld by man. They encompassed an angel sitting in the midst of a shooting fountain of heavenly water. I nodded my head in approval of our selections. The Romans had *did* this.

Opting for adjoining, deluxe executive suites, I loved the hell out Quincy. Almost strangling him after he had surprised me with five stacks, enough to upgrade from the standard room to these and have more spending money. Outside of that, he had been doing well by his come up. We had been to the bank to open various certificates in random amounts under nine hundred ninety nine dollars. He was ensuring his money made money and flew under the Feds radar.

Settling in, we hit the *Qua Spa* located in the hotel. I selected the Thai massage, designed to help achieve mental and physical release. Releasing tension in every muscle, my mind was so liberated after the eighty minutes, I battled the urge not to pay another two hundred fifty five dollars for the service. Finishing up, we chatted in the spa room about the rest of our plans for the day. I took off my robe and basked in the water that fell from a shower head in the ceiling into a pool. This was the way I was supposed to live. I closed my eyes and an inner peace came over me that I had never experienced in my life.

"Krissett?" Schtanya called me back to reality to the fluorescent lit, plush white chairs that sat around the area. I turned in her direction.

"You ready to see the rest of Vegas?" She stood up, rubbing her fingers together in a gesture of being ready to spend money.

"Hell yeah!" I hopped out of the pool.

It was warm for late October. The semi-cloudy temperature wasn't doing a great job of blocking the heat that beamed off the concrete pavement. Light sweat formed on my forehead as we headed to the Miracle Mile Shops at Planet Hollywood. Shopping was number one on my itinerary on any vacation I took.

Grabbing a bite to eat at Cheeseburger of Vegas, I found myself twitching to spend more after using every penny of my five hundred dollar budget. Delta would already charge enough airline additional baggage fees for the ones that were at my feet. I needed at least twenty five hundred dollars to blow in the casino on the craps tables and half of that would probably be returned.

Getting ready to paint the town, my phone rang.

"Krissett?" Quameer questioned like someone else would answer my phone.

"What's wrong?" I panicked, hearing Na'Siah screaming. There was a woman in the background trying to comfort him, but the distress in his voice increased.

"I need Na'Siah's policy number for the registration lady." He informed me they were at University Hospital.

Na'Siah had accidentally been burned on his arm and hand. Mariah was cooking dinner when he tripped over a rug and ran into the stove. The pot she was preparing to move from the front burner fell and the boiling water spilled all over him. My pressure went sky high wondering why the hell they would have a pot on the front burner with a child in the house. Na'Siah ran everywhere, so even I knew better and I only had him three nights a week.

"Let me talk to my son, Quameer," I demanded in aggravation. Lord knows had I been home I would have tried to whip his ass with my one good arm.

Loud whimpering sounds took over the line signaling that Quameer had given my baby the phone.

"You are mommy's big boy, right?" Tears began to trickle from my eyes at my baby's pain.

I could tell his little chest heaved up and down by the deep pauses he took to catch his breath. It had to be serious, because my baby didn't cry like that. I did my best to soothe him over the phone, but he kept repeating that he wanted me to come get him. I knew that wasn't possible for more than one reason, but I promised him that we would have the weekend together.

"I love you, baby." My heart was tearing into a million pieces, trying to contain my emotions for him.

"I love you, too, mommy," he finally managed to get out.

"What the fuck you called that bitch for?" I heard Mariah scream into the background.

83

That ho had to be out of her fucking mind to question why he would call me about my son. "Can you put your daddy back on the phone, please?" The next thing I said wasn't for his ears.

"What's good?" I heard the shuffling of the phone before Quameer came back.

"Is that bitch out of her motherfucking mind questioning you about calling me regarding my fucking son? You better get that bitch in line, pulling shit like she don't know who I am. Make sure you call me…"

"Give me the fucking phone," I heard Mariah blow as the phone disconnected. I called back and the phone went straight to voicemail. Pulling out my laptop, I began searching for a flight back home to beat the piss out that ho.

Meishelle came into the room in her little black tube top dress and chandelier earrings, ready for our first night at the casino.

"What is going on?" Meishelle could see something was wrong.

"My baby got burned some kind of way and that bitch is playing with me," I raged. Her trashy, trailer park ass would sell her soul to be Na'Siah's mother.

"What the fuck happened?"

"Girl, I couldn't get all the details." The words got caught in my throat. This was that shit that would get her purged from the earth. I already had one bitch under my belt.

"Say no more." She pulled out her phone and we checked into the ticket prices together. Our tickets had been cheap because we ordered them nonrefundable, but anything going home now was a grand or better. The tears I tried to hold back began to fall. That shit was just too much.

Meishelle suggested we call my mom and ask her to go to the hospital to check on them. She didn't hesitate. Schtanya came in and they sat on each side of me while I cried. Knowing my child was in pain and I was powerless to take it away from him was like watching someone slashing my lungs. I struggled for my breath, my baby being my lifeline. He was my one weakness, no matter how hard my heart became toward the world.

Forty-five minutes later my momma called, rattled and upset. Craig had to intercede between her and Mariah at the hospital. According to

Mariah, it was Na'Siah's fault for running through the kitchen after she told him to stop.

Disrespect my momma *and* act like my baby had burned himself? She should've known better than to fuck with my momma, but a hard head made a soft ass and I was going to tear her up whenever we met again.

The doctor said it was a second degree burn and would heal with the possibility of leaving some permanent scarring. Promising to keep me informed on his status, my momma encouraged me to stay and enjoy myself, because my coming home angry would only end up making the situation worse.

Ordering a bottle to the room, the girls did their best to cheer me up. I sporadically called Quameer's phone, which repeatedly went to voicemail. Taking myriads of shots to the head, I eventually passed out from the room spinning, Meishelle and Schtanya were right beside me.

The next morning we got dressed to see one of the Seven Wonders of the World, the North Rim of the Grand Canyon. My breath fogged the window of the small flight as we flew over the Hoover Dam and Lake Mead. The breathtaking ability of Mother Nature to mold rock into a path that water could flow over was astonishing. Stone mountains and crystal waters extended as far as the eye could see, erasing my fear of heights. The plane allowed us a moment at the top where we took goofy pictures, having a blast.

Na'Siah was still heavy on my mind. One day I would take my baby to see sites like that. I wanted him to experience every site the world had to offer him. That was definitely the life. I would never suffer again with mania if I was able to behold scenes like that on a permanent basis. It was soul healing.

My spirit obviously more broken after taking in a Seventh Wonder of the World, the girls offered to order in room service and a movie, but it was unfair to have them spending their vacation inside with me. Knowing they wouldn't leave me alone, I got up and dragged to pop my Lithium with three Somas. Opening my Lithium bottle, I needed a refill. Adding it to the list of things to handle, I would need to brainstorm on what to say because sharing my true thoughts would have me committed.

"I'm ready." I announced to Meishelle and Schtanya who had been waiting for me at least twenty minutes.

Making our rounds, the casino was swarming with people. Buying in on the crap table, I counted out my eight hundred dollar allotment for the night and purchased my chips. The waitress came over shortly thereafter and collected my drink order for two shots of Crown. They made sure not to serve unless you were spending. Assuring them that I was fine, Meishelle headed to the slot machines and Schtanya went to the blackjack table, agreeing to meet within two hours in the center of the casino.

My money fluctuated, but I eventually walked away up two thousand dollars. I briefly went back to the room before meeting the girls to see the strip that night. Vegas at night was gorgeous. The various neon-colored bright lights, illuminating the casino strip mesmerized a person into wanting to lose thousands. *The Bellagio* and *Mirage* captivated us the most, lady luck gifted me another three thousand dollars.

Back at the hotel, I looked at my phone for the hundredth time for a call from Quameer. His phone was ringing, but no one would answer. My blood boiled when my mom called to tell me she had been to the house to check on him, but no one would answer the door.

God was raining blessings on Quameer and Mariah without them even realizing it. Had there been an available flight home, I would have been the first one on it. This was the last time I flew Spirit's one flight a day airline. Shit made no damn sense.

Agitated, I tossed my phone on the bed and went to check on Meishelle in the bathroom. She was stretched out in front the toilet, never having the ability to hold her liquor. I helped her up and into the bed, placing the garbage can in front of her. She would've never made it back to the bathroom. She mumbled a thank you, her breath reeking of alcohol.

"You sleep?" Schtanya peeked her head through the door. I had taken a long, hot shower, hoping to bring sleep. It had been stressful worrying about my little man, but tomorrow I would find out what the deal was.

"Nah, not yet. What's up?" I roamed through the TV channels.

"We haven't had much chance to really talk since you told me what happened between you and Stone." She flopped onto the bed. "I just really wanted to apologize if it was my advice regarding the threesome and he ended up cheating with her after."

During me and Meishelle's disagreement about Janasia being in the wedding, Schtanya had been my confidante in Atlanta. I had taken the getaway to ponder Stone's proposition of having a threesome and discovered that Schtanya had done one with her husband, Bryan, prior to them tying the knot. Never having gotten around to telling her we did not go through with it or exactly who Stone had cheated with, she assumed it was Cionna.

"No worries. It was a blast from his past anyway. I suspected it from day one, but didn't follow my gut." The other secret would remain just that. Even though it was good, it left me with an uneasy feeling the day after.

"Oh. That's a good thing." She paused. I could tell something was up because the silence was awkward. Selfish, I had my own shit I was dealing with, I didn't want to invite the possibility of new drama by someone else. However, Schtanya was here for me now trying to take my mind off the Na'Siah situation back home. If nothing else, I owed her.

"What's the deal?" I offered my listening ear.

"I don't know where to begin." She sighed in exasperation.

"At the beginning is a start." I rolled my eyes jokingly to lighten the mood.

"Well, I stepped out on Bryan with a chick."

"Huh?" Her confession took me back. Based on our conversations in Atlanta, I knew she enjoyed women, but within the confinements of her marriage. I had always envisioned Schtanya living the happiest married life of anyone I knew.

"It was just one time though. I need to tell someone. It is eating me up. Since you already know I've gone there once…"

"Get it off your chest." I opened the floor for her to spill all the tea.

Apparently, they had a car accident on the interstate. She was initially suspicious because the woman lived out of state, but in a hurry to get to court for a case, they agreed to resolve the issue between themselves and exchanged information. The damage didn't appear

87

extensive so if she didn't make good on the offer it was something she could handle. Their schedules always clashed because she was out of state, but they kept in contact and a few weeks later they met at a body shop to have the repairs assessed. The place crowded so the woman offered her lunch while they waited. Their conversation flowed and they discovered they had a lot in common. The repairs were more than expected so it took an additional month or two for the woman to get the money together, but she made good on her word. By then a small friendship had developed and one thing led to another, which I didn't quite understand.

The mind-blowing description of the sensuality and passion they had shared put Cionna on my mind for a brief minute. It quickly dissipated when I thought about the fact that she still struggled with our friendship even after lunch at Acme. The conversation went on for hours before Schtanya thanked me for listening and retreated to her room.

On our last day, we decided to rent a car and head across the border to California. The bright green and pure white street sign clearly read Rodeo Drive. Signs there looked like those in New Orleans the day they were installed. Like they were perfectly depicted in the movies, Tourists peered through high end retailer's glass windows that advertised their most expensive items available.

The affluent sat around under umbrellas sipping pricy lemonade and eating sandwiches on croissants. Never had I seen a Lamborghini, Ferrari, and Bugatti line the same side of the street. I spun around in amazement down the paved pathway that held Chanel, Prada, and the mini blue box from the store of my dreams, Tiffany and Co.

There was no way I could pass the white building with the grey blocked archway without beholding the insides. I slid my finger along the silver, metal bar, eyes wide at all the gems. The middle-aged black salesperson was extremely friendly. For the commission she made, I would have been, too.

With the additional money that I won returning to the casino with Schtanya in the middle of the night, I purchased a silver linked bracelet for Na'Siah. The engraving would take the standard business days, but would be shipped to the house. The rest of the money I was saving to show him a fabulous time when I got home, hopefully to take his injuries off his mind.

We took a trolley ride through the rest of Beverly Hills, finally catching the Hollywood sign before heading back.

My momma made another trip to check on Na'Siah and let me talk to him. He sounded like himself, and I admired his resiliency.

We went to dinner and headed to the casino. My instincts fooled me and I lost a grand. Overall, I had a great time. Finishing up with one last massage, my body tensed up at what awaited me. Outside of Na'Siah, everything else was in shambles. Wishing I could take my baby boy with me and just disappear, I frowned, waving bye to Vegas from the runway of the airport.

Chapter 11

I had got off the plane in Houston to catch my connecting flight to New Orleans more ready than ever to deal with Mariah and Quameer, but due to our plane being delayed an additional hour, Na'Siah was already waiting for me by Hattie Mae. The moment I opened the door he dashed over to me hugging my waist. He probably would have jumped into my arms, but the sling reminded him that he couldn't. My arm function was coming back great with the extra weekly sessions, but I still used it occasionally if the pain showed up. I planted kisses all over his forehead.

Na'Siah ate ice cream while calling out his wish list of things he wanted to do over the weekend. So far I had the Children's Museum, Zoo and a Saints game. Tapping into the Vegas funds I set aside, his wish was mommy's command. Excusing himself to play his video games, Meishelle, Hattie Mae and I sat around talking until it was time to change his bandage. We all were anxious to see just how bad the burn truly was.

Using the aftercare instructions and changing supplies, I held my breath unwrapping his dressed arm. Unveiling what lay beneath, I couldn't bring myself to do it. My baby's skin was completely incinerated, leaving his bright pink flesh exposed. The back of his hand had a shiny, rubbery appearance with small blisters scattered on the inside of his hand where water must have splashed.

Quameer was too damn reckless in this situation. Fuck an explanation, because accident or not, someone was going to pay for this shit. I asked Meishelle to take pictures before excusing myself from the room to gain my composure. First thing Monday morning I was calling my lawyer to report their asses and his pediatrician for an aftercare follow up. It appeared that he hadn't been taking the medicine that the doctor prescribed which I figured, since they wouldn't answer the door for my mother.

Drying my eyes and taking a deep breath, I went back into the kitchen when I believed they were finished. Na'Siah tried to go back to his game, but came back shortly later complaining that his arm was bothering him. I gave him some Motrin and held my baby in my arms until we fell asleep.

Bright and early the next morning, the damn rooster Hattie Mae had inherited from someone in the neighborhood was sounding off under my window. Offering Na'Siah a hearty breakfast, he declined for a bowl of cereal and milk. His eyes were slightly droopy indicating he wasn't one hundred percent, but he was fighting it off. Not having Frosted Flakes or milk we headed for a quick run to Walgreens and Sammy's to get breakfast for me and Hattie Mae.

"Frosted Flakes, they're *grreeaatt*!" He mimicked Tony the Tiger, picking the box off of the shelf.

"Come on, Tiger. Let's go get some milk." I burst out laughing at his impression. This little boy was something else.

After getting the milk, Na'Siah managed to detour us to the bubble bath and toy aisle. Making his selection of Sponge Bob suds and a noisy instrument sure to drive me crazy, we headed to the pharmacy to pay.

"Hey y'all. What's going on lil' man and Ms. Baptiste?" Hollow called out to us from the medicine aisle.

"Nothing much. Trying to get us home to breakfast." I had no time for his foolishness. My food was probably ice cold from Na'Siah's field trip around the pharmacy.

"You have time to help a friend out? My son is sick and I don't know what to get him." He stood facing the various products on the wall.

He said his youngest son, Xavier, had a stomach ache and fever of 101. Quickly pointing to the Motrin, Pedialyte and Gatorade I allowed Na'Siah to offer his expert opinion on the flavors to purchase.

"Na'Siah, make sure you remind her about Xavier's party at Laser Tag next weekend." Hollow dapped him off for his help.

I shot him a dirty look for exploiting Na'Siah. Na'Siah would hound hell out of me about going and thus I would have to call Hollow for details to bring him. I could try to bribe him with something else, but I knew it wouldn't stand a chance.

"Ok!" He screamed in excitement.

Finishing up breakfast we got together for Na'Siah's choice activity of the day, The Children's Museum. While inside, Quameer called to arrange a lunch date during the week where we could discuss holiday arrangements for Na'Siah. I texted him to gladly confirm as I had a few very choice words for him and his bitch about my son.

My opportunity to bless his soul would present itself long before though. Saturday night we ended up in Children's Hospital emergency room because Na'Siah had a small fever and diarrhea. The doctor said his burn was infected and blood pressure was on the high side, so they would be admitting him to the hospital at least overnight.

"You need to call Quameer and let him know what is going on with Na'Siah." Hattie Mae urged me with a stern look.

I stood in defiance for a moment before complying. Technically, I didn't owe that motherfucker one thing. Had it not been for him and that simple minded trick ignoring my momma's knocks with the medicine, we wouldn't be in this situation.

"Dial the number and give me the phone, Krissett," Hattie Mae commanded, stretching her hand out for my phone.

Of course, the son of a bitch had it where the phone was still going to voicemail. Hattie Mae left a message with all the details of what was going on. Never returning the call, he appeared within an hour, Mariah right on his heels.

"No, ma'am. Only family is allowed. Wanna be parents don't count." I motioned for the nurse to dismiss Mariah's ass from the room.

"Excuse me!" Mariah bucked from behind the nurse's back.

"Don't make me skull drag your ass out of here." I gritted through squinted eyes.

Mariah already had one coming to her for hanging up on me at the hospital and disrespecting my momma once again. I wanted her to try the shit tonight when my momma got there. The bitch would already be right where she needed to be when I was done.

Temporarily forgetting Hattie Mae was in the room, she cleared her throat to call order in the room and remind me to watch my language in her presence.

"Mariah, step out and let me handle this. I'll come get you shortly." Quameer requested that she comply.

"Don't make promises that you can't keep," I replied sharply. He was skating on thin ice himself being there.

She mumbled something under her breathe as the nurse escorted her from the room. I know her blood boiled wondering what was going on in the room from the waiting area.

"So, it's clear my baby never got his medication by the appearance of his arm." The moment the door closed I went for answers.

"Man, my phone is broke, Krissett. Your momma never came through with the medicine." Quameer began his excuses and lies.

"Nigga, you are a mother…"

"Krissett!" Hattie Mae barked, noticeably fed up with my mouth.

"You are a lie! My momma came to the house with the medicine the day after Na'Siah was released from the hospital. No one answered the door." I barked, rephrasing my words to respect Hattie Mae.

"It had to be while I was at a job interview, but Mariah was home. I checked my voicemail and didn't have any. Your mom's number is in my phone and I didn't have it." He almost had me believing that he cared for Na'Siah.

"Well, there's only one common factor in all of this and I'll handle that at my earliest convenience." I made a break for the door, but he blocked me.

Playing with my child wasn't an option for anyone that walked the face of the earth.

"Nah. My girl don't play like that. Mariah loves Na'Siah as her own. She ain't doing no type of foul stuff on that level. I'm not about to play with my son, Krissett. That's my all right there." He swore by it.

"Don't let me find out. You walked out on that same "all" you are referring to a few years ago without a care in the world." I turned my back and left the conversation at that.

We sat around the bed watching Na'Siah sleep. He opened his droopy eyes momentarily and gave a small smile. It was evident that he was putting on a show for us. I sat by the bedside holding his little hand in mine, saying silent prayers for his pain to go away. Quameer parked his ass in the corner behind Hattie Mae looking stupid as fuck.

"Excuse me, Mr. Johnson." The nurse knocked before entering. "Your wife said that she would like to speak with you please, outside."

"That ain't his wife." I huffed.

"Ok. Let her know that I will be there in a minute, please." He spoke over me so that Mariah could hear him.

She was standing with her arms folded against the wall on the other side of the hallway staring daggers through the room. Quameer's sudden onset of niceness toward me had that bitch feeling some insecurities. I could never understand a woman who gloated while her man disrespected another female. In her deranged mind, it probably gave her some type of security that he wasn't going anywhere. While Quameer was the last man on my mind, they say the way you get a man is how you lose him. The pauper was knocking and she was buckling before she knew his price.

"I'm going to try to come back. If I can't, I'll call to talk to him. What's the number here?"

I ignored him. Hattie Mae flipped over the receiver and gave it to him.

"I hope to see you for lunch on Thursday, if I don't speak to you before." He kissed Na'Siah on the forehead and left.

By Wednesday Na'Siah was doing well enough to go home. He cried to come with me instead, but of course Mariah was hell bent on him going to their house so she could play mommy. However, neither one of their pitiful asses had the money for his medicine. I didn't trust their asses, whatsoever, to give them the cash for it, so Quincy and I went to drop it off and head by my mom's until it was ready for pick up.

Standing at the counter for assistance, two older ladies chatted in the lobby seats about their pastor's church anniversary. I handed the lady at the counter the prescription and waited for her to tell me if the medication was in stock.

A sudden surge of pain shot through my shoulder and back as I hit the linoleum floor.

"Yeah, bitch! I told you I would catch you in the street." Takiesha was looking up at me.

She went in, arms flailing to land punches. I began kicking wildly to stop her from being able to land any blows. The women in the chairs screamed hysterically for us to break it up. Field goal kicking her in the pussy, the bitch hooked over like a man with balls. I quickly got up off the floor and slung bags of Epsom Salt that was sitting next to the counter at her. They burst open, riddling the floor with small crystals until one of the bags knocked the bitch dead upside her head.

"Miss, stop it!" The store manager grabbed me by the arm in midstream of humming another one at her. He stood in between us as she continued to try and come for me. The pharmacy manager came from behind the counter to restrain her hands.

"Sir, that lady attacked her." The elderly women came to my defense, picking Takiesha out of an imaginary police lineup.

The manager took me by the hands, escorting me past her to the door. I was going to get a last hit in for good measure though. Doing a ballerina pirouette, I kicked Takiesha in her back with the strength to cave in her spine. Her mouth sounded off making impact with the tan counter as she fell forward.

"Ma'am, if you don't stop I am going to call the police." He damn near yanked my good shoulder out of the socket.

Turning back in hopes that the bitch was unconscious, she was standing, holding a bloody mouth. I could see two teeth on the floor. I jerked away from him satisfied with the result.

"Catch you next time, you stupid ho!" I laughed hysterically.

"What the fuck happened?" Quincy immediately met me at the walkway at the sight of wrestling with the store manager for possession of my arm.

"That ho, Takiesha, came at me while my back was turned to get my baby's stuff!" I shrieked.

He thanked the manager assuring him that he would be back without me to pick up the medication.

"The hell you will. That's my baby's shit!" I yelled.

Quincy ushered me off from making a further scene. He attempted to peel out the parking lot, nervous that the manager would change his mind and call the police after I continued my rant all the way to the car. Headed out the parking lot, I noticed Deborah sitting in a car that I didn't recognize.

Without a second thought I grabbed the tire rod he kept for protection on the passenger side and flew out of the moving car. Dashing over to the vehicle, I smashed the window and windshield on the driver side where she was sitting. She hollered bloody murder, begging for her life with her eyes.

Quincy ran up and seized the tire iron before I could make the second strike to bash her fucking dome in. Blood trickled from the nick in her forehead where the iron had caught her on the first swing.

"Are you out of your fucking mind?" His big ass was damn near wheezing after having to dash over.

"It ain't over you, old trifling bitch." Quincy struggled to carry me off.

I could hear her screaming into the phone at Stone about what I had done. That's about all she would do. That ho would be much too afraid of Stone's spot possibly being blown up to call the police, although I had no idea if one existed.

Securing the child locks, Quincy tossed me into the car and pulled off. Before we could get to the corner the calls and messages began to roll in from Stone. Those three motherfuckers had flames coming out my head.

Stone 5:15 p.m.: Bitch what in the fuck?!

Krissett 5:16 p.m.: Fuck all you motherfuckers you low down dirty bitch.!!!

Once by my momma's, I retreated to the bathroom to inspect my face. Grabbing some concealer I covered the spots where she had torn miniature pieces of my skin.

Underestimating Takiesha's boldness, I could promise it would be the very last time she caught me with my guard down. First, the ho tried to take my life and now she felt I was some fucking wimp. Calling in a favor from my cousin who was the police officer for her jurisdiction, he was out of the office on vacation. For now the sun would continue shining on her world.

We dropped off the medicine by Quameer's and headed to Hattie Mae's. At the door, there was a long brown box with a huge red bow. Examining the label it was addressed to me with no sender's name, but I knew that I hadn't ordered anything. Bringing it inside I found Hattie Mae was in her usual spot, her recliner with the TV on, but her eyes closed.

"Why is this always where I find you?" I laughed and kissed her on the cheek.

"Because it is the most comfortable place in my house." She opened her eyes. "What's that?" She inquired about the box in my hand.

"Something for me." I went into the kitchen, sitting the box on the table and getting a knife.

Because I love you so much... was the message on the card that rested on top of the white tissue paper.

I checked the back of the card for the sender, but no one wanted to take credit for the gift. Unfolding the wrapping, there were three dozen black roses bound together individually by the dozen, a tag sitting upright.

It is only right that I wish you well in the afterlife.

Always and Forever, Stone.

The bitch had transferred his negative energy this way, but I was about to give it back. My fingers were rapidly texting him when a call came in from Cionna. She must have had a person on psychic to tell her when my body tensed up and needed a release. Being Speedy Gonzales, I inadvertently hit the accept button in mid-stride of typing the message.

"Hello. Hello." I heard her voice through the speaker. I fumbled with the idea if I should sex this girl again, but hey no harm, no foul. We had an agreement that we weren't checking for anything and that made the shit even better.

"What's up?" I replied.

"You ok? I been calling for about a week now," she resentfully replied.

"Yeah, I'm cool. My son has been sick."

"Oh. Wanna meet me at my apartment in thirty minutes?" She offered me a method of stress relief. Tonight she had caught me in a willing spirit.

"See you there." I could feel the heat of her mouth on my clit, moisture formed in the tunnel as I hung up the phone.

Before leaving the kitchen, I pressed the button to send the draft message to Stone.

7:45 p.m. Thanks for the flowers. I'll be sure to set at least half to the side for your coffin.

Chapter 12

The following Tuesday I sat at the kitchen table surrounded by the ladies in my family, sharing a huge pot of cabbage, pot roast and cornbread that Hattie Mae had prepared. All of us looked forward to the late October annual holiday menu meeting. This year it had been pushed back to the first week in November due to the shooting death of my cousin a few days after I came back from Vegas.

The gathering gave us an evening of food, fun and women talk while discussing the dish we would bring for each holiday. Each of us would volunteer to cook something to be a good sport about it, but have a random excuse to back out at the last minute. The unspoken truth was that none of us dared try our hand at a dish Hattie Mae had already prepared on a previous occasion.

This year was the first time that I could honestly say I wasn't looking forward to the holidays. Shit was all over the place for me. Contrary to my belief, my arm was not healing correctly. It was probably my fault from busting windows, fighting and strangling people. Deborah's hateful behind had the lights and water to my house cut off. Based on the description of the person each office had given, she identified herself as my grandmother producing a fake death certificate to disconnect my service. Stone had sent two anonymous additional packages by Hattie Mae's, both containing dead animals body parts.

Even worse, without my pain pills life was becoming unbearable. The constant nausea, muscle aches and cold sweats were driving me nuts. It was too obvious to ask the doctor for more medication so I was gobbling down Hattie Mae's and buying a few off the street to make it from appointment to appointment. Tonight though I was going to do something that would make me feel much better.

After everyone left, Meishelle hung around to help clean up before we headed out to take care of business. Staking out Stone's whereabouts for weeks, it was time to give him my second taste of payback. We chilled in her newly upgraded E class Benz across the street from Deborah's home listening to *Ready for Whatever*. She had pulled the temporary plate off before we left the house and put a small piece of duct tape on the windshield so the VIN number couldn't be deciphered. The darkness would conceal the fact we were riding dirty as fuck.

An area for lower income families, Deborah's repulsive two story, Pepto Bismouth colored house stood out from the surrounding houses. High school children had more maturity than that old, petty bitch. She was having another room and connecting garage built next onto the house where the abandoned house Stone had purchased was.

"Man, this bitch need to hurry his ass on." I huffed getting hot in the damn black hoodie and gloves.

The car clock changed to two a.m. and Stone had yet to show up. Any other night that we had been staking out, he was inside by midnight. If it wouldn't have fucked up the plan I would have called Takiesha and asked why Stone wasn't laid up under her as she claimed.

"We have time. You got everything, huh?" Meishelle bobbed her head to the music.

"Yeah." My patience was growing shorter by the minute.

"Something is up with your brother. I have this feeling he is cheating on me, but I'm not 100%. I want to believe I am making something out of nothing." Meishelle blurted out of nowhere, turning down the radio.

"What gives you that idea?" I was taken aback.

Meishelle could only be referring to Janasia's antics. When Quincy told me Janasia was getting out of control with the calling I knew it would only be a matter of time before Meishelle became suspicious. A woman's intuition was real and proven later to be fact 99% of the time.

"He's getting calls that he claims is for work." She mimicked quotation marks. "His checks show some overtime, but the way he handles the calls, I sense it isn't no damn job."

"Well, if the checks match with the calls, just leave it alone for right now."

The voice of my conscious echoed disloyalty. This was the downside of having Meishelle as a best friend and sister-in-law. She had been more loyal than some of my blood, but the decision on who to uphold was never easy. The one thing that was certain was I never wanted to see my girl hurting. Quincy had better reel his bitch back in.

"True that." She appeared to place it into her file cabinet memory.

Sleep was heavy on my eyes when Stone finally pulled up at three a.m. He emerged from his truck, holding a black duffle bag in one hand and the other at waist height. Another confirmation for me that he was back in the game. Setting the alarm on his truck, he went inside to take a shower. No matter what time he got home, he had to take a shower. Giving him time to get settled and into the bathroom, I disarmed the alarm with my key chain.

"You ready?" I glanced over at Meishelle after she didn't respond within a few seconds.

She didn't answer, but instead held up her spray bottle in cheers to a successful mission. Cutting off the interior lights and leaving our car doors slightly cracked, we crept over to the vehicle with the liquid concoction I had mixed. Meishelle took Deborah's cars while I took Stone's. Unfortunately, time wasn't on my side to do both of their asses in by my lonesome.

Close upon the truck, I noticed Stone must have had it painted recently. The dark brown shade he had shown up with by Hattie Mae's was now money green. He had graciously helped me make the damage I was about to cause more obvious. Squeezing the trigger, my eyes twinkled watching the mist of industrial paint stripper and boric acid eradicate the hue from the vehicle. My senses heightened, I could hear the drops of paint from Stone and Deborah's car a few feet away splatter to the ground. A dull silver metal emerged in scattered spots on the truck.

With the white concrete stained with paint, I moved to the final stage of my plan. Opening the gas cap, I emptied the sparkling green antifreeze into the gas tank before resealing the cap. Able to get the full container in, I assumed his tank had to be on empty. The cars would definitely have to be stripped and painted, although I hoped more for the maximum possibility of the vehicles having to be replaced. With more time I would have drained the fuel and replaced it all with antifreeze to make sure his damn motor locked up. To leave my signature without writing my name, I scattered a few of the black rose petals on the ground in front of the car.

Meishelle had already finished and was waiting for me back at the car. With a small amount left, I sprayed Deborah's trunk with the word TRICK. Living off her children and grandchildren was her only means of support. Their fraudulent asses collected more money in social security

101

checks than a board room executive. Our fine American system at work. *Laugh at that, you old bitch.* Covering my mouth, I snickered like a bad school kid.

I jumped in the car and we held our doors open until we reached the corner before slamming them shut. While on our way to the airport, we stripped out of the clothes and trashed everything in a dumpster that sat on a random, pothole ridden street that was under construction. The minor revenge helped me sleep the soundest that I ever had.

Chapter 13

With time to kill before meeting Quameer, I pulled up at Home Depot on Veterans Boulevard. My morning had been off to a great start, especially for the middle of the week. I had awakened at 8:25 a.m. to Stone's discovery of my art work and to continue, I cruised the aisles to settle on a definite fuck over for my next victim, Takiesha. My momma and Hattie Mae would have a fit if they knew I had started driving again, but being chauffeured was getting on my damn nerves.

Most of the wooden cubbies that served as shelves that held something that seemed perfect: screwdriver, hammer, garden plows. Those would have probably killed her, but what I really wanted was for her to have to remain on the earth and suffer. It was the one regret I had begun to have about Nija. I could imagine that strangulation had to be painful, but only until she couldn't feel anymore. My point was that these hos would have to live in misery.

Two aisles over, the divider's held the perfect tool, a box cutter. Knowing a lady accessorizes, I picked up a pack of fresh razors, rope and duct tape. The minute my cousin provided me her address I was serving that bitch. Jovially swinging my shopping bags, my next destination was Bone Fish Grill.

"Hey there." Cionna walked up the parking row waving.

"Hey, what's going on?" I was surprised to see her way out here.

"Nothing much. The door put a hole in the wall that I needed to patch up."

"Man, that's messed up." My gut told me it wasn't a coincidence. She had passed up a Lowe's near her house.

"I can grab this and maybe we can head to lunch." She offered.

"Actually, I have a lunch date today. Maybe we can hook up some other time."

"Yeah, maybe so." She rolled her eyes and walked off.

So much for a fuck and run. I turned around to make sure she went into the store. Exiting the parking lot and doubling back in the other entrance, I saw her peep out the store before exiting empty handed. Our sexscapade had officially come to an end.

Grabbing a glass of Merlot, I sat at the bar waiting on Quameer to arrive. My mind wondered how Cionna knew where I was. *Was it Stone who had sent those dead animal parts to Hattie Mae?* Stone had put bullets in people, but he hated animals. Shit had my mind going a million miles together. In lieu of her actions today, it seemed I had been so busy stalking other people, I neglected to notice that I might be being watched myself.

"So, what's been happening with ya?" Quameer startled me from behind.

"Nothing much. You wanted to talk." I got up to get a table. The hostess wouldn't seat me until he arrived.

"I'm coolin.' I wanted us to talk about some things concerning Na'Siah."

I motioned for him to continue.

"Well, some things have changed on the home front," he began.

My eyebrow furrowed. He had better not be trying to ditch my baby because Mariah was pregnant. It would be news to my ears personally, but would crush Na'Siah. My baby wasn't a damn doll to be played with and then placed on a shelf.

"Na'Siah isn't in any danger, however, on the next court date I'll have my lawyer petition for us to have joint custody of Na'Siah. Maybe we can share six months out the year, a few days out the week or something like that. I'm sure we can work that out between us." He quickly eased my concerns.

I choked on my wine. I wanted to jump up and give him the biggest hug ever. Sole guardianship would have been better, but small progress was good.

Why so suddenly though?

"Quameer, while I am thrilled that we can come to a mutual decision about Na'Siah, I have to know why you've been so nice to me lately. I enjoy us not being at each other's throats, but it was so sudden." Curiosity was killing me, so I asked the looming question in my mind.

The Bank of Krissett was closed for business permanently. Before he bribed me, I would take my chances in court. He had been way too damn nice since the day he saw me come outside Hattie Mae's house with my arm in the sling.

"Krissett, I never hated you or no shit like that. I don't get off on us beefing or nothing. You been chill and so I been the same. Real talk, I know I did you wrong. It's about my son, period, and I don't need any money or whatever, because I know that's what you thinking." He wore a genuine expression.

Quameer's answer had me absolutely convinced that his kindness would come with a price. I could deceive or be deceived by the jackass that sat before me. Never having lived by the codes of being fake or phony, this situation called for an exception to my rule. The old wives' saying was that you caught more flies with honey than with vinegar, so I would see what I came up with.

"Alright then. That's what's up." I took a bite of the Bang Bang Shrimp. The perfectly seasoned, fried, velvety shrimp were the best under creation.

He agreed to give me Na'Siah for Thanksgiving and Christmas. Craig's parents were coming in town, so he agreed to bring his gifts to my mom's house. Mariah's trashy ass would be parading her ass around the house ruining my time of good cheer. Holidays were about family, not thots that wanted to be a part of it.

Na'Siah had already begun writing his Christmas shopping list based on commercials that came on TV. He darted into whatever room I was in at the time to make sure I knew it was a must have. Out of fairness, it was split down the middle based on the cost of each item. This year I had the tablet, bike and a few video games. Quameer took the notebook, travel DVD player and other video games. I had tried to explain to Na'Siah that a tablet and notebook did about the same thing, but of course he didn't see my logic.

"Can you please separate the check?" I reached into my purse to retrieve my credit card for the waiter to split the check.

"Nah. You good. Here you go." I snickered while Quameer handed the waiter his card. He was fronting like his money was long on her dime. Lunch on her low down, trifling ass sounded great to me though.

"I appreciate it." I thanked Quameer for his generosity.

"Don't mention it." Quameer signed the receipt. I took some cash out my purse to leave the tip.

He grabbed my bag and walked me to my car.

"Yo, last thing. Na'Siah mentioned that he hasn't been seeing Stone and your ring finger is empty now. I ain't going to press you, because you not going to tell me anyway, but if you having trouble with that nigga let me know. I need you here for Na'Siah." He winked at me. I knew damn well he wasn't going to do shit, because he had been a punk all his life, but the gesture was nice of him.

"I'm good, but thanks." I opened my car door and got in.

I smelled a damn rat named Quameer. There was no way he would be willing to give up partial custody of Na'Siah without a price. He would be giving up the child support, plus any extra he was collecting from me. Mariah worked at City Hall making roughly thirty thousand after taxes. She maintained all the household expenses, gas, cell phone and had just paid for my meal at Bone Fish Grill. I needed to find out what he had up his sleeve and quick.

Chapter 14

"I dressed myself for the party, momma." Na'Siah came into my room Saturday morning, wearing an orange, mismatched button down shirt, lime green jogging pants and multicolored Durant's on the wrong feet.

Screaming into my pillow, Na'Siah looked at me like I needed a strait jacket when I raised by head. After offers of Chuckie Cheese and Laser Tag on another day were rejected, it was apparent Na'Siah's heart was set on the birthday party. I gathered my thoughts before messaging Hollow about the party.

My little man was the total opposite of me, being extremely sociable. With Meishelle being childless and my only friend that lived in the city, he had little interaction with children outside of school. I could suck it up for a few hours for his sake. It was unfair for him to suffer due to my looney ass ways. While I waited for Hollows' reply, Na'Siah and I went over other possible clothing selections.

We left early enough for him to pick out a clearance bucket gift from the electronics department at Toys R Us. He tried to persuade me to get Madden '15 for himself and Xavier, but for a child who wasn't mine, I'd be damned if I would spend that amount of money. They were lucky we were showing up with anything.

At the curb of the parking lot, Na'Siah broke from my hand and ran to the Laser Tag. He struggled to pull the handle, but the door weighed more than him. The inside was crowded with kids of all ages running around freely from video games to interactive games. Na'Siah jumped up and down in anticipation at the sight of teenagers emerging from the Laser Tag rooms with their masks and gun drawers ready for more action.

"Hey, man. What's going on?" Hollow turned around and dapped him off in the celebration room.

"This is for Xavier." Na'Siah held up the Happy Birthday gift bag with blue tissue.

Hollow introduced Na'Siah to his children along with a few smaller kids closer to his age.

Meishelle and I took seats in the back, catching inquiring eyes from the women in the room. She had been gracious enough to meet me there and keep me company. Na'Siah shot out the room with the other children after tokens were equally disbursed among them. His smile was wider than the Pillsbury dough boy.

"Thanks for bringing Na'Siah." Hollow came over while Meishelle stepped out to take a call.

"No problem." I dryly replied.

"Don't mention it." He took a seat. "I won't push the subject anymore after this, but I'm asking you to at least consider a friendship between us. I can't front that I don't want you back in my life and understand that you have other stuff going on. I can respect that. There's nothing wrong though with allowing yourself to like me again. You did at one time, remember?" Scooping the cheese with his index finger, he dabbed it on the end of my nose.

Over the years he had definitely developed persistence.

"Yeah and that got me nothing, but heartache." I wiped my nose with a napkin, not wanting to make a scene at his son's birthday party.

"You just won't cut me a break." He chuckled. "Anyway, I'm giving a BBQ at the house tomorrow to end the weekend out. You and Na'Siah are welcome." He excused himself to speak with the party host.

Meishelle returned and our conversation continued where it had left us. She had dismissed her initial suspicions of Quincy's infidelity and they had decided to begin their own family. I was glad to hear her distrust had been eased, but they weren't out the clear. A woman like Janasia wasn't one who would just go away.

Meishelle grinned when Hollow returned requesting I assist with passing out ice cream to the kids after singing happy birthday. I swore that is what they paid the hostess to do. Making up an off the wall excuse, I declined his offer. Out of all these damn women giving me the side eye, I was sure another was willing to help.

"Go ahead and help the man." Meishelle whispered, jokingly nudging me on.

"The hell with that man. I did this just for my son." I shook my head.

"Then see what he has to offer him." She rubbed her fingers together symbolizing money. "It's time you give these niggas a taste of their own medicine. The opportunity at revenge don't come every day."

While Meishelle had been one of Hollow's biggest supporters in our younger days, she couldn't stand the ground that he walked on since our breakup. To hear her encourage me to use someone was a new one to me. She did have a valid point though.

Maybe it was time to see how worthwhile this friendship could be for me. Christmas was around the corner and Na'Siah had mounting expenses. My ideas at vengeance had included inflicting maximum pain, scaring or targeting what seemed to matter the most. Hollow had flown below the radar on my list thus far, because of the consistent antics of Stone, Deborah and Takiesha, but he wouldn't keep offering the chance for catch back through his friendship forever.

Revenge on Hollow seemed to be through his heart, so I might as well increase my pockets, too. After all, back in the day he used my naïveté to strip me of my virginity and then a piece of my life. He could never fully repay, but he could provide some restitution. Tomorrow would be the perfect way to begin.

At the conclusion of the party, Hollow stood at the door with Xavier, distributing the thank you bags to the kids in attendance. Na'Siah had a handful of items after his remaining tickets weren't enough for a prize, so my money filled in the rest.

"We will be there. Text me your address." I flashed him my pearly whites, accepting the bag and his earlier offer for the following day.

6:12 p.m.: Hello. My phone vibrated on the console.

Thinking it was Hollow, extra disgust set on my face when I realized the message was from Cionna.

It was the millionth time she had texted me since seeing her at Home Depot. Battling with my gut or the option to continue getting great head, I had cut off all communications after our coincidental run in at Home Depot.

Na'Siah went silent about ten minutes into the ride, forcing me to try and lug his heavy butt back into the garage. Descending from the garage, Stone's behind pulled up in the driveway. I would have to rethink the idea of the garage door being solely accessible from inside the house.

"Man, what is this?" He approached me with a brown, manila envelope as I proceeded up the driveway to the house.

I was in no mood to entertain asinine questions. It was apparent by the broken seal that he had seen what was in the package. The lawyer informed me last week he would be served by his grandmother with the divorce papers for our first court date in February.

Staring at him in remarkable disbelief, I went to walk around him, but he blocked me. Deborah's DNA definitely ran through his veins. Any other man with an inch of common sense would have been sailing above the heavens at the thought of getting rid of this situation and moving on with his life.

"Let me make this clear to you, Krissett, because you seem to not get it. The problem with women is that they act out of emotion. All the shit you doing means nothing to a nigga like me. I'm still standing strong. You can't truly hurt me. But this won't happen unless you ready to depart the face of the earth." He shoved the divorce papers into my purse flashing me the .9 millimeter in his waist to reinforce his seriousness.

"Move, so I can get inside with my son." I responded fearlessly, losing count of how many times he had made fruitless threats on my life. Seeing was believing.

Na'Siah stirring in my arms, finally interrupted the confrontation.

"Don't forgot what I said, ma. Those roses are cheaper than you think." Stone referenced the black roses he had sent by Hattie Mae's before kissing my cheek and walked away.

I watched him pull off from the porch before I unlocked the door and went into the house. Engaging the alarm, I picked up the house phone and went into my room closet so Na'Siah wouldn't hear me. I would show his ass about fear and fucking with me. No bitch intimidated me at this point in my life.

"911." The operator came on the line.

"Please help me." I shrieked interrupting her script. "My husband just hit and threatened to kill me. Please send someone." I shouted hysterically.

"Ma'am is he still there?" The operator earnestly sounded concerned.

"I'm not sure. I just ran inside and locked the door. I'm hovered in the closet with my son. Please come quick." My voice rattled with terror. Damn, I should have been an actress. This acting job was Grammy worthy.

Hanging up after she collected Stone's information, I cracked the door and stepped back to the far wall of the closet. Hurtling myself into the door, I stumbled in confusion seeing multiple stars from the impact. Ramming my right arm into the edge, my shoulder dislodged from its place. For extra measure I tore the skin on my forearm as if Stone's nails had done it while I tried to pull away.

The Soma had faintly taken effect on the pain in my arm. Eventually, satisfied that the swelling had gotten to the just the right point, I sat with an ice pack covering my eye and the bridge of my nose. I'm sure the police would have been suspicious if I had made no attempts to nurse the inflicted wounds.

It's about fucking time.

Typical to New Orleans two hours later the shadows of the circling blue lights in my driveway announced the arrival of the NOPD. I knew damn well the 911 operator's pledge of a quick response time was a hoax.

Show time.

I rose from the sofa and dropped a few of the Visine drops I found in the cabinet into my eyes. Standing behind the door, I awaited their knock.

"Who is it?" I questioned timidly.

At their response, I opened the door and allowed them inside. The two male officers took their report and assured me that they would put out a warrant for Stone's arrest. Informing me that his last known address in the database was mine, I nervously scribbled down Deborah's address for them. They offered to call the paramedics for my arm before leaving, but I told them that I would have my best friend come over to watch my son so that I did not scare him more.

"Ok, well lock up the doors, put on the alarm, if you have one, and call us immediately if he comes back." They instructed me before leaving the porch.

Seeing them out, I locked my door and went back into the closet to perform the agonizing task of snapping my arm back into place. Burying my head into a pillow I braced to the wall, my screams ricocheted off the walls. Soaking in warm water to minimize the resonating ache of my shoulder, my phone vibrated on the TV stand as I joined Na'Siah in the bed.

10:22 p.m.: 12 Avoyelles Pl, New Orleans, LA 70129.

The text from my cousin with Takiesha's address brought a smile to span the ocean across my face.

***

Opening my car door at Hollow's house, the smell of fresh meat on the grill made me think the situation might not be so bad at all. The compensation had better be worth my time.

Hollow's oldest son, Jai'Shon, showed us to the back yard where Hollow sat with his feet propped up on an elongated chair, Heineken in hand. With Thanksgiving a week away, the temperatures averaging in the upper fifties, we welcomed the heat coming off the BBQ pit.

"Hey!" Na'Siah announced our presence.

Hollow took his attention off the Saints game. He gave Na'Siah dap and embraced me in a tight hug. The tension in my body melted away into his powerful, muscular grip and I sunk into his arms.

No ma'am. This is for a purpose, I reminded myself breaking his lock.

Xavier had walked to Dollar General with his friends to buy paper products for us to eat. Na'Siah ran around outside while we sat around and talked. Hollow had a bunch of questions now that he was a single father. Some I had the answers to, but most I didn't. He was raising teenagers and I only had five years experience. The conversation dwindled into my marriage situation. I could tell by some of his questions Hattie Mae had turned to a partial informant on me. I played the damsel in distress role momentarily, pausing in between a few tears as if I was choked up with emotion about the whole situation.

"Man, I told you if you needed something to hit me. I got you." Hollow brushed his hand along my cheek.

"I can handle my own and even if I couldn't, I wouldn't have come to you. You have three kids to provide for." I sat back. Hollow's hand fell into my lap.

Hollow called Xavier, who had returned from the store to come and show Na'Siah to the bathroom. Na'Siah had been so involved in playing that he held it until the last minute, as usual. After going, he returned asking if he could go back inside to play the game with Xavier and to add a PlayStation 4 like it to his still ever growing Christmas list. Quameer and I had divided at least five extra items a piece since our meeting.

"Check this. What else does Na'Siah want for Christmas?"

"We good." I knew he would offer again.

"Confidence is sexy as fuck, but I'll get the information from the source then." Hollow waited until the food was ready and we sat around fixing plates at the table.

Na'Siah enthusiastically ran off the items that he could remember, asking for my assistance on the ones he couldn't. Finishing up our meal, the kids went back to their individual activities while I helped Hollow clean up the dishes. We took our time, distracted by the Sunday night game. I could never get enough of watching the Falcons get stomped.

"I'll get the bike and half of the video games. Can you handle the rest?" Hollow spoke up in between commercials.

"I told you we are good." I took the dish from his hand.

"My portion wasn't up for negotiating." He handed me the next dish to dry.

My insides were beaming. Hell stringing men for money could be an interesting side hustle.

Chapter 15

Hattie Mae's Thanksgiving tradition mandated morning church service followed by food preparation at my momma's house.

9:24 a.m.: Happy Thanksgiving to you and your family. Cionna's message was one among many, most of whom I didn't recognize the number.

10:50 a.m: Same to you!

Fresh out of service, I put my Christian-like qualities to use and returned her Happy Thanksgiving text, wishing her the same.

The men immediately retreated to the man cave for football, while the kids settled in the living room with cartoons. The cold front that had come through during the week rendered the overcast, high thirty degree weather too cold for them to be outside.

Once the other ladies had cooked their dish, under Hattie Mae's supervision, I grabbed Quincy for a quick backyard conversation. We had been playing hit or miss ever since I had received the doctor's clearance to drive. They were still monitoring my arm pretty closely, but needed to see what my true range of motion was before making any other treatment recommendations.

I suggested he quickly put a muzzle on his mistress, warning him that the pauper would come knocking for his payment soon. Meishelle was already onto him and Janasia wouldn't play seconds too much longer. All the years hadn't taught Janasia a damn thing. She seemed to think there was some badge of honor that came with taking someone else's man.

"Honestly, I fucked up. Period. There is no win. It's lose my wife, my freedom or both." Quincy hunched over, shaking his head.

I personally felt Quincy would be better taking his chances to trust Meishelle with his secret than letting this ho blackmail him.

"That will never go down, if I have anything to do with it." I pledged whatever it would take not only for his sake, but Meishelle's.

"I know you got personal beef with this chick, Krissett, but don't do it, sis. You letting these people destroy you more. The revenge won't heal shit."

Hattie Mae would always say it was time that healed all wounds. In my opinion, it only allowed time for infection to set in when compiled with constant repeats of heartache.

"Krissett, your phone is ringing." My momma held my phone out the patio doors.

Hollow called to make sure I would still meet him later at the house for Na'Siah's gifts. He had gotten the kids gifts out the way early to avoid Christmas shoppers. By the time I reached the phone he had hung up and I took a deep breath before calling him back. It had already been agreed after church that I would stop by his house. Doubts were setting in that I could tolerate someone for money.

Wrapping up with Hollow, Quincy and I chatted for a minute more about his Christmas gift to Hattie Mae. He needed me to purchase the building and renovate it with the last of the money he had stashed for Hattie Mae to open her own soul food restaurant. I was in total agreement with the great idea. It would encourage her to get out of her chair, be more active while doing something she loved, and most importantly continue taking her medicine. Since my last plea weeks before, she had been taking them on a regular schedule.

"Krissett, it's time to come in and begin to prepare plates. I know ya'll out here up to something, but it will have to wait." Hattie Mae laughed, closing the door.

After arranging the feast, Hattie Mae graced us with a beautiful prayer, reminding us of just how blessed we were to be in each other's company. We sat around the table sharing stories about my grandfather, who was said to be quite a character. I had little recollection of him, being only five or six when he died, but Quincy remembered well. Hattie Mae shook her head at his childlike spirit as my mom and aunts shared their memories of his attempts to tap dance like Sammy Davis and be a comedian like Richard Pryor. Many times, Hattie Mae would have to be the disciplinarian, because they could never take him seriously. Forty-six years of great times until death did them part.

"I can't wait to see that man again." Hattie Mae's head rolled back in laughter.

The men interrupted our good time, scattering like roaches at Craig's announcement that it was time for the next game. For the first year ever,

Hattie Mae made an exception allowing cell phones at the table so they could at least get the last games stats. Cleaning the children up, the women withdrew to the kitchen for light conversation and dish duty.

My cousins started leaving at sunset to take the final shift for the Black Friday sale. They wanted some item that was on Walmart's ten p.m. ad listing. Checking my phone, Hollow texted me that he and the kids had made it home, so I decided to leave behind them. Na'Siah decided he wanted to spend the night with my cousin's kids that my mom had agreed to keep.

My earlier friendliness to Cionna was a prime example of why it didn't pay to be nice to certain people. A simple return message had led to a chain of text messages that ranged from checking on me to spazzing out that she wasn't the one I wanted to fuck with.

I shook my head at the power of pussy, it could really make a motherfucker go insane and forget about any agreements in place. A few weeks ago an occasional fuck was alright with her.

Since Na'Siah was with my mother, it was the perfect night for me to visit Hollow and get his gifts. I sat in his driveway for a minute, grabbed my purse, hopped out and rung Hollow's doorbell.

"Where are the kids?" I walked in, Hollow tenderly kissed me on the cheek.

"In their rooms. They don't fool with me unless they hands out." He joked, invited me to have a seat.

I would hang around for a minute, so it wouldn't be too obvious. Retrieving a bottle of wine and two glasses from his wet bar, he poured glasses of Merlot.

"This is for you." He leaned over the arm of the sofa and handed me a sparkly red bag.

I thanked him as he called Jai'Shon and Xavier out their rooms to put Na'Siah's gifts in my car.

"I need to see your face tonight, so if you would please?" He ushered me to open the bag.

Playfully sighing like it would be such a hard task, I allowed more anticipation to build. The idea of an unexpected gift excited me.

The perfectly square navy blue box had a huge green bow securing it.

The two women that will always have a place in my heart, Krissett and Ketoyia. The card was handwritten in beautiful silver monogrammed font.

Inside the box a platinum heart with the diamond initials "K & K" in the middle rested on a miniature satin pillow.

"How did you know her name?" I gazed upon it, overwhelmed with emotion.

Without him present, I couldn't place his name on the birth certificate. Outside of those who attended the service, I never told anyone my baby girl's name.

"I had my ways. I didn't lie to you when I told you I have constantly thought about you." He brought my face to his.

The ice around my guarded center melted for a minute and streamed down my face.

Without thinking, I stood to my feet and embraced his neck firmly. Thank you just didn't seem to fit.

Hollow buried his head into my neck, locking our body together in his arms. Deeply inhaling his cologne, I melted into the tight embrace. Wrapped in his powerful grip gave me protection from the cruelty of the outside world. He delicately brushed his lips along my neckline in waves, the fine hairs on my back stood up from arousal.

"I'm sorry." He came up passionately sucking on my bottom lip.

Parting my mouth our tongues entangled fervently as he guided me to the bedroom. The nozzle to my outlet dribbled. Secured in one arm, he pinned me to the door while he searched for the handle. He tenderly laid me on the mattress, our exchange continuing, as he unbuttoned my blouse, running his finger over my stomach.

"Sssshhh." I wriggled as the sensuality of his touch inflamed me. He reintroduced himself to my body driving me to near delirium. Returning to the top, he traced my nipples before drawing them into his mouth. My tunnel seeped its juices onto the sheets. I tugged his shirt off wanting to feel his skin on mine. Our eyes communicated the lust that we felt as he came up to lift it over his head.

"I'm going to make this right." He continued treating each part of my body like an aphrodisiac.

Licking my inner thighs, he applied pressure to my canal which was almost ready to burst. Celestial flashes appeared from the heat he employed to the wetness that spilled over. I shook my head in denial that anything could feel so fucking good. Squishing sounds of saturation filled the room. Inserting two fingers, he rotated them wildly ricocheting against my walls.

"Fuck." I grabbed a pillow to bottle my howls of hysteria. Trying to control my orgasm, I pushed my body away from him.

"Uhh un." Hollow clasped me into a handstand position gorging on my sweet treat. His head maneuvered feverishly like a lion devouring fresh prey. Pushing back the hood of my clit, he directly focused on the shot that laid underneath. The swivel of his tongue mixed with the warmness of his mouth transformed the room to a magical land of enchantment.

"Got damn it!" My legs shook uncontrollably from the tension that screamed to be released. No longer able to hold on, I released my honey onto his tongue.

He affectionately kissed up my body, unfastening his pants. Already at attention, I spread my legs beckoning him to enter my furrow. He lapped up the sweet reward from earlier as I took the doggie style position.

"I want to look into your eyes." He turned me over onto my back. Teasing my canal he rubbed his rod in the pool of wetness from our foreplay. My pussy muscles yearned to constrict his dick inside of me. He eased the head in before gradually submerging himself into my lake. I fastened my legs behind his back in indian style fashion to ensure he went deep sea diving in me. He muttered as my pussy increasingly moistened from his titillating stabs. His body repeatedly rubbed against my pearl tongue. The poking of my canal and stimulation of my clit drove me insane.

"Mmhh." I groaned. He slowly stroked my insides, treasuring the moment. Grabbing my love handles, he freed himself to get control. Our eyes became fixated and we peered into the other's soul. I could see the genuine love he had for me. Caught in the moment I had given myself to him with no regrets. Bodies in perfect rhythm with the other, I lost

119

muscle control. He broke our stare, affectionately grazing his lips over every inch of my upper being.

"Fuck, Krissett!" My body was pulling at him.

No longer able to resist, he let go.

"Ahh!" He landed on top of me.

Sleepy, I pulled into my driveway to bring these gifts inside. Hollow had definitely matured in at least one area. Unlike the first time, the sex did everything but hurt. Only wanting to make one trip inside I hung up with him momentarily to grab my plates and the gifts the boys had loaded into the car.

Click.

With my hands weighed down to capacity, I fidgeted with the key in the lock and tired to locate the door handle of memory.

About time.

My eyes bulged out my sockets, suddenly my feet left the ground and someone's hand was covering my mouth. The packages fell to the floor as the assailant slammed the door shut. My heart hammered as I bucked wildly, kicking and screaming into the hand.

"You fuck over me, my grandmother, my shit and now you out here fucking bitches. You forgot who I am, huh?" Stone snarled like a mad man, hitting me across the face.

Roughly maneuvering me to my bedroom with his hand still over my mouth, he hacked the door off the hinge with his foot and threw me onto the bed. I leaped up to dash for the gun in my closet, but the punch across my face had me seeing stars.

The room spun as he ripped my skirt, pushing my thong to the side. Hearing his zipper, I tried again to make a mad getaway, but his elbow sent me back to the mattress.

"Move again, motherfucker." Trickles of spit landed in my face.

He rammed inside me vehemently, my pussy burning from his thrust. The dryness of my tunnel seemed to cause him to seethe more. He mumbled obscenities, continuing to inhumanely pulverizing me.

"Stone, please." I tried to wriggle. My arms pinned to the bed, I lay helplessly under his crushing weight, imploring him to stop.

"Shut the fuck up! I'm going to make you remember how this dick feel. You'll never look at another ho, for what I can give." He thrashed himself in and out harder, reprimanding me for my transgressions.

I stared at the ceiling wondering when he would be finished. He choked me and bit into my breast almost breaking the skin. The increasing pain became unbearable and my burrow went numb. He let out a loud grumble falling onto me as he reached his climax.

He lay there snoring in my ear, his dead weight pinned me to the bed. I was able to move just enough to breathe with him on top of me. He slept for about two hours before he got up again, hammering my pussy. His last nut he wanted in my mouth.

"You better act like this motherfucker is the best chocolate stick in the world." He threatened pulling the gun off his waistline and putting it to my temple.

This shit can't be real, I thought, horrified.

I obeyed his command opening my mouth. Allowing droplets of spit to trickle down his pole onto the shaft, his staff dissipated under the heat of my mouth, drifting my tongue over his head on the way up.

I sped up the motions, my neck wildly moving enough to cause whiplash. The roof of my mouth and tongue gave his head a deep tissue massage. He gripped the back of my ponytail. Tears came to my eyes from me gagging from his forceful thrusts to the back of my throat.

"Oh shit." He mumbled, the beginnings of his semen spilling into my mouth. I wriggled my tongue onto his spout to make sure that I got every drop.

I hurried my pace for him to cum. Flickering my tongue over his balls, I sucked each one in rotation. My hands worked overtime, his pole pulsated in satisfaction at my head game. I returned my attention to his rod, sloppily guzzling down ready for action.

"Fuck. Come on and give me that pussy." I stared up at him, licking his lips. I sunk my teeth into the rim of his head.

"Motherfucker!" He tried to jump up, but I had lock jawed onto it. The taste of his tearing flesh sent me into a frenzy. In rabid dog mode, saliva appeared to be foam as I shook my head, attempting to rip that bitch clean off his body. He dislodged me with a blow to the face that sent me flying into the dresser.

"Bitch, I should blow your fucking head off!" The tears in his eyes glowed.

"Fuck you, Stone! You lucky that bitch is still attached." I spat into the barrel of his gun.

He let off a shot off next to my ear that sent my ear ringing. My ear drum felt as if it had exploded. I remained quiet, picking myself up off the floor. The cylinder of the gun brushed against my face.

He hammered the butt of his gun into my jaw. I fell to the carpet, the crack of my jaw told me the bitch had been dislocated. My gun fell from my hand as I searched around on the carpet. He approached, hitting me with a vicious combo that had me seeing stars.

Paralyzed from the aching, I stayed in place. Pants around his ankles, I heard the water in the hallway bathroom running.

"Oh. Don't waste your time even calling the people. My fam is back at work and taking care of me." Stone had only caught his bid because his people was out on leave due to an on the job injury when he got busted. It was some kind of way his IT ass had figured out to wipe certain files out. He could only do it on warrants, charges pending prior to arrest or court appearances. By the time he came back, the charges had already made their way to court and couldn't magically vanish in the middle of the case. My cousin that was also on the force couldn't figure out the shit and since he rolled dirty on another level, he kept it under wraps.

The house eventually went silent as I heard the front door slam and his truck peel down the street.

Hours seemed to pass before I closed the door that Stone had left unlocked. He had apparently rummaged through his boxes which were shredded to pieces.

Running some bath water to soak in, I checked the mirror of the bathroom. Applying ice to the small bruise next to my eye and busted lip, I reclined in the water to soothe by soreness. Closing my eyes, I wondered should I really be thankful for this life.

Chapter 16

Cionna had magically vanished for about a week. She claimed a moment of insanity from her past provoked her to action. I made her feel cheap and she apologized for allowing her feelings to take her there. Little did she know I already knew she had been behind it. Stone had the audacity to forward me a picture the following morning that she had texted him of me and her lying naked in the bed the first night we were together. That's why I only fucked with a certain few. The right time, place and method was all I was waiting on to deal with that bitch. She would find out what my insanity looked like.

The ringing in my ears subsided after a few days and my jaw was seriously swollen, but not dislocated. A few days of additional rounds of concealer and foundation covered it nicely.

Two weeks before Christmas, I was about to make this holiday one that would be etched into Takiesha's memory for life.

I sat in the raggedy, non-licensed plated car rasping my black gloved hands on the steering wheel impatiently waiting for Takiesha to arrive. Quincy finally honored my pleas, securing the car from the old chop shop owner he did jobs for.

"Here is half now and we will go to get the other half when you're done, ok?" I handed my dope fiend assistant a small portion of the product that I took from Stone.

"Ok." He eagerly agreed, his yellow teeth illuminating the dark street.

"Do we need to go over the plan again?" I couldn't risk a fuck up.

"No. I got it." He shook his head confidently.

For a bitch who talked so much shit, one would think Takiesha lived in a better neighborhood. Stone put me in a three bedroom house in a nice neighborhood with a back yard. This ho was living in two bedroom home in an almost lifeless neighborhood. Only angels could hear her ass scream. Checking my watch, it was eleven, so I knew that Takiesha should be pulling up any minute. Trailing her moves for the past week, it took Takiesha approximately ten minutes to get home from her gas station job a few blocks away.

Knowing that she should arrive any minute, my assistant took his position ducking down on the side of the car.

Takiesha arrived an hour later than expected and got out grabbing a couple of bags. *Looks like someone planned to give gifts this season.* I chuckled. Moving at tasmanian devil speed, my helper aided her inside with use of a jagged blade. Securing the voice distorter under my ski-mask, I headed inside to join them.

I proceeded down the hallway, peeping in the other rooms to ensure they were clear. In the bedroom, I located my colleague standing at Takiesha's side with the knife still in place at her throat. Her whimpers and the wet stain in the crotch of her pants was a clear indication that she was scared shitless.

Her pissy ass was quiet as a church mouse.

I pointed my gun at her head and tossed the strip of rubber on the bed.

"Tie yourself off." He demanded.

"Please, don't kill me." Takiesha sobbed, finally able to muster up words.

"We won't take it, but you may wish we did." I promised. The white contacts gave me the appearance of Satan himself.

Snap!

The crackle of the rubber band around her arm immediately caused her vein to protrude.

Suddenly, my plans changed midstream. Laying eyes upon her, my slight sympathy to allow her minor sedation disappeared. This bitch needed to feel my wrath and ultimate pain.

Removing a clear plastic bag from my sweatshirt pocket I handed over the razor blade leaving the pre-filled syringe of cocaine untouched. My assistant's eyes questioned me. I shook my head to let him know there would be no tranquilizing agent.

"Here." He commanded.

"What is this for?" Her tears streamed heavier for her unknown fate.

"You're face." He replied.

"I'm not about to…" Takiesha's belligerence ceased at the click of the safety off the stolen .22.

Obedience or death were the only two options available. My preference was that she complied, but I had no problem with sending a bullet through her heart.

"Please, don't make me do this." She muttered one last plea. I gave my response by approaching the bed with my finger on the trigger.

"It's do or die, bitch." I handed down final judgement.

Her hands quivered in contemplation while my patience wore thin. The clip holding three bullets, I stepped forward pressing the barrel against the trigger. We would see if lady luck would be in her favor.

"Alright." She screamed at the click of the trigger.

Her life obviously more important to her than disfiguration. The empty chamber worked in her favor.

Grabbing a handkerchief that laid on the night stand, my assistant tied her mouth. He stepped up to help her begin the task. The cloth almost failed to trap the crippling shrieks as they slithered the double-edged, stainless steel blade against her skin together.

My eyes widened at the gruesome sight. Blood seeped from the incisions and dripped off her chin like droplets from melting icicles. Excitement raced through my veins as her pink and white tissue surfaced from under the layers of shedding skin. Passing out from the slaughtering pain, her hand jerked, severing a strip of face that fell onto her arm like the rind of an orange.

"Let's go." He held his hands over her body to avoid the blood dripping onto the carpet.

Collecting his gloves, they replaced the syringe in the plastic bag. He retreated to the living room appearing to have some last minute compassion for Takiesha. Now that she had felt every agonizing minute, there needed to be some sign to police that she might be delusional. Cocaine in her system would cause her to lose any creditability that she might have.

Using her hand, I pushed the plunger introducing the liquid poison into her opposite arm that was still tied off. Once all the contents had been extracted, I allowed the syringe to fall at her side of the bed.

Scooting my foot against the carpet to erase any shoe prints, I did an individual room check to make sure there was no evidence of foul play. Satisfied that no one could be implicated in her acts, I rushed to the door turning the lock on the knob behind me. Praying fully she would come through with all the blood loss in enough time to reach out for medical assistance.

My helper was in the car anxiously awaiting his second half of payment.

"How far do we have to go?" He returned to a fiend quickly at the thought of his second portion of payment.

Glancing at him, he greedily licked his chapped lips. I despised a gluttonous person. Driving a few blocks down, the street became aligned with secluded wooded areas. A short distance from the interstate ramp, I pulled over into deserted section.

"What's wrong?" He looked over at me.

"Nothing. This is where the other half is stashed." I reached for the flashlight under the seat.

"Why out there?" He fearfully glared over into the woods.

"I'm not stupid to ride with a heap load of that shit in stolen shit." I pulling the mask back down to conceal my identity.

"What's the mask for?" His suspicions were becoming heightened.

"Possible street cameras. I ain't taking any chances." I got out and stepped around to the passenger side.

Through the back windshield, I could see his head scanning the surroundings. The inner fiend voice egging him to trust me was battling his intuition that something was up.

"Hello, you want it or not?" I rasped on his window.

Someone was bound to eventually pass if his ass didn't come on. Then I would have to just shoot him through the car window.

"Forget it then. It's your high." I began to go back around the car.

"How far?" He slung the door open and got out. Addiction was clearly a motherfuckin' monkey to have on your back.

"About fifty feet." I flicked on my flashlight.

The sound of owls, crickets and leaves rustled under our feet signaled we had entered into uncivilized territory. My senses on one thousand, I occasionally pointed my flashlight toward the ground for any sight of rodents. Snakes and alligators were known to freely roam the dirt-filled swamp area.

"Over there." I pointed to a space approximately thirty feet ahead discerning it as the spot.

He hungrily searched for the dust that would take him to another world while I extracted the gun from my waistline.

"I don't see it." He called out, turning around to make sure I had given him the right directive.

"I know. There's nothing there." I bluntly stated once again with the .22 in my hand.

He should have trusted his gut with this one. Ordering him to get naked, two of the three bullets were for him. The other just in case Takiesha refused to cooperate at any point.

His pleas fell on deaf ears. He looked around for any method of escape, but his fate had been sealed. Taking his chances he tried a mad dash, but the barrel of my gun halted him. Death was his sole way out.

"I won't tell..." He must have thought complying with my request might spare his life.

Without hesitation I let a shot off. Condensation formed off the hot lead as it traveled, hitting him through his open mouth. His body would make some gators a real good treat.

Leave no witnesses. I stood over him and put one in his head just to make sure he was gone. I tucked the gun in my waist, emerging from behind the trees at the sight of no cars.

Continuing to my next stop, I stood on the concrete stairs of the lake staring at the rough and choppy water crash against them. The wind howled the secret that I was about to share with the tributary. Pitching knife, gun and razor I watched the gigantic upsurge swallow them whole.

Comfortable that they disappeared, I headed to take the vehicle back to the chop shop for disposal. In the garbage can they kept ablaze for certain car parts, I discarded of all the clothes I had worn. To make me have a bulkier frame I had added a few garments. Sliding through the back alley Quincy was waiting for me on the other side.

"Let's roll." I removed my face covering inside the car and put them into a metal lunch box. Quincy would dump them in the scrap yard.

Chapter 17

Meishelle and I got up bright and early Christmas Eve morning to finish the last grocery shopping for tomorrow. We needed to be by my momma's before dark so I was able to claim my stool right in front of the counter. I was guaranteed to be the taste tester to all my favorites Hattie Mae would prepare, namely the cake bowl. I was still a big kid wanting to scoop the mix out the bowl with my finger.

Following my routine for two weeks, the jury was still out on Takiesha's life. I had tried calling the hospitals, but a few wouldn't release any information regarding her patient status if she was there. Desperately, I resorted to the news for any information on whether Takiesha had lived or died.

Another hour wasted. I came up empty with word on her status.

I felt cold, droplets sliding down my face. Red beads of blood fell onto my beige carpet. Grabbing tissue from the bathroom, I threw my head back and counted to ten.

Having them frequently after losing Ketoyia, the doctor had diagnosed me with high blood pressure. He recommended counseling rather than medication to handle the grief. The psychiatrist ultimately concluded that I had mania.

I had to stop worrying about this bitch and everyone else.

Na'Siah had everything he had asked for plus more. Stone had a replacement tablet sent by Hattie Mae for the one damaged on Thanksgiving night. I threw it away, buying my own. There was no making up for what he had done.

Hollow texted me as we were sitting in the drive-thru of Popeyes getting chicken for us to snack on tonight. We had been getting in some time lately when it was worth my while, but sex had been off the table for us since Stone violated me.

4:08 p.m.: Hey Beautiful. I rolled my eyes. He had better be talking about coins or the conversation would end.

4:10 p.m.: What's up?

4:11 p.m.: Thinking about you. We are opening our gifts tonight at about 6:00 p.m. and I got something else for y'all. You passing through?

4:15 p.m.: I'll be there. Money was calling and I never disappointed with the voicemail.

***

No more than forty-five minutes after I laid down, Na'Siah came busting through the bedroom door, dragging me to the living room in anticipation of what awaited him.

Last night when I went to retrieve our additional Christmas gifts, Hollow wanted to cuddle after dropping those eight letters, I Love You, that most men were allergic to. Keeping the money in the forefront of my mind, I reciprocated the sentiment and hung around. I also had to admit there was a gleam of satisfaction in being the one fucking over his heart this go round.

Hattie Mae joined us first, followed by my momma, Craig, Quincy and Meishelle to shower him with more presents than he could play with in ten years.

By one o'clock the extended family came pouring through, including Quameer toting way more presents than what we had divided on the list. Na'Siah opened a few before Quameer took him back outside, along with a few of his cousins, to play football.

Mariah arrived about an hour later to ruin my day. The red capris, black halter top and gold six inch heels were beyond inappropriate for the occasion and weather, especially considering her grandparents were there.

"Would you all like a plate, drink, or something?" Hattie Mae extended her Southern hospitality.

"No, thank you, Mrs. Hattie Mae." Mariah sat next to her grandparents in the living room, who also declined.

Every holiday she strutted her unwanted ass across the door seal. I know she had to be miserable sitting on the sofa looking at my family interact. She had long ago stopped speaking to her mother and from what I heard by Quameer's mother, she was completely ostracized. His mother had a strong distaste for interracial relationships and no matter how hard Mariah tried, her ass remained white trash. For the most part, Quameer played with Na'Siah the entire day. Maybe this is what the lonely did at Christmas. Some company had to be better than none, I guess.

"Hey, love." Hollow announced himself and the kids, grazing my face gently with his lips.

An uncomfortable knot formed in my stomach at the display in front of my family. I caught a glimpse of my nosey ass cousins exchanging a look.

I doubted his claim that he came through just for a plate of food. Hattie Mae had sent me by him with plenty of plates last holiday. I'm sure he felt slighted after opening up his feelings to me last night and not being invited to my family's Christmas celebration.

In the midst of helping to get Hollow's plates together, the kids burst through the door, converting the dining room into a frenzied school cafeteria. Quameer went into the living room to talk to Mariah's grandparents while we got the kids out of the way first.

"Quameer!" I called out to him once the children had their plates.

Mariah accompanied him to the doorway, intensely eyeing our exchange. Her ass should be starving by now, but I would have been fucked if I fixed her a plate. One of the best gifts of the day would be to irritate her.

"What can I get for you?" I flirtatiously awaited his choice of selections.

"Macaroni, greens, turkey…" He pointed at items farther to the right of me.

Leaning over him, I allowed a perfect view of my cleavage through my draped blouse. I felt his gaze penetrating my perky, supple breasts.

"Mmmh." Mariah cleared her throat to break his hypnosis. "Get me a piece of ham, please." The bitch needed a tan for her flushed tone.

"Some ham, too, please." Quameer repeated the request.

I continued bending over the table to finish his plate, wishing Mariah to say one fucking word to me. I still had it on my mind for Na'Siah getting burned and her disrespect to my mother.

"Let me heat this up for you and get the potato salad." I caught a glimpse of the hard that had risen in his pants.

Mariah snatched the ham off the plate as I begin my usual task of cleaning up. My insides bubbled over with laughter. Giving her a break for now I would think of a way to murder her remaining feelings on the way out the door.

With my first bag of garbage in my hands, I headed to the can on the curb.

"What's up, Mrs. Robertson?" I wished I had a brick or anything that would bash his skull. I couldn't lie that Thanksgiving had shaken the shit out of me. Going into my house, I turned around at least ten times to make sure I did not let my guard down again.

I had to give it to Stone. He had way more balls than most niggas to show up at my momma's house and make a small scene. He conveniently wasn't home when the police went with the warrant to arrest him. New Orleans police definitely weren't known their follow up abilities either. If it wouldn't have brought the issue to Quincy's attention, I wouldn't hesitate to dial 911 and have him picked up.

The distance to the door seemed infinite. I briskly headed up the walkway trying to slam the door. He pushed back sending the door knob through the wall as the door crashed against it.

"My bad, mother-in-law. I'll have that repaired." He apologized to my momma and Hattie Mae who had come out the kitchen to see what had happened.

The expression of disgust on my mom's face displayed the mean tongue lashing she was holding back. She had been filled in on what landed me in the hospital and saw straight through the concealer following Thanksgiving. The old excuse of running into the door didn't cut it for her. She rolled her eyes mumbling to herself as she returned to the kitchen.

"I wanted to give your ass a gift and see lil' man on the holiday, but you always have to show your fucking ass." Stone clenched his teeth.

"Nah, we good." I refused looking him square in the eye. My momma was so scary she didn't allow any weapons in the house. After today it warranted some serious reconsideration.

"You can make this easy or hard on yourself." He wrung my arm like a dish towel. "If anybody step wrong because you wasting time, their blood is on your hands." He pulled me back to feel the weapon he was packing.

Understanding that the situation would only escalate more, I jerked away from him to get Na'Siah. I sure knew how to pick men. Something had to be wrong for me to consistently attract users, abusers and deficient thinking motherfuckers like Stone. I couldn't wait until after Christmas to tell my attorney, Ms. Populus, about this mess. Calling the people had proven to be a joke. They had yet to make good on any warrants. Shit, I had stalked Stone to fuck up his car and learned his patterns. You couldn't tell me the police were incapable of picking him up.

Na'Siah ran up thrilled to see Stone. Giving him dap, Stone handed over the Game Stop bag containing the Play Station 4. Na'Siah darted to the back, announcing what Stone had brought.

"Alright. You gave him the present now leave." I knew now it was only a matter of time before Quincy appeared.

"This one is yours." He handed me a long rectangular box.

"Ok." I snatched the box from his hand.

Hearing a commotion arising in the kitchen, I realized Na'Siah's announcement had reached the back of the house. I could hear my mom, Meishelle and Hattie Mae trying to reason with Quincy.

"Hey, babe. Everything good?" Hollow dodged all the uproar coming through the dining room.

Shit was about to get real. Hollow and Stone both had that same pride. Neither one of these niggas was going to back down.

"Babe?" Stone crooked his head to the side, stepping up close. "Apparently, this disrespectful nigga don't know who I am." He approached Hollow.

"I'm standing right here, nigga. You ain't got to address her. I know who you are. I just don't give a fuck about it." Hollow met Stone halfway.

Hattie Mae left Meishelle and my momma to tend to Quincy, noticing that Hollow had made it past them.

Stone remained unmoved. He and Hollow engaged in an old Western stare down.

"Gregory, out of respect for me, I'm going to please ask you to leave and not ruin the holiday. You and Krissett can discuss whatever needs to be by me this week. Pick any day you choose." She slid herself in between them.

"Only on the strength of you, Mrs. Hattie Mae, and I do mean only. I back down from no man." Stone never took his eyes off Hollow. "A discussion will definitely happen between me and my wife though and long before then." He nodded.

"Nothin' is guaranteed, bruh. If she want to talk, we'll see you. Give the day and time." Hollow gritted.

Hattie Mae grabbed Stone's arms in hers to walk him out. She disappeared for a while, I assume talking Stone down, but no one gave a fuck about him. Bitch had cheated on our whole relationship and was having a tantrum when the shoe was on the other foot. Fuck him!

"Come on." Hollow took my waist, guiding me into the kitchen.

Hollow had done good and proved usual for another purpose. Piss Stone the fuck off. Honestly, they could have killed each other and I would have shown up at neither funeral.

Mariah sat on the sofa smirking at the drama that had taken place. Out of respect, I bit my tongue. I wondered how much she would smile at a video of her man fucking me senseless. Coming to a phone near her soon.

Chapter 18

Tonight was the first night since Christmas Na'Siah and I had the house to ourselves. Hollow and the kids had made themselves temporary tenants since Christmas, with Stone's threats. Stone had been surprisingly quiet since Christmas, but he was on the way back. He didn't even answer Hattie Mae's call for us to meet at her house.

With Na'Siah fed and bathed, I packed his bag to head back by Quameer. He had called during the week to announce he and Mariah had made plans to take Na'Siah to Disneyworld for New Years. The thought of not seeing him to bring in another year slightly agitated me, but he had given me two holidays in a row.

To add to the irritation, my leave of absence officially came to an end tomorrow. Why my doctor signed for me to go back to work New Years' Eve, I couldn't understand.

Dropping Na'Siah off that morning, Quameer came outside dressed and ready to go. I got an extra tight hug and kiss from him, since I wouldn't be bringing in the New Year with him.

"Come back after you do that." I pleasantly invited, having finally thought of my plan to get him all to myself.

"Sure thing." Quameer put the bag I packed into the trunk and brought Na'Siah inside.

Hollow had actually given me the idea for how I could get Quameer alone. Exhibiting OCD symptoms, he was fixated on assembling Na'Siah's toys as if they were calling his name. I came home one evening to catch him pulling the drum set out the box to spread it among the other nuts, screws and bolts that had been laid out.

"Can you come hook up Na'Siah's drum set when you get back?" I made an excuse to get him alone.

"Yeah, I can take care of that for you." Quameer humoredly hesitated.

"Thank you." I rolled up my window. Na'Siah was in the door waving.

By the time I arrived to work my mood was gone to the left. The early morning traffic had me in a cranky mood stepping out the elevator to work. The lunch date I had planned with my defense attorney, Mrs.

Populus, probably wouldn't make it any better. Expecting the worse, I hoped for the best. She had already informed me that Takiesha was fully cooperating with the prosecution on my case. The District Attorney's office had opted to proceed with the second charge of manslaughter although Stone was not cooperating, because he felt the case was of a domestic nature.

In the midst of cleaning out e-mails, my boss knocked on the door notifying me that we would be having a working lunch today. I almost grabbed my purse and flipped him the deuces on the way out the door. It was my first day back to come at me with the bullshit of giving up my damn personal time.

Shooting my attorney an email to inform her of my unexpected change of plans, I asked if we could arrange something at my home later in the week.

Coming back later that evening she had replied that she was on vacation, but could meet with me the week after next. In the meantime she had reviewed the case file and recommended that I take anger management classes. She felt it might please the court to show that I was being proactive in getting a handle on my aggressive behavior. The income based classes took place on Tuesday and Thursday in Uptown New Orleans. Calling on my way home, the receptionist informed me they weren't scheduling anything until after the New Year.

Go figure.

Bringing in the New Year alone for the first time since I was a teenager felt strange. Between my cousin's funeral, the holidays and drama, my mind had been too occupied. Thinking back, I had been without my medication since shortly after Vegas. Everyone had invited me somewhere, but I opted to watch fireworks on the River. The strangers in the crowd brought more peace. Close to the stroke of midnight, Na'Siah called me to scream Happy New Year, rekindling the notion that he wasn't there with me.

Suddenly, I needed a drink. Joining the massive crowd on Bourbon Street, the rest became a blur and I woke up with some man who wasn't even my type next to me in a cheap motel. Jumping up, I dressed and ran away from the room confused as to what I had done and whether it had been consensual. It was time to make the call.

Bright and early that Wednesday morning, I phoned my psychologist and gynecologist office. Waking up with a perfect stranger had haunted me for the past two days and I desperately needed to be checked. Had he given me a communicable disease that required reporting I couldn't even give his name as a previous partner that I could have contracted the disease from. Regrettably, my psychologist was out of the office and the gynecologist's office was closed for the remainer of the week.

The receptionist at the psychologist office tried to scold me for running out of medication, citing I should be more responsible in managing my condition. Nastily. She obnoxiously offered me appointments with the other doctors available, but I didn't discuss my business with strangers. It had taken me long enough to get comfortable with her. After a fuck you, I disconnected the call in her face.

In an attempt to ease my mind, I headed to the door for therapy through retail outlets. Taking an hour ride, I found myself at the Gonzales Factory Outlet ready to blow some serious cash. It was a great thing that my income was in a high bracket. Over twenty bags of all sizes in hand from stores like Coach, Nike, Ralph Lauren Polo, I loaded the car and headed back to the house.

Restless and unable to sleep, I decided to spend the night by Hattie Mae's. She slept so much in the recliner during the day when she claimed her eyes were just closed, that they stayed open all night.

We spent the majority of the time having girl talk and planning for the restaurant over late night TV shows. Quincy had brought the building and paid for most of the renovations. He had surprised her Christmas morning when we were all gathered in the living room. She had signed me up for the weekend breakfast crew shift. The conversation ended over breakfast the following morning.

Chapter 19

Meishelle dropped me off after our night of skating. She wanted to ease the bombshell that she and Quincy were moving to Tennessee. Her company was opening another division and was promoting her to Director of her department.

"At least now you and Na'Siah will always have a vacation spot." She attempted to lighten to the situation.

"Uh huh." I replied.

It was bittersweet. She would be getting rid of the constant stress that her evil ass boss had her under, yet at the same time my best friend would be over five hundred miles away.

"So, you coming to dinner when I make the formal announcement? I'm going to have Hattie Mae cook my favorite meal."

"Of course. I wouldn't miss this reaction for the world." I chuckled, closing the car door. Meishelle or Quincy hadn't told my momma or anyone else yet.

"Call me." She hollered through the window.

In the morning. I had some plans for the evening.

"Want something to drink?" I offered Quameer while I poured myself a shot of Jamaican Rum.

He made it over about nine o'clock. Mariah had gone out with some friends and Na'Siah was by his mom's for the night.

The one hundred fifty proof alcohol burned a hole in my chest going down. It would help the second dose of pain pills I had taken to kick in. They had become my way of managing the mania without prescription drugs. I refused the numerous calls of my psychologist. I figured I had been handling my mania this long so I could continue by my lonesome.

"I'll take a hit of what you're having." He accepted the glass from my hand, sneaking a peek at the short fitted dress I had slipped into.

"You can set the drum set up in here." We headed to the living room from the kitchen.

I brought the bottles of liquor and some punch along to keep us company, as well. Quameer probably would have sexed me sober, but if I remembered correctly, he couldn't fight off anything drunk. To stall and allow for that to happen, I had already peeked into the box and removed one of the final tools needed to put everything together.

Over light conversation and rum punch, we discussed him working offshore and that meant he would have less time with Na'Siah than ever. That could have only meant his joint custody would include weekends and some holidays. There was no way that bitch would get her hands on my son alone.

By the seventh glass he was having trouble reading the instructions. *Lucky seven*. When he reached the part of the install that required the hidden tool, I took an extra fifteen minutes in the garage to find something comparable. He slightly stumbled over to me to retrieve it.

"It's getting a little hot in here." I rose off the sofa and slipped off my dress.

"Yeah it..." He stopped mid-sentence at the sight of my body in the lace bra and g-string set. Resuming my seat, I folded my legs on the coffee table.

I laughed as he tried to hold his focus, but the desire in his eyes said something different. His ass wanted me so bad.

Growing impatient with the obvious battle he was having to take the pussy, I brought another drink over to help him out.

"Last one for the night." I offered the glass to him, strategically placing my pussy in his face. He took it, downing it with no thought.

"So, now you going to take this shit or keep playing like you don't want it?" I candidly suggested. Enough was enough.

He gave his answer with a handful of my ass cheeks. Apparently his dick had begun doing the thinking.

"Shit!" I seethed at the stinging of his strong grip.

He towered over me once on his feet. His dick print rested perfectly on my ass as he nibbled on my ear.

"Stand your ass right here and arch your back." Quameer pinned me to the sofa.

His fingers found their position onto my pearl button, rotating over it in circular motions. Sinking his teeth savagely into my neck, he whiffed his tongue down my body all the way to the small of my back before reaching my ass cheeks. The vibration of him jingling my ass cheeks stimulated my pussy, causing it to bubble forth.

"Motherfucker!" I mumbled from the sweltering heat of his tongue glutinously indulging on my aphrodisiac. Practice had made his ass perfect when it came to eating pussy. My forehead braced the back of the sofa, securing my stance. He moaned enjoying the taste of my honey pot. Curling his fingers into a hook, he added to the pleasure inserting them in and out my tunnel. My cave clinched them, rejecting their wish to leave.

"Let them go!" He commanded with a stinging slap to my ass. I hissed from the pain and pleasure impulses that soared the length of me. His multitasking ability to brutishly fuck my tunnel, passionately sucking my love knob and wriggling his tongue over my pearl simultaneously was off the Richter scale. My knees quivered, locking up to grant him even more access.

"Shit, I'm about to cum!"

He tapped my engorged pressure box to tame it down while he came up momentarily for oxygen. Clinching my love handles, he guided me to a bedroom. I grabbed my phone from the end table. Shoving me onto the bed of the guest room, he yanked my legs forward and continued devouring me where he left off.

Lights, camera, action my video began. He was going so hard in my pussy he failed to notice the footage being recorded.

"Fuck, Quameer!"

His head shook violently back and forth, trying to extract the juices I fought to hold inside. My toes curled like the wicked witch of the West. Unable to hold back any longer, I rewarded his spectacular work by squirting my sprinkler system into his mouth. Quameer's ass had learned a few tricks in the past couple of years. My nerves ran rampant, causing convulsions throughout my body. Quameer smiled wickedly in satisfaction.

"Bring your ass here." He ordered ready for me to ride the wave.

Taking my position above him, I swiveled my hips to build anticipation. Midway in the air, Quameer almost knocked my ass over making a mad dash from the bathroom. It was a good thing that he wasn't in the middle of eating my shit when the moment caught him up.

"I have an extra toothbrush in the drawer for when you're done." I called out to him callously.

He answered by heaving more of his stomach's contents into the toilet.

At least I did get my video and a nut.

During my nightly bathroom trip, I discovered Quameer's naked ass still stretched out across my floor sleeping. I had laid in the guest room listening to his punk ass lose his soul in my bathroom for I don't know how long under the assumption he would see himself out at some point. It was clear I would have to take matters into my own hands. Retrieving a bucket from the garage I filled it with cold water in the tub before dousing it on him.

"What the fuck?" He jumped up with his dick hanging limply.

"That's what you were supposed to do, but didn't. It's time for you to roll up out of here," I calmly replied.

He brushed past me with an obviously bruised ego that he couldn't fulfill my expectations. While he got dressed I swallowed four Tylenol for the impeding headache that I now felt coming on. By the time I let him out, the lukewarm water I had used to take the pills had reared its ugly head and I found myself replacing him right on the bathroom floor. That damn Jamaican Rum wasn't my friend either.

Chapter 20

By week's end, we were having dinner at Hattie Mae's. Meishelle couldn't hold good news two minutes. I had taken a half day because Hattie Mae had an ophthalmologist appointment for her glaucoma. She flopped down in her recliner to catch her breath.

"Can you pick me up some Popeyes on the way back from the store?" Hattie Mae handed me a list of other items she needed to make dinner.

"Yes, ma'am." I looked over the sheet of paper. It had everything to make both Meishelle and Quincy's favorite meal. It was a pretty quick one of cabbage with turkey wings and cornbread.

"While you are out, I am going to take my pressure pill and go lay down for a little nap."

I stuck my chest out proud that she was following doctor's orders for a change.

Calling the gynecologist office again, they had reopened from the holiday, but were out to lunch. My pussy had developed an extra clear discharge in the last week. I was worried the unfamiliar person from the hotel had given me something.

Putting the groceries on the kitchen table, I went to check on Hattie Mae. Her back to me, she was sleeping soundly. She had a while before she would have to start dinner, so I tiptoed down the hallway back to the living room. When Dr. Oz came on, I knew it was time for her to get up. She must have run to the bathroom while I was out, because she hadn't been up once since I got back.

"Hattie Mae, it's time to get up and start dinner." I went into the kitchen to start getting everything together for her.

I called out again as I walked down the hall to her room. She found it hilarious to scare the shit out of me.

"You know I am not going anywhere. You never let me get peace since you started walking. Always calling out to me." She would tease. I would walk in to find her sitting up or laying on her side. The blinking always gave her away.

"We both already know you are not going anywhere." I laughed, walking towards her room.

"Hattie Mae," I called her again, but she still laid on her side. "Come on now. This really isn't funny."

I approached the bed. Leaning over her, I expected to find her eyes open, playing possum with me. Her eyes were closed and still. I nudged her slightly, but she didn't budge.

My heart rate accelerated and hands shook nervously. Something wasn't right.

"Hattie Mae, wake up!" I commanded, shaking her forcefully.

Her body rocked bath and forth. She was somewhat stiff and her lips had the beginning of a reddish, purple hue to them. Her chest was motionless. Pressing my index finger into her neck, she had no pulse.

"Please get up. This isn't funny. You said you weren't going anywhere!" I screamed, angry that she would not awake. Tears began clouding my vision.

Repeating my pleas rapidly, I squeezed my eyes tightly, praying that God would be merciful and grant this one request for me. I promised Him I would ask for nothing else, except on the behalf of Na'Siah. I gasped trying to take in the air that was being sucked out of the room. The beating of my heart ached and my chest threatened to cave in.

"*Please! Please*! You promised me!" I howled, my words became lodged in my throat. A part of my soul left my body. She couldn't leave me.

Realizing my prayers were falling on deaf ears, my anguish turned to rage. Why would God continue to do this to me? Hadn't I suffered enough in misery? Why were bad things continuing to happen to me?

I climbed into the bed wedging myself between her and the wall. She had been my lifeline, support, encouragement, my any and everything. Who would be there for me now?

The sheet stuck to my face, saturated from my tears. Hearing knocks on the door, I used her arms to cover me, remaining unmoved. Wrapped in her embrace, I sobbed until my wells had finally run dry.

This was all my damn fault. I should have checked on her when I first came in, instead of foolishly believing that she was just napping. Maybe then I could have saved her.

"Where's all the good food?" Quincy shouted from the kitchen.

"Mrs. Hattie Mae? Krissett?" Meishelle hovered over us instantly, noticing what was wrong. "Oh my God! Quincy, come here!" Meishelle shrieked.

I heard Quincy's heavy steps sprinting down the hall.

"Krissett, sweetie." I snatched my arm back as Meishelle reached out to touch me.

"Meishelle, call my momma and 911." Meishelle followed Quincy's directive.

"Sis, come on." Quincy kneeled onto the mattress and ripped me from Hattie Mae's arms.

"Quincy, let me go! *Let me go!*" I rebelliously kicked and screamed.

Placing me outside the door, he used his body to block the entrance. "Please, Quincy!" I landed several punches in his chest for refusing.

The police arrived before my mother, along with the paramedics. I could hear my mother's wails outside the windows from the porch. Craig brought us into my room while the coroner came to remove the body.

When the house was finally clear, Quincy came into the room, offering me a choice of where I wanted to stay, temporarily.

Nothing mattered anymore. Remaining nonresponsive, he made an executive decision that I would stay in the spare room at his house. I was convinced the whole deal was playing a cruel prank with my heart and I wasn't sure how much more I could bear.

My stomach felt queasy and I darted for the bathroom, losing my Popeyes and everything else in the toilet, until all my stomach contents had been emptied.

"Just let me be with her." I cried to the heavens to remove the pain.

Chapter 21

Instead of celebrating her birthday February 2nd we found ourselves laying Hattie Mae to rest on January 26th, exactly two months after she thanked God for our family being able to come together on Thanksgiving. Holidays would never, ever be the same. My spirit battled with attending the funeral, but after everything she had been through with me, paying my respects was mandatory.

The coroner found that Hattie Mae had died about two hours before I arrived at the house. Her taking the fluid pill was too little, too late. The swelling of her feet and hands had been just what I thought, fluid backing up on her. When she went to take a nap that day it suffocated her while she was sleeping.

As the days progressed, whimpers had become the strongest cries that I could muster. The bags under my eyes told the severe sleep deprivation and crying spells I had been through.

"I thought you might need some help." Meishelle was sitting on the bed when I emerged from the bathroom.

Shaking my head to decline, I eyeballed the suit she had pressed for today with contempt, blaming it for what was happening today.

Quameer had dropped Na'Siah off by my momma's to ride with us to the service. For the first time since I lost custody of Na'Siah I hadn't gotten him for visitation. Meishelle called to inform Quameer of what happened, since I had been mute since Hattie Mae passed and made arrangements for us to get him.

My little man looked so cute in his black three piece suit with vest and tie, along with his shiny black church shoes. He came to me and gave me a hug.

"Mommy, daddy says Sugar Momma went to live with the angels."

"Umm." I replied.

It was not my personal belief that people went to heaven when they died, but I did not want to confuse him. The Bible says for dust you are and to dust you shall return.

The funeral director stood outside awaiting us to offer condolences. My momma had opted for us to have a moment with Hattie Mae prior to the service. He promptly showed us to the service room, Hattie Mae's silhouette could be seen through the stained glass, double doors.

"You ready?" He glanced for our individual consent to proceed.

How do you prepare to lose a piece of yourself?

"Yes, sir." My mother spoke up, Craig massaging her shoulders.

Quincy stood between me and Meishelle, his arms around our shoulders. I squeezed Quincy's hand for strength.

"I got you, sis." He whispered in my ear, kissing my cheek.

I took a deep breath when the door swung open and I beheld her in the black, open coffin. I forgot how to walk mid-aisle and crashed to my knees.

My momma turned around to come back to me, but Meishelle took her to the front. Na'Siah still held onto my hand while Quincy and Craig attempted to lift my anchored weight off the floor. I bowed my head and shook it defiantly. I just couldn't do it.

"Mommy, please get up." The terror in Na'Siah's voice brought me back.

He already would have a hard enough time understanding what was going on, so to frighten him would only make it worse.

I can do this.

I rose and slid my feet to the front row.

From my seat, she seemed to be sleeping peacefully, captivating attention as she always had. My mother had picked out a lovely two piece coral suit with an off white pearl button down blouse. The complimenting veiled pill box hat that I had given her for Christmas adorned her head, hanging right above her eye.

I wore a blank expression while people stopped to offer condolences for our loss. The shaking hands, kisses and whispers became distorted and I entered into my own world. Losing Hattie Mae was the beginning of a tribulation for me.

"I'm here for you today and always." A gentle kiss on the check caught a falling tear unlocked from my eyes. I recognized Hollow's voice in my ear.

He grasped my hand. With no fight left, I permitted it to be, sensing his pain. Blinking through my drenched eyelashes to regain my sight I could see the devastation in his bloodshot red eyes. She'd been like a mother to him.

My momma arranged a true homegoing remembrance. Schtanya sat behind me, rubbing my shoulder, while the soloist's rendition of *A Child of the King* caused people to catch the spirit. Pastors who attended the funeral from various area churches reminisced about the woman who wore a smile that lit up the room. Her wisdom, happiness and good-heartedness was something a person encountered once in a lifetime.

Extending the final opportunity to view the body, mourners made their way to the front for one last glance of the most genuine soul to ever walk the face of the earth. I couldn't take anymore.

"My condolences to you and your nigga." Stone stood before me. Hollow's grip on my hand cut off my blood flow.

"Hey, Stone." Na'Siah's eyes lit up, unaware of the true situation.

"Hey, lil' man. What's good? I miss you." He glanced over in Na'Siah's direction.

"Say, dude, it ain't the time or place." Hollow warned him with a look of death. Meishelle placed her arm in front of Quincy to stop him from rising from his seat.

"I hear you, bruh. I'mma get at you for sure this time, Krissett." He laughed and walked off.

At the coffins appearance on the funeral home's steps, the Hot 8 brass band blew her favorite song, *We Are One* by Frankie Beverly & Maze. Funeral goers erupted into dancing, bucking and dipping to the music, waving the handkerchiefs imprinted with Hattie Mae's picture high in the air. My cousin did his tribute from the roof of the establishment.

The Lady Buck Jumpers, a well-known social and pleasure club of the city showed out in memory of one of their original Divas. They were infamous for killing the scene from head to toe. Displaying their "fancy footwork," they wafted feathered and rhinestone hand fans around the pall bearers, commanding attention to the woman of the hour. If she could have risen from the dead, Hattie Mae would have torn the cement of the streets right with them.

The sun's reflection off the shiny black coffin, I stood horrified at the idea I would never lay eyes on my Hattie Mae again. Glancing up at the open space in the cement wall, the preacher said the final few words while the casket sat on the mechanical lifter at Mount Olivet. She was being placed with my grandfather and Ketoyia. My hand refused to close around the stem of the white rose the funeral director distributed.

Watching the mourners return to their cars, for the second time a hard thump hit me in the chest, collapsing my heart and locking my wind pipe. Struggling to breathe, the universe became uncertain and strange.

Chapter 22

For the second time in less than eight months I woke up in a hospital bed. IV needle in my left arm, the small emergency room area contained my immediate family. Hollow's and Stone's unwanted behinds had shown up, as well.

"Good afternoon, Mrs. Robertson." An Indian doctor drew the curtain back and greeted me. She was accompanied by a younger resident.

"Miss Baptiste, please." I corrected her. My voice was raspy, not having spoken in a while.

Stone brushed his nose, chuckling at my refusal to acknowledge his name.

Requesting to discuss my information, I asked for only immediate family to remain. Stone left shooting me an evil facial expression that said he had a lot more he wanted to say. Hollow excused himself to pick up his kids.

The doctor told me everything I already knew. My blood work had come back normal and they wanted to keep me for observation. I was extremely dehydrated and a little malnourished. Being unable to hold anything down would do that to a person. Quincy had been prying my mouth open to intake liquids which my body outright rejected.

"It's important for you to take care of yourself, especially being pregnant." She continued reading off other tests she was ordering.

It couldn't be right!

"I'm sorry, doctor, you must be mistaken. I'm not pregnant." My results had apparently gotten switched with another room.

"Blood test don't typically lie, Ms. Baptiste. I'll call in an OB consult to confirm. Do you have any questions for me?"

I trusted the radiologists when he said my tubes were blocked. The entire time I had been with Stone no babies and now when my life was all over the place I was being "blessed."

Dumbfounded and speechless, I had no idea where to start. My head swarmed with a million questions, predominantly how could this happen. There had to be some mistake.

Quincy announced an emergency call from his job in the form of Janasia and had to leave. Meishelle sucked her teeth, obviously not falling for his alibi to get by Janasia. She had really gotten on my very last nerves.

The obstetrician came a few hours later with a fetal heart monitor and ultrasound machine in tow. Feeling my uterus, she estimated that I was approximately eight to ten weeks along.

"Oh my God!" Meishelle screamed, hugging my neck as the physician drew a circle around the image on the kumquat size egg growing inside of me.

"My baby having another baby." My momma sobbed happy tears at the strong heartbeat blaring from the fetal monitor.

The specialist removed her gloves, mentioning some concerns about my weight and encouraged me to seek a regular obstetrician immediately.

There was no doubt I was becoming a mommy, however the question remaining who was the daddy. Based upon the approximation, conception had to happen Thanksgiving night when I had two sexual partners, Hollow and Stone.

The evening lagged on into a sleepless night. I took a deep breath. Nothing in my life could be clear cut and fill me with happiness. A short time ago I had been devastated to find out that I lacked the ability to conceive. We bury Hattie Mae, my life is in all kind of confusion and I'm miraculously blessed with the gift of child. This baby would be another obstacle in my already complicated world.

Never understanding the concept of abortion as a teenager, I went forward with my pregnant. You reaped what you sowed. Giving up my virginity at a young age resulted in me becoming a teenage mother. Now it was the only solution my mind could think of. There was not a damn thing I had done to deserve the possibility of Stone being this child's father.

My baby was supposed to be born in a two parent household of love. Neither of which I had for Hollow or Stone. Had Stone's barbaric behind not raped me his DNA wouldn't have been in the fucking fertilization pool. A baby meant a lifelong connection and constant reminder of what we had been at one time, good and bad. The divorce proceedings would be extended to require separation for an entire year and introduce the messiness of family court to establish custody. Stone was too vindictive to keep my baby without some fight.

Undisputedly, a baby would bring Hollow the ultimate joy, giving him a chance to right a transgression from years before. His sole purpose was as a human ATM. Outside of that I could barely stomach his ass. Just like today at the funeral, I had let momentary emotions get me caught up over probably a cheap ass trinket. I hadn't worn the thing yet. It was exactly why I said at the beginning of my plan that I had to keep them in check. He didn't deserve second chances where I was concerned.

The point of my revenge was to get back at them and move past it not relive my demons on a daily basis. I would have to get with my doctor about medications. The doctor said that the baby was ok, but drug dependency couldn't be determined this early. Those Somas had been getting me by sometimes, getting me high enough to at least tune my surroundings out. Shit required major thought. I knew Hattie Mae and Ketoyia were probably looking down on me wondering what the hell was I thinking, but they had reached their eternal peace and left me to deal with this hell called earth all alone.

Chapter 23

Schtanya arranged to stay in town a few more days and came with Meishelle to pick me up from the hospital.

After a spoiled appetite at the Trolley Café, due to consistent talk about the baby, I went to work cleaning the house. Paying two hundred dollars for another lock, Quincy warned me about keeping the spare key hidden in the backyard. Stone graciously left the new wardrobe of Versace, True Religion and other brand designers scattered on the bed while I had been away.

It was definitely time to surrender and move. Time was of the essence, though, so I would settle for a luxury two bedroom condo or even apartment in a nice neighborhood. Making my selections, I typed the prospects that I spoke to agents about into a note on my phone. I would use the two days off from the office to check them out.

Checking the peephole when the bell rung, I had Schtanya and Meishelle park in the garage for our girls' slumber party. We stayed up half the morning pillow fighting, giggling and watching movies like teenage girls over a bowl of popcorn with hot sauce.

"So, what's the deal with you and Hollow? I saw him holding your hand at the funeral and then he came to the hospital." Meishelle nosily inquired.

"Not one damn thing." I emphasized my words.

"Wait, the hospital, too? Somebody trying to make their way back." Schtanya jested.

"Girl, bye. Allegiance is something unknown to a man." They said amen in unison to my comment.

I deviated from the original plan of sleeping on pallets on the floor of the living room by sinking into the soft sofa cushion. With the girls sleeping, Hattie Mae and I talked until I had to make a mad dash to the bathroom. Burying my head in the toilet bowl, I made a mental note that popcorn and hot sauce were off my list of pregnancy food.

Crossing the door frame, the loud shattering of a window startled me. Meishelle and Schtanya joined me in the hallway.

Scared shitless, we huddled in the hallway thinking of our next move. There was no sense in running outside, because we had no idea who or what was waiting for us.

"Call the police." Meishelle whispered to Schtanya who returned to the living room.

Deciding that three might overpower one, we walked down the hallway, throwing open each door to see what the deal was. In Na'Siah's room I grabbed his baseball bat ready to Hank Aaron the motherfucker vandalizing my damn house.

Counting to three, I flung open the door to my room, the knob crashing through the wall.

"You lock me out of my shit again? Are you out your fucking mind?" Stone was pushing Takiesha's feet through the window. The girl was stupid as the fuck.

He apparently must have endeavored to use his key in the lock. Meishelle and Schtanya had been snoring so damn loud, he probably would have gotten in had it been the same.

"You must be out your motherfucking mind!" I rushed over to the window, swinging the Louisville slugger. The bat grazed Takiesha's forehead. Her face hit the crease of the window busting her mouth.

Meishelle and Schtanya rushed over to restrain me from leaping out the window.

"Stone, why don't you take you and your trash away from here?" Meishelle barked.

"Bitch, who you calling trash?" Takiesha bucked back spitting blood to the ground.

By the streetlight, I got a firsthand view on my work. Shit was unreal. The brown foundation powder sunk into the multiple dents that stretched the length her forehead, cheeks and chin where stiches had obviously been used to fuse her skin back together. A naked eye wouldn't notice the smaller chips and notches that sat below her eyes and the remainder of her face, but a painter always knew the most intricate parts of her work.

"This is my shit here." Stone roared.

Bringing this ho to my house, breaking up in my shit and then want to talk reckless, notions of him having her all up and through this bitch, christening my fucking rooms while I had been mourning the loss of my grandmother, had me feeling some kinda way.

"You right, so let me give you your due share of it." I dropped the bat and scrambled through the closet.

Meishelle and Schtanya argued with Takiesha's trifling behind.

Going to my guns, they weren't where I had stashed them. God was working miracles every day for these two assholes. A bullet in the ass or a crack upside the head, they would feel my rage. Fuck calling the people, sure enough as Stone said my cousin verified the shit had disappeared. Shit was self-defense. They came through my motherfucking window.

Grabbing the bat off the carpet, I emerged onto the lawn with my attention directed at the common denominator, Stone. He immediately abandoned Takiesha to bolt for his truck. Aiming for his head, I pitched a brick that lined the flower bed, hitting him in the crease of his knee, causing it to buckle. I raced over to him and whacked him in the back.

"When I get up I'm going to fuck you up." He turned over to face me.

"You have to get up first." I brought the bat down bashing his knee caps. It would take him a moment to get to the truck without his legs.

One down, one to go.

Meishelle, Schtanya and Takiesha were still going back and forth like a bunch of cackling hens. I was the one that would have the last word in this dispute. Parting them like the Red Sea, I swung the bat clean across her mouth, dislocating her jaw.

"Say something else, bitch." I bashed her in the side.

Takiesha cowered against the house hollering bloody murder as I pummeled her body, screaming different obscenities at her.

Schtanya and Meishelle finally interceded when porch lights flickered on and the neighbors began surfacing in their robes to see the disturbance taking place.

"I wish I would have this motherfucking baby." I thundered, slamming the front door.

Meishelle picked up her phone to call Quincy about repairing the window. Instructing her to put it down I used an extra 2 by 4 that was in the backyard from the shed we built to patch up the window until morning.

"Krissett, I know you're upset, but please don't do it. Hattie Mae would be upset to even know you are thinking about it." Meishelle randomly blurted out. None of us could sleep after the incident that had taken place.

"Not now." I retorted. She was leaning on my last nerve.

"Me and Quincy would raise the baby. I'm begging you to think about the blessing you are about to destroy."

"Meishelle, allow me to actually live my motherfucking life for once with no opinions and sidebars about my damn decisions, ok?" My eyes shot her a warning not to say another word.

Schtanya shook her head, unable to comprehend my mindset. The room fell silent, the ladies visibly upset by my decision. I certainly didn't expect two happily married women to understand the plight of a scorned woman on the verge of divorce.

Politely cursing the police out for not showing up until ten o'clock in the morning, Schtanya and Meishelle prepared to leave. Neither had uttered a word to me since handing down my verdict on the baby. I had been through rougher times than this to concern myself with it.

Chapter 24

Driving to my realty appointments, I contacted the hospital to fax over the paperwork that would extend my FMLA. Using my remote access, I had business to take care of and the scheduled meetings wouldn't allow it. I narrowed down my choices to a condo in Slidell that would be ready in a couple of months. It would give us a chance to get acclimated and speak more about what to expect.

Arriving about one o'clock, Mrs. Populus got straight down to business.

"First things first. The preliminary trial has been pushed back again due to reassignment to another section of court. Our date is now mid-March I believe." She had left her appointment book at the office.

Clarifying some vague details in the report, she seemed to be optimistic about the case. She inquired if I had registered for the anger management classes. Totally slipping my mind, it shot back up to a top priority on the list. I promised her I would call tomorrow. She stressed the importance of making a good impression with this judge. He was one of the toughest when it came to sentences.

"So, what is the worst case scenario here?" I was glad she had brought up the subject.

"The charges you face are felonies, of course. Most times it holds a sentence for up to a year, probation and fines. The average sentence is about ten months. Your criminal history is not positive and judges have been known to change charges to ones that hold stiffer penalties. Hopefully, the history of mental illness and taking the anger management class can counter that." She gave me a small smile.

Recalling my Central Lockup experience, I wouldn't make it a day inside that place much less months. The idea of being away from Na'Siah, my family, my every action being controlled disturbed me.

Following up on the anger management, the classes actually started that night at seven o'clock, leaving me a few hours to spare. I changed into some sweats and submerged my feet into my spa tub. My psychologist's office called to confirm my appointment for Friday evening and Quincy called about our meeting with the contractor on tomorrow regarding the restaurant. He and Meishelle had temporarily postponed their move for a few months until we could get the restaurant property finished. We were considering turning the property into a small community kitchen to feed the homeless called Hattie Mae's. Since Hattie Mae had been so giving, I felt it would be a great way to honor her memory.

My momma made a surprise pop up with Chinese food for me and a letter Hattie Mae had written me from her will reading. I sat it down on the table, not ready to see what it said.

The event seemed so final. I couldn't bring myself to go. People sitting around to see what their come up would be when someone died. I already knew she had left me the money that she had hidden in her mattress and savings account. The amount didn't matter. I would trade it all to have her back.

"Everything will work out, Krissett. Momma promises." She stroked my hair. I already knew Meishelle had opened her damn mouth about what I told them, because normally she would just call.

I continued watching the CSI Marathon without a response. Blocking out anyone else's opinion, I had approximately two weeks to come to my own decision.

Using the lesser estimation of eight weeks I should be almost ten weeks now and by the time I saw my obstetrician, Dr. Bacchus, almost twelve. That was the soonest appointment that the office had. It would give me only another two weeks to go through the paperwork and process of the procedure. By fourteen weeks I would have to be induced and go through a small labor. It would dredge up too many memories of what I went through with Ketoyia and adoption would become my single option.

My momma and Craig had a dinner date with an upcoming NFL prospect he was hoping to manage. I got up myself to head Uptown for the courses.

"You make sure you call me for anything." She looked at me from the bottom of the porch.

"Yes, ma'am." I came out to the meet the UPS man.

I wasn't even sure that I wanted the contents of the package any-more. Tracking my Zulu Ball gown I knew it should arrive today. Mardi Gras was right around the corner. I had ordered the dress from China a little before Christmas to make sure they could make and ship it prior to the Chinese New Year. It always occurred during our Carnival season and I was adamant not to pay three hundred dollars on a dress.

Tossing the package into the car, I headed out to the session. Hollow texted me while I was sitting in traffic due to an accident. His ass had been tearing my shit up since the hospital. I wasn't in the mood for much conversation, but he could pay for these classes. Finding out he was at work and had the money, I took a quick detour to pass over for the cash.

The courses turned out to be a complete waste of money. It would have been better served paying my cell phone bill that Hollow was ringing off the hook. The instructor basically gave us packets to read over and complete about how to manage getting upset. Shit was no different than my psychologist encouraging me to write down my thoughts.

Linnea

Chapter 25

I lay across the bed to rest my eyes before getting something to eat, but was awakened by pounding on my door. Checking the clock it was 11:10 p.m. Going into the closet I had something hot for whoever's ass this was banging on my fucking door. It had taken me a week to locate the bitches after he hid them in the bottom of his watch drawer.

"Who the fuck it is?" I yelled.

The banging subsided the closer I got to the door.

"Mommy!" I heard Na'Siah's panicky voice through the window, crying and hollering my name on the porch. I hid the gun in the couch cushion and zoomed to the door.

Fidgeting with the door, my sweaty palms seemed to slip off the locks. Swinging open the door, Quameer fell to the floor on his side. He was bleeding and barely conscious. Na'Siah ran into me, immediately hugging my body.

"Help daddy, mommy!" He was hysterical.

I stiffened at the scene not sure what the hell was going on and why he would come to my house. Everything in me wanted to drag his ass onto the porch and shut the door, but Na'Siah's screams tugged at me to help. Bad as I wanted revenge, I couldn't look my baby in the eyes and explain if I allowed his father to die and did nothing.

"Na'Siah, go get mommy the phone." I instructed him trying to remain calm.

"Quameer!" I bent down to grab his arm.

My hands were covered in blood from his left arm that was slashed to shreds. He peered at me, his words inaudible.

Putting his arm back into his side, I noticed a wound to his back as well. Blood seeped from his mouth. Grabbing the arm that wasn't bleeding, I tried to drag him fully into the house, but his body was dead weight.

Na'Siah returned, handing me the phone and I quickly dialed 911, giving the dispatch my address and telephone number. Handing Na'Siah the phone, I resumed trying to get Quameer inside.

"I told you I would kill you and this bitch if I ever found out." Mariah advanced up the walkway with a ten inch chef knife in tow.

163

Her face was covered in Quameer's blood spatter. I hadn't managed to get Quameer far enough inside for me to slam the door.

"Go into your room and lock the door, Na'Siah." I commanded my baby. He didn't need to see this.

Sprinting to the sofa, the gun had slipped deeper between the cushions. My short arms struggled to reach the handle of the gun. Finally securing it I rushed back to the door. She had crossed the door seal, repeatedly raising the knife high above her head and coming down into Quameer's side. Quameer moaned, but didn't budge.

"Why do you keep taking everything from me? I hate you!" She screamed, her attention fixated on me.

There was no point in trying to reason with a woman who was on one. If I had to kill the bitch, I would make it as painful as possible. Her head would be the final shot.

Removing the safety, I let one off in her arm. The knife fell to the ground. She reached down to pick it up with her other arm. Letting off another shot, I hit her in the wrist of her other arm. It burst open, spilling flesh. Even treacherous people bled the same.

Rising to her feet, the ensuing bullets went through her foot and ankles.

"Freeze! Get on your knees!" The police demanded with guns drawn.

I dropped the gun at me feet and obeyed.

"I'm the one who called you." I blurted out. "They brought this mess to my house."

The police cuffed me and sat me on the sofa. I asked the female officer to check on Na'Siah in his room. She found him crying under the bed. EMS came to collect Quameer and Mariah. Unluckily, neither was dead.

After verifying that I was defending me and mine, they left me alone with my blood stained floor and foyer in a total disarray. I threw towels over the stains, deciding to deal with them tomorrow. I needed to see about my baby and relax my nerves which were on high alert.

"Will my daddy be ok?" The sadness in his dough eyes almost caused me to cry.

"I think so. Would you like to sleep with me tonight?" I offered.

"Yes." He nodded his head.

I washed both of us up and snuggled with my lil' man in the bed. I was desperate to know what had really happened between Quameer and Mariah, in addition to what in the world possessed him to come to my door. The only thing that came to mind was that I was the closest place for help. His family and the nearest hospital was downtown.

"I'm here. Everything is ok. Mommy has you." I rubbed his arms to soothe him to sleep.

Na'Siah remained home the following day. He had nightmares all night about the violent episode. By the time we awoke the next morning, the blood had become permanently embedded into the floor. It would have to be replaced.

Meishelle was still in her feelings, so staying with her and Quincy was out. I concluded my momma's house would be the better choice. She and Craig had taken a spur of the moment trip out of town until the weekend. The flooring guy said it would be at least a week for him to rip everything up and replace it. This condo in Slidell couldn't be ready fast enough. The haunted memories in this house were mounting.

The idea that I could handle all this shit alone reached the breaking point. I called the psychiatrist's office for a same day emergency appointment. The receptionist immediately checked her attitude hearing my brusque demeanor and accommodated my request.

Bringing Na'Siah with me, I took my seat in the waiting area, ready to tell the doctor everything on my mind. Composing a list of the most important: Hattie Mae, my medication, and the pregnancy. I only had an hour and needed every minute. Stone and Takiesha's name had made the list initially then I changed my mind. Sharing my thoughts with her might incriminate me later. Attorneys could find a way around client and patient privilege.

Dr. Bourgeois called my name to step into her office. The receptionist offered to keep an eye on Na'Siah while I spoke to the doctor. I ensured he was ok with it.

"I'm a big boy, mommy." He took his tablet from me.

Spilling out all the bullet points on my list, Dr. Bourgeois paid close attention and gauged my feelings on the issue before dropping the bad news.

"Ok, we have a decision to make then regarding managing your condition." She closed my medical file.

"What do you mean?" I asked with a raised brow. I had never considered doing research on my medication.

"There are some present and future effects to consider if you decide to keep the baby."

She explained that Lithium held risks, such as congenital malformations and low birth weight in the baby. In addition, there were greater chances of a mania episode that could negativity impact me and the baby. I told her I was willing to take the chance, but she handed me a small pamphlet of information to read with instructions to call her within a week with my decision. Defeated, I left the office, head hung low.

Chapter 26

For the first two weeks it was really difficult managing Na'Siah and being pregnant. I still hadn't been able to return to work. Calling Dr. Bourgeois with my decision to continue Lithium, she opted to try an alternative form of therapy and medication. Encouraging me to see her at least twice monthly, she prescribed some medication that I could never remember the name of. I knew it did absolutely nothing for me.

Na'Siah continued to have nightmares and his behavior had drastically changed. His usual sweet personality was full of screaming, tantrums and battles. After a week home with me, I brought him back to school, thinking the interaction with kids would be good. Contrary to my beliefs, the teacher called taking notice of his increased aggression toward the children and extreme defiance when given instructions. I asked him to talk to me, but he just froze up, I think out of fear for Quameer and Mariah.

The fatigue and stress of constantly having to run to school had me on the verge of a depression stage. Only reason I hadn't slit my wrist or swallowed a whole bottle of pills was I didn't want to traumatize Na'Siah more than he already was. Dr. Bourgeois suggested that I arrange an appointment with a social worker. Maybe through drawing pictures they could get the root cause of what really happened.

On top of all else, it was time for my first divorce hearing.

"I'll make you a deal. If you can behave today and think of mommy when you get mad, I will bring you to Chuckie Cheese this evening. Deal?" I knew I shouldn't bribe him, but I had no idea how long I would be at court today.

My momma, Meishelle or Quincy would have no problem leaving to go get him, but I had been hell bent on doing it alone.

Hattie Mae's demise had taught me to become really independent, never knowing when someone might be called home.

"Yes." He accepted. We sealed the agreement intertwining our pinkies.

Standing on the steps of Civil District Court, I had been waiting to see the old rusty building on Loyola Avenue for about five months now. I etched this day, February 25th, in my mind. Hopefully, the judge would set a date thirty days from now in which I would no longer be Mrs. Krissett Robertson.

Soaking up some sun, my divorce lawyer called to tell me she was running behind a few minutes. I checked my voicemail to see what the realtor had to say about the condo in Slidell. She had called on my way to drop Na'Siah at school. For an early morning laugh, I listened to the message Stone had left last week.

"I let you live because of several fuck ups on my part. Now you playing with my life, fucking up my work. *Game over!*" He came through the speaker blowing.

I smirked figuring he had discovered his dope was short. He must have counted it before whatever he had to do, because had he been in the process of a deal, shit would have popped off, no questions asked. I cleared it and kept it pushing. I hadn't done anything yet.

A short while later I saw Ms. White dashing across Poydras toward the building. She paused, noticing the pudge in my belly. On my third child, my stomach poked out sooner than expected. I thought my clothing selection had concealed it well, but I think the baggier shirt made it more obvious.

"It's not his." It wasn't a full lie since I had no clue who the baby's father was.

"Ok." She took a deep breathe. "This should be pretty quick. The judge should divide any property and set a date for the divorce to be finalized since there are no kids involved. He has filed for the home." She quickly summed up what to expect.

"He can have it." The realtor indicated the condo would be ready in thirty days or less.

"Then this should be even quicker since there are no real assets to divide."

"Great." Today could continue to be one of my better days.

Going into the building, I hoped the rather long line of people was a last second rush of the jury duty pool. After weeks of waiting for the doctor's appointment to come, I didn't want to miss it. Getting off the elevators, my optimism deflated at the sight of the wooden benches jammed packed with people. Last time I came it had been a damn ghost town.

Checking in, my attorney informed me we had about an hour and a half wait. We elected to head across the street for breakfast, the one meal this baby wouldn't let me skip.

Enthralled at the thought of food I attempted to board the elevator without paying attention, bumping into Stone on his way out. He wore a smirk on his face with his ugly ass grandmother by his side. I ignored both of their silly looking asses and got into the elevator.

We timed court practically to the minute. Approaching the court section a male I assumed to be Stone's attorney requested to speak with my attorney, but the clerk called us for the case.

The clerk handed her the court file and she briefly glanced over the information after the other formalities had been completed.

The judge's summation of the case sounded acceptable. I had considered seeking alimony, but I wouldn't get anything since I brought in the majority of the substantiated income.

"Your Honor, my client is willing to relinquish the home to Mr. Robertson as he had originally requested." My attorney rose to her feet.

"Actually, Your Honor, it has been brought to my client's attention that Mrs. Robertson is pregnant. The defendant believes that he is the father and will seek joint custody of the child through family court." Stone's attorney rose to his feet.

I held my head low, massaging my forehead. This motherfucker refused to leave well enough alone. He must have heard my announcement as I slammed the door the night I came home from the hospital.

"Your Honor, my client is one hundred percent certain that the Defendant is not the father," Ms. White rebutted.

Stone's attorney leaned over toward him and they had a brief discussion before he responded. He rose to his feet requesting that the divorce not be granted until paternity could be established and the judge sided with them.

I sat dumbfounded by what just happened. Most niggas would have been ecstatic that they had beat the responsibility of a child, but not his bitch ass. From what I could tell he was back on the streets, so why waste time playing these games when two of his retirement options was a life sentence or death.

"You ready?" My lawyer gathered her things. Stone's attorney told him something and then walked out the courtroom.

In the hallway she discussed what to expect. Inhaling, to my dismay Stone and Deborah waited for me at the end of the elongated hall, probably to rub the slight victory in my face. The baby pushing on my bladder, I debated whether I could hold it until I got home, but that wasn't going to work. My attorney checked her watch. She was running late for a lunch engagement with another client.

"Perjury could land you in jail. You know damn well that's my baby." He spoke as I brushed past him pressing the elevator button.

Hopefully, the results would show favor to me and speak differently.

"It doesn't matter. You all should still be married by the time she goes in. The baby automatically gets your last name and is assumed to be yours by the court. Results wouldn't mean shit." Deborah chimed in behind me.

"Sad that a woman who gave birth to two children won't have any of them. I'll make sure her ass doesn't see this one unless I can come back home." He hissed into my neck causing the hairs on my neck to stand up.

Ignore him. A court building isn't the place, I repeatedly reminded myself.

"Nah. Let her watch your woman, Takiesha, raise the baby like she watching that white ho do."

That remark I wasn't about to let go. Turning around, I hocked spit into her face.

"I'll kill this baby myself before I let you bitches have it." I furiously pushed past them, knocking Deborah on her ass.

I could hear Deborah crying out to Stone about letting me get away with handling her like that.

Holding back tears, heading for the steps would be good exercise for my expanding thighs. I swore that woman just could not help herself. Every time I saw her some negative shit was coming out her mouth toward me. She had to be the world's oldest petty bitch alive. I had something that might humble that ho.

Chapter 27

My momma had a fit that we arrived fifteen minutes before my scheduled appointment. She and Craig believed anything less than thirty minutes prior made someone late for anything. Dr. Marcel Bacchus, my gynecologist and temporary obstetrician had been so wonderful with Na'Siah I stuck with him after. He gave me the real deal upfront, cutting no corners and was known for successful deliveries, if one was to take place.

I fidgeted impatiently waiting for my turn playing Candy Crush until the nurse took my weight and a urine sample, before directing us to the room. By the waiting room it was clear why I had to wait three weeks for a second of his time. If I went through with it, my abortion certainly wouldn't hurt the population.

Examining my uterus, he determined I was eleven weeks and my due date of August 30th. That gave me an extra week to decide on the abortion. He did a preliminary ultrasound to ensure everything was ok, circling the pea-sized ball.

Dr. Bacchus went through his usual pregnancy talk about diet, exercise and keeping active in general. Expressing my concern about the discharge and nosebleeds, he told me those were most likely caused by the pregnancy, but he took a vaginal culture for testing. He wanted me to gain a slight bit of weight since I was down twenty-five pounds from last year and see him next month to monitor my progress. The nurse handed me the order for some blood work, my prenatal vitamins and iron pill prescription before he excused himself from the room.

He about faced at the door and said, "Remember, all weight…"

"Isn't baby weight." I finished the thought I remember he told me when I had Na'Siah.

Quameer's mother called while I was in the doctor's office. He had finally agreed to let Na'Siah come to see him. Mariah had really done him in, inflicting life threatening injuries. We had tried to call, but since his financial well-being depended on Mariah, the phone had been disconnected. The news was better than Chuckie Cheese to Na'Siah when I picked him up from school. He had been constantly asking about him and tomorrow I was going back to work, leaving minimal time on weeknights.

Na'Siah immediately bombarded him with a million and one questions that Quameer wasn't ready to answer. Quameer's mom stepped in and offered to take him for a snack to allow us time to talk. He invited me to have a seat next to the bed.

"You looking a little round there." Quameer motioned at my stomach. This shirt wasn't an option anymore.

"So, how you feeling? What's going on?" I pointed the conversation into the right direction.

"Docs say they can't tell me much yet. The knife damaged my spinal cord, so they aren't sure if I'll walk and my kidneys were badly damaged." His voice was laced with pain.

I felt a strong sense of satisfaction in my gut. We could have been a family doing our own thing, but instead he wanted those other bitches.

"What happened between y'all that brought you to my door?" I wondered why he never called 9-1-1 instead of showing up on my doorstep.

Mariah had been suspicious we were fucking around since the day he brought Na'Siah's bag inside. Convinced after he called me when Na'Siah was burned at the hospital, she took his phone. It was designed to keep us from communicating and force him to remain inside during the week. The house phone became his only communication.

She had given it back only when he began to get job interviews. When she caught him on Christmas checking me out, it began all over again. The night we hooked up, he had no idea that I had used the phone to make a video.

Oh shit! I had grabbed the wrong damn phone off the sofa. His must have fell off the clip in the middle of us doing our thing.

While he was in the shower, she decided to go through the phone.

Seek and you shall find. She discovered some random chick sending him photos of her pussy before coming across the video. She swore that it was a fake Facebook page I had created. In actuality, he didn't know the woman on the account. He had deleted the texts and phone calls from the chick he was dealing with.

In the midst of the heated argument when he came, she confessed Na'Siah's burns weren't accidental. They were punishment for my hoeish ways. Sensing he was out with me, when in actuality it was the other woman, she tied my baby to a chair and poured the scolding hot water on him.

He lost control and started tossing her ass around the room, trying to break every bone in her body. Na'Siah came in screaming for them to stop. He packed Na'Siah a bag to bring him to me and attempted to leave. At the bottom of the stairs she went to stab Na'Siah with the knife and he blocked it with his arm. She came down again, hitting him in the back. This bitch was on borrowed time for real now.

"Basically, my lil' man is home with you where he belongs. Don't bring him here anymore. My momma leaves her cell phone, so he can call that number to talk to me." He had tears in his eyes.

"Are you exiting back out of his life again? Because if so, do it now. He don't deserve it, Quameer." As much as I couldn't stand him, Na'Siah was going through enough adjustments to have his little world shaken up again.

"Nah, I'm not. Just need some time to get my head around everything. Na'Siah looking at me like this ain't helping shit, but I love my dude, Krissett. Can't cut him off. " He was speaking from his heart.

"Ok, then." I took the number and waited for his mother to bring Na'Siah back.

He gave Quameer a big hug, dap and we left. His momma asked me if she could come get him on some weekends and I was fine with that.

Picking up McDonald's, we headed home for our routine of home after school, bath and bed. He gobbled down his food in the car, anxious to get the toy I had stashed in my purse.

"Look, mommy, another box." He sat his Happy Meal bag on the swing in exchange for the package.

"Come on. Let's put them with the rest." I slowed my steps, exhausted with Stone's newfound way to aggravate.

Almost every other day I received a shipment of something for the baby.

I want my seed to be raised with their mom and dad. It was a cold day in hell before that happened.

173

When they first started coming, I refused the package, but he reordered them once the refunds were reflected in his account. It was too much wasted energy, so I just kept them tucked in a closet as possible gifts if I was invited to a baby shower.

At some point this week I would be calling to arrange my consultation for the abortion and placing an order for some bullet ants. Deborah had something coming for her.

Chapter 28

My boss came by to see if I had made the decision of what staff members I would have to let go. The company had cut our budget due to a new energy tax increase that was denied in the recent election. My employees were all exceptional, so I had yet to determine how to even narrow the pool down. Years on the job was my first idea, but Human Resources advised that they were all on the list. I needed to select additional employees outside of them.

11:58 a.m.: Guess who needs three tickets for the Zulu Ball this year.

Schtanya hadn't been back for Mardi Gras since she had moved away to attend college.

12:00 p.m.: You coming down for Mardi Gras?

Texting back and forth, I discovered it was business related, which explained everything. She or Meishelle still hadn't really spoken to me much since the abortion conversation.

Schtanya had been thinking about expanding to the entertainment industry and had someone who was possibly interested in retaining her. They were from out east so knew nothing about Fat Tuesday, as Mardi Gras was also known.

I shot Meishelle a message to contact Schtanya about the seat availability. I knew no more than six of us sat at the ten seat table on years when my mom and Craig wanted to attend. They probably would this year, because Pattie Labelle was the entertainment.

Taking a break from the elimination process, I phoned the abortion clinic on General Pershing Street for their next available appointment. Scheduling for the end of the week, only seventy-two more hours and I could call my attorney to tell her the abortion was complete. I requested Thursday off to attend the required twenty-four hour physician consultation prior to the procedure on Friday morning. Mrs. Williams had already asked for Na'Siah to spend the weekend, so it would give me time to two days of rest.

I quickly gathered my things at the conclusion of the last minute meeting request and made a beeline for my car. All I could think about was a nap to get me through the evening. The red button to indicate voicemails blinked on my phone, but I dismissed them until later.

"Mrs. Robertson." Exiting through the lobby, I spun around to correct the receptionist calling my name from the desk.

Hollow was directly in my face. I wanted to run out of the building, but it was no use. His eyes roamed my frame, focusing on the protruding belly that showed through my tight, pencil skirt.

"I came to surprise you with lunch, but looks like you have one for me." Hollow put his hand on the bulge.

If this wasn't my place of employment I would have slapped his hand off me. I had been limiting our contact to text messages since I picked up the money for the anger management class. My wish was that I could duck him until after the abortion. What he didn't know couldn't hurt him.

With the cat out the bag, I figured we might as well have a sit down about it. There was no stopping the plans that had been finalized. The prying ass receptionist had taken off her headphones to hear every word of our conversation. I'd be damned if my business would be the talk of the break room.

Grabbing his hand, I escorted him to the elevator for lunch downstairs.

"So, now I know why you have been dodging me. What's the deal?" Hollow began his questions the minute we were seated.

I requested just a second to at least get my salad. "I believe it's pretty apparent." I took a seat.

"So, you weren't going to tell me you're having my baby?" He inquired.

"Honestly, I didn't see the need, Hollow. I'm not having the baby." I announced.

"So, you killing our baby?" I guess he needed confirmation of my previous statement.

"Well, I don't see much of a difference from when your baby momma did it. They say history repeats itself, right?" I was trying to keep my voice down.

I could tell by the contempt in his eyes he wanted to choke the fuck out of me. This nigga thought he could really come back and pick up

176

where he left off with no consequences. It wasn't the facts of life. I had been out of middle school for over a decade. Now that his heart was tied to it, I was supposed to be ready to settle down and have a family.

Get the fuck out of here with that shit.

All I wanted was his money. The rest he could keep. What he wouldn't contribute another man would.

"That's some fucked up shit." He finally spoke.

"It's a fucked up world, sweetie. Besides, I don't recall saying it was yours anyway." I blurted matter-of-factly.

He loudly hit the table with his fist. His nostrils began to flare like a bull. The other patrons stared at the table, ready to see a scene take place. I sat back taking a sip of my water.

Hollow took out his wallet and threw two twenties on the table.

"Thanks. I'll put it on the procedure." I slid the money into my purse. He shook his head before walking off.

Upon my arrival at the Women's Health Care Center, I was escorted to a room with an informational DVD designed to give alternative services and options available for pregnant women. Adoption had crossed my mind, but I couldn't live with myself allowing someone else to raise my responsibility. If my child ever found me, there was no way to explain why I kept Na'Siah and gave him or her away.

Confident I was making the best decision, I signed after the doctor reviewed all the complications and risks involved. Turning my head during the ultrasound she drew my blood and returned with paperwork for me to have the procedure in the morning. Reminding me that someone would have to drive me, my plan was to catch a cab home with no one to ask for a ride.

By the time I arrived home, I went through the same procedure of masking my IP address and purchasing the ants from some random unknown site. Using another fake credit card under someone else's social, I hope they were legitimate. I could only use these cards multiple times in one day.

Dr. Bacchus nurse called the house phone to tell me I had a small vaginal infection. It had probably been from the soap I used cleaning my toys off. Immediately dialing his office, I left an emergency message about the situation. His medical assistant called back and advised Dr.

Bacchus had prescribed a seven day antibiotic. Explaining that I couldn't wait that long, she told me there were no other available options. She scheduled a follow up culture with me the following week to make sure that it had cleared up.

I called the clinic and the nurse advised me that they would not be able to complete the procedure until the infection had cleared up. I slammed the phone down on the coffee table, driving my hand right through it. My laptop hit the floor cracking half of the screen.

I wasn't having this baby.

Chapter 29

Despite a minimal amount of depression, I was amped for the night of the ball. My plan was to be baby bump free in my dress, but it didn't pan out that way. Picking it up at the last minute, this second alteration would have to do. If this baby decided to grow anymore in these next few hours we would have a problem. Even sporting a belly, the cut out double split gown made me look like a Nubian goddess. Trimmed with rhinestones, it would definitely make me one of the best dressed tonight.

Meishelle and I had gotten everything and were on our way to the nail shop. We had started speaking here and there, but it wasn't like we had been.

We were the last clients for our nail tech, Sasha, who would be joining us at the ball. She had done the last minute favor and did our nails for Meishelle's wedding. She turned out to be good people and she easily became one of the girls. Every other week when she came in from Houston we had a standing appointment.

"Where is Schtanya?" Meishelle asked.

"In her business meeting. She passed by last night in her rental to pick up the tickets. Mika will take care of her right before the ball."

Our table had filled up for the first time in the many years we had been going.

"Oh cool. Baby, I can't wait for tonight. We going to kill 'em." Meishelle excitedly bounced to the music on the radio.

The nail salon where Sasha rented a space was jammed packed with people. Almost everyone in the city lived for the ball.

"Hey, belly." Sasha rubbed on my tummy.

"Uh. Don't remind me." I grunted in disgust.

While Meishelle went first, we chatted about Sasha's new house in Houston. The new gated subdivision had some bad ass houses from the pictures she showed us, including hers. It was crazy how much more land a person got for her money away from New Orleans.

"Giirrrl, I knew there was something I wanted to tell you. Why I saw Stone at one of my neighbor's houses ago a few nights with some chick. Her face was all fucked up and shit."

My lips curled in satisfaction. Finally, confirmation that my artwork could be seen. I had been so busy beating her ass that night at my house I didn't pay attention. Last time I had driven by her house there was a for rent sign on the lawn. I heard through the grapevine she had moved in with Deborah and Stone.

"Fuck Stone. I ain't even trying to ruin my night with talk about him unless ole boy is about murder for hire." I unbuttoned my pants to eat the macaroni and honey baked wings from the Pie Man.

"Well, if he keeps it up, you may get your wish. He have to be dealing, because the dude is a supplier of product."

The dude next door loved to floss and thought divulging his profession would impress her, but it did just the opposite. He had manipulated check stubs to an offshore company that his cousin worked in Human Resources for to get the house.

They say a nigga couldn't hide who he really was forever. Stone truly had no damn spine when it came to Deborah. True she had been there for him when his mom wasn't, but he was sacrificing his life for her. The most she had sacrificed was her pussy.

"My policy premiums are up to date." He could fuck around and get killed. I would get the big pay out and they would never see a dime.

***

Na'Siah played with his game in the living room while I got dressed for the ball. Quameer and his mother were keeping him for me.

When I emerged from my room, he was sitting on the edge of the sofa with his feet kicked up on the end table. He had picked up on Hollow's bad habit.

"Mommy, you look pretty." He gave me the once over before returning to his game.

I nudged his legs off the table. Coming down my feet knocked the book sitting on my table to the floor.

"What's that, momma?" The two page letter from Hattie Mae separated as it slid out of its envelope. I had picked it up numerous times, but never had the courage to read it.

Picking it up, the letter unfolded exposing her handwriting.

Dear Baby Girl,

If you're reading this letter then it means my time on earth has come to an end. I was certain it would come one day. No one can live forever, baby.

You, Krissett, were the most precious gift the Lord could have ever bestowed upon me. When I looked into your eyes on the day you were born I saw God giving me the baby I lost back in another body. You are a strong, beautiful, educated and talented young woman with much yet to give the world. Enjoy your blessings, no matter how nontraditionally they may come.

Believe in the abilities you have been given. Remember, there is no person under the sun without imperfections or weaknesses. Some may mask them better than others, but they always exist.

Don't force love, but allow it to blossom and flourish into what it should be. Shut no one out. We each love people in our own way. Accept those people that come for a reason, season or lifetime. Know when their time is up and let them go. If it's meant to be, you will be directed back to it.

No matter how hard it gets, keep pushing forward. Use your past to fuel your future. Each challenge presents the opportunity for a lesson and furnishes strength for the next obstacle. Follow your heart and look back with no regrets. Give no one the ability to control your outlook on the world. You are the solo captain on the ship of your life. It ends with the path you have selected for it. When the water of life looks rough, know God is at His best. Question not, but allow the storm to lead you to the sunny, calmer waters that are ahead.

In life or death the love I have for you will never, ever fade. Hold onto those memories that we shared. Kiss my great grandbaby and tell him daily how much I love him.

Always,

Hattie Mae/Sugar Momma

I wiped the tears that poured down my face uncontrollably. It was a good thing Mika had cancelled my makeup appointment until right before the ball.

By the time I arrived, I had to walk about a mile to enter the convention center. Schtanya finally responded to the text I sent in the car. She was getting the final touches put on her hair and then would get dressed. That meant she had at least another two hours or more. Good thing I had followed my first mind and drove myself.

Hitting the edge of the elongated building, this was the New Orleans version of the Players' Ball. All the men were required to wear black tuxes, a few going all out with the matching vests and ties. Besides a good smelling man, a well-groomed one was the next best thing. Females strutted like models in their long silky floor length gowns of all sorts, colors and styles that ranged from classy to trashy. Many stood outside trying to floss by snapping pics outside of limos, stretch Hummers and cars with 24" rims.

The inside of the building appeared to be struggling to hold all the attendees. It had never been this packed before. I gave up on pleasantries, such as excuse me, and made my way through the massive crowd.

My damn feet were barking by the time I arrived at the seat. Meishelle grabbed my arm to go walking before I could get comfortable. She had some coworkers and associates she wanted to find in the Kings section. Struggling through people, several trampled on my dress train almost tripping me directly onto my stomach. Hell, I might not need the abortion clinic by the following week.

"I am ready to go sit my ass back down." I hollered at Meishelle walking ahead of me.

"We almost there." She tilted her head back. "Come on."

I huffed and continued with her. She had about two minutes to get there or I was just going to leave her ass. She knew her way back to the damn table.

"Look, they are right there." She directed my attention to a section that sat behind barricades.

We went around to the side and got them to meet us at the barricades for entrance. Offering us food and drink, I helped myself to the fruit and cheese tray before taking my seat.

Enjoying the second line parading across the convention, my view was interrupted by Janasia strolling her ugly ass over. Conniving intentions at the forefront of her mind, her attention was focused directly on Meishelle.

"Hold on, bitch. Not tonight." I stepped in front of her.

182

She could start some shit if she wanted. There were no police to stop me from whipping her ass. It was time for this gorilla to be caged up.

"How you did that?" She pointed at my stomach. I know she was drove to see me pregnant, after gloating in my sterility.

"It's called a man who loves me. Something your ass will never know about." Baby or not I could stomp her down.

"You better get the fuck out of my way." She peeked over my shoulder to Meishelle.

"I wish the fuck I would. Show me the bad ho that you think you are." I grabbed the Jack Daniel's bottle off the table, standing my ground.

From knowing her throughout the years, deep down Janasia really wanted a man to call her own and love her. Her problem was that she had this idea that there was some grandeur in stealing someone else's. You could never find happiness on the misery of another woman. Karma would see to that personally.

She peeked over my shoulder eyeing Meishelle engaged in laughter and a good time. The constant rejection she encountered had turned her into a bitter bitch that fed off the hurt in someone's eyes at having their heart broken. She needed them to feel the misery she did. Embarrassing them in the midst of others was an additional pleasure. Somebody was going to murk her ass with the games she played.

"You can't hide her from the truth anyway. I'll catch her soon enough." She sucked her teeth and headed back to the hole she crawled from.

I hated to admit it, Janasia was right. What was done in the dark would come to light.

I resumed my snacking while waiting for Meishelle to finish up. After the extremely long coronation ceremony, she ended her conversation. The performances would be starting soon. By the time we got back to the table, Schtanya had arrived with her guests. One of them looked strangely familiar.

"Hey!" She rose for introductions. "I want you to meet Cionna and my future client, Derrick."

Derrick rose to shake my hand.

I had sworn that Schtanya said her clients were coming when she texted me for tickets. Cionna wasn't a damn entertainer unless you needed a motherfucker short of a full deck. I balled up my fist wanting to sock the ho dead in her mouth. Texting my damn phone almost every day and fucking my cousin.

"Cionna is the one I told you about in Vegas." She whispered into my ear.

All the ways for Cionna to get to her mother in Tennessee, Cionna coincidentally went through Georgia and ended up meeting my cousin. Red flags flew up even more. Something about this chick seriously wasn't right.

"Well, isn't it a small world indeed." I sarcastically replied.

Schtanya glanced back and forth between us waiting on an explanation of how we would know each other.

"Yeah. Nice to see you again. I don't remembering you being that round when I interviewed with you." Cionna joked.

I found no amusement in her humor. Had she not been a damn psycho bitch and sent that information to Stone, I might not be knocked up. Then again, her knowing Schtanya might not be such a bad idea. I would work on a plan. Catch back fever was in the air.

I took my seat for a moment, the wheels in my head already were turning on a plan for Cionna.

Chapter 30

Na'Siah called two hours after I got in from the ball to make sure I was on my way to take him to the parades. I woke up out of my sleep in a cold sweat screaming at Hattie Mae and Ketoyia who had been inhabiting my dreams since I read the letter.

"You're given nothing you can't bear," Hattie Mae responded.

"I'm not ready, I can't do it with them." I cried out in my head referring to Hollow and Stone.

"Give me a second chance." Ketoyia pleaded.

"I'm sorry. Please forgive me." I repeatedly apologized for what I was about to do.

The parades were almost better than Christmas to him. My tradition was to roll from that Friday to Tuesday with almost no sleep, but Na'Siah had it take place way earlier.

Quameer asked me to help take Na'Siah to some parades during the less crowded weeknights, because he wasn't coming out for Mardi Gras. I think he was ashamed of his appearance and wheelchair-bound status though. The damage to his spinal cord seemed to be permanent and his kidneys were failing, leaving him to take dialysis every other day.

6:35 a.m.: I heard pregnant pussy is so much wetter. Can I get a taste? Cionna's message came through while I was in the bathroom.

Dinner and death did sound like a good combination. A taste of my pussy I wouldn't give her if we were the last two people on earth. I made a mental note to find a substance that would poison her in one ingestion.

BBQ pits, DJs, vendors and parade goers lined up under the bridge on Mardi Gras Boulevard waiting to scream "throw me something mister" at the painted, decorated trucks on wheels that rolled through the street. While the crowds waited, we filled the streets dancing to old school New Orleans hits.

"Where dey at? Look for 'em. Where dey at? Look for 'em." Partners in Crime blared through the speakers. Meishelle and I motioned like explorers.

This song always brought back memories from the high school talent shows throughout the city. Schtanya came running up from out of nowhere and joined in to dance on the last part of the song.

185

Taking a break after the Wobble, I let my nose lead me to the nearby food truck for a sausage dog fresh off the grill. Meishelle had gone off to see if Quincy and Na'Siah wanted something. They were playing football in an open field with some of the other families on the parade route.

Schtanya struck up a conversation by asking what I thought about her and Cionna.

"I didn't know that she was important enough for consideration."

It was comical that she was worrying about what I felt about Cionna and she was concerned about tasting my pussy.

"I mean we just hook up and do our thing, but you met her before in an interview. I was in town without my family, so I figured it couldn't hurt to play. Business and pleasure can be a good combo."

That didn't even add up. Flings were just something to do in someone's spare time. They weren't seen in public nor brought around to meet family. In lieu of those two things, Cionna automatically disqualified as passing time with. The shit Schtanya had pulled last night was disrespectful as fuck to her husband and her children. On top of it all, she was dealing with a lunatic.

"I hear you. Being real with you, I'm not the biggest fan of what you doing. Personally, I saw her as fake and decided not to hire her." I hoped that might send up some red flags on her radar.

Schtanya was one of my best friends, but the only people that I would give a straight up warning to was Meishelle and Quincy. Some things people had to find out on their own. Even Meishelle had limits if it meant exposing my brother. People would confuse your help with ulterior motives, especially women. Every person's experience with another was different and with grace from above, Schtanya's would be.

"I feel you, but I got this. We are the only ones who know what the deal is."

"Ok. You better make sure that the feeling is mutual."

Schtanya stepped away to take a call from Derrick as Meishelle came back with Quincy and Na'Siah's greedy order.

As the floats rolled, children beamed with pride at being gifted teddy bears, swords and other trinkets. Derrick made it about midway through the parade with some of his people. A few caught my eye.

186

"What's up, Ms. Krissett?" He attempted to sound smooth.

"Nothing much." I held my hands up to avoid being stung by beads being pitched in my direction.

Talking to him, I realized Derrick had to be at least five years younger than me, if not more. He struck up conversation about what he and his friends get into. Originally from out east, he and his family had moved to the city a few months ago. It was his first Mardi Gras experience and he wanted to make the most of it. Advising him that Bourbon Street would jump up from the night until the morning, Canal would be the best place to catch everything.

"You seem to be the person I need to find out everything from. How about you give me your number?"

We exchanged numbers and he excused himself to talk to Schtanya. It seemed to be more a come on than a friendly gesture. The first chat was free, but any others would have a price attached if he was trying to get at me.

Na'Siah came over on Quincy's shoulders to bring me an additional bag of throws that he had been given. Clearly, Quincy was taking half of this stuff with him.

"We need to have a sit down conversation and real soon, matter of fact A.S.A.P." I hadn't gotten a chance to talk to him yet about Janasia.

"About what?" Quincy examined.

I answered with my touted up lips and bucked eyes. Na'Siah was at the parrot stage where anything you said was bound to be repeated in the company of the wrong person.

"Ok. I'll pass by tomorrow or Monday. Make sure you cook something, too. You owe me for this."

"Nuh uh. You want to be a daddy, remember? This is free practice." I giggled.

Na'siah was bouncing up and down to catch the next approaching float.

***

With all the activities that had consumed my weekend, by Monday evening I was too damn exhausted to cook.

187

Sitting the plate from Triangle Deli into the microwave, I quickly got Na'Siah into the bed. Tomorrow would be a long day.

Quameer called to inform me that he wouldn't be riding on the truck floats this year. He was preparing for a kidney transplant. His sister had matched and she was donating one of hers.

Texting Quincy about 7:30 p.m. to be on his way, I laid with Na'Siah until he was fast asleep. Headed to the kitchen to heat up Quincy's food, he scared the shit out of me already sitting on my sofa tearing the food up.

"Boy, don't do that shit. Announce yourself when you come in my damn house." I knocked his feet off the table.

"The King is here!" He hollered facetiously.

"Shiiidd! The closest thing to a king in this castle is sleeping." I plopped down next to him and took a fork full of macaroni and cheese. "Anyway, how did your ass get here so damn quick?" Had he been at home, it would have normally taken him an hour to pry himself from Meishelle.

"You already know why. Had to deal with that bitch." He sneered, referring to Janasia.

"I tell you this! What you had better do is get that motherfucker under some type of control. The dumb bitch tried to approach Meishelle at the Zulu Ball in front a crowd of people. I could see the malice in her heart."

"Man, I told you she is on some other shit. She thinks if she tells Meishelle I will be with her duck ass. I gotta find a way to do something about her. Real talk."

"Well, how you want to handle it?" I was 'bout that vengeance life.

Quincy refused to tell me. Little did he know, she was already on my list. Outside of Stone's, I wanted Janasia's to be the most gruesome for all the shit she had pulled. Fortunately for her, Deborah was up to bat. The stun gun had been purchased and the four farms of ants had arrived today at another randomly selected abandoned house in the city.

"You don't have to share. That ho has personally fucked with me and her day is coming. Now, do you need something to drink?" I rose from the sofa, leaving him with that thought.

188

Chapter 31

The burning aroma of the grill distinguished itself from the morning fog, welcoming us as we pulled up to the neutral ground on St. Charles. Families filled the street coming to claim their spots for the day. Helping us unload the pans of food from the car, my cousin left after camping out on the parade route all night to take a shower and change clothes.

Sweaty by 7:30 a.m., I walked a few blocks to my aunt's house to change me and Na'Siah. He was full of chili from the hot dogs and beans. The humidity mixed with the sun gave way to a beautiful Mardi Gras day on the horizon. The Zulu Witch Doctor had done a good job this year.

Returning to the avenue felt like a huge family reunion. Na'Siah eagerly ran up to the Batman and Saints whistle garbed in costume for pictures. The multitudes danced to local bounce artist D.J. Jubilee's song, *I Wanna Coconut,* screaming insanely at the float riders. Some held up handwritten signs or held up their state IDs to let them know the thousands of miles they traveled for the infamous plastic possession.

Quincy left Na'Siah to talk to an old classmate and he stood next to me, pleading and pouting for me help to get one. Struggling to balance my center of gravity with him and the protruding baby bump on my hip I had until the end of the week before he would be an only child again. Meishelle stepped in and volunteered.

Summoned by one of the male riders with the spray painted black faces, Na'Siah approached with his eyes and hands outreached for his coconut. Out of nowhere a woman came up, attempting to snatch it from his grasp. With the strength of Samson, I threw my elbow in her direction. The woman hollered in pain as it landed directly in her nose. No one was about to play with me and mine.

"Bitch, are you crazy?" She screamed, holding the bridge of her nose. It appeared to be dislocated.

"Nah, but you must be. What I know is you saw that coconut was for my nephew," Meishelle blasted.

"All I saw was the motherfucker hanging from the float." She bucked, stepping into Meishelle's face.

I took Na'Siah and placed him on the ground. She was about to get a double serving of ass whipping.

"Mommy." Na'Siah tried to get my attention.

"Not right now, baby." I pushed him behind me. My nostrils flared. I had a short temper when it came to talking. It was wasted energy that could have been used to whip a bitch ass.

"Nah. It can't go down like this." Quincy came up in between us and saved the woman's ass.

By noon, Zulu had passed and we packed up to head by Craig's family. From one side of the city to another, they gathered downtown yearly at their family house on Ursuline Avenue. The atmosphere was much like St. Charles Avenue with ten times the amount of people.

The minute we arrived, Meishelle and I prepared to head under the bridge for the concert. Local artists performed for a few hours before the headliner came on. It happened to be Charlie Wilson this year.

Men lined the sidewalk tugging at my arms with the tired ass line to "let me holla at you for a minute." The last dude caused me to almost snatch my damn shoulder out of place trying to get away from him. Hearing the announcer calling Charlie to the stage, I began a brisk walk to make sure that I didn't miss one moment.

"What the fuck?" I swung my fist aiming for whoever's face it would connect with.

Someone grabbed my arm for the last time. I guaranteed they would learn today. Hollow ducked at the right moment to avoid my wrath.

"Damn. My bad, love." He held his hands up, signaling that he wanted no trouble.

Filling him in on all the harassment we had endured along the way, Meishelle made small talk with him briefly. Somewhere between Christmas, the funeral and the hospital Meishelle claimed to have seen a changed man. Having seen people being able to put on airs in a ten year relationship, I wasn't a sucker for the hype. He introduced us to his boys that sat on the porch steps, giving me the title of his future wife, clowning that he would come with us down the block to defend our honor. I could handle my own battles.

"You decided to keep the baby." Charlie was in the middle of *Outstanding* when we arrived and wiggled our way to the middle.

190

In the overcrowded space, I dodged Hollow's attempts at kissing my check and sing into my ear.

"Appointment at the end of the week." I tried to maneuver away from him.

"Give me a chance to make this right, please." He latched onto my shirt like I was breastfeeding him. I ignored his request as Charlie Wilson crooned *Suppa Sexy*.

The sidewalk overflowed with people as the crowd disbursed for the evening. The bass of the music giving me a headache, feet burning and back was killing me, I needed to use the bathroom at least thirty minutes ago I was exhausted with the invasion of my space all day by strangers.

Meishelle clowned the half-naked women laboring and toiling to show off their designer corn chip shorts and top with six-inch stiletto heels for the stunners. A couple almost broke their ankles that gave way into the terribly paved streets. They almost gave themselves whiplash when they heard a horn honking, searching for the source.

"Krissett, somebody is calling your name." Meishelle called out as if I was hearing impaired. Hollow searched the swarm of people for the source.

I recognized Stone's damn voice from anywhere. The relentless gifts, phone calls and texts was enough torment. He must have given up and kept rolling, because there was a sudden halt in my name being called.

Reaching the house, I rushed inside to the bathroom. Meishelle went to the backyard to help Quincy with the grill and Hollow to the kitchen for my momma to fix him a plate of food. He called his boys on the way back to let them know he would catch up with them later.

"Krissett!" Craig's sister called out to me from the living room. I heard a child crying and thought maybe Na'Siah had been hurt. Instead, Stone stood at the bottom of the steps.

This motherfucker believed in seizing an opportunity, knowing damn well I wouldn't give him trouble in front of Craig's family. While I had been around them the majority of my life they weren't my true blood, but were Mariah's.

Leaving out the bathroom I overheard Mariah's aunt discussing her in the bedroom. She was going through physical therapy due to surgery

191

on her knees. The bullets that I put through them had fucked the ligaments and tendons in them up. In the meantime, she had been committed to Kindred Hospital in hopes that her mind would snap back to reality. The doctor's said she experienced a form of psychosis that night and was still residing on the dark side. Karma took care of those bastards quite nicely for me with little effort.

Gathering my car keys I played as if he had stopped by for something.

"Why is your ass here?" I gritted through my teeth, yanking him away from the home.

"Man, I been trying to check on you and my seed. You won't take a nigga calls and when I come by you calling the people on me. So here I am." He reached out to touch my belly.

I knocked his hand off me.

"Look. I moved on, fucked someone else and made a family with them. Now waste your time waiting to find out this baby ain't yours."

Within a split second, he snapped and snatched me up. Wrapping his arms around my neck, he effortlessly applied pressure to my windpipe.

"Anything you attempted to start with another nigga is done. Fuck with me and I will cut my baby out your stomach. I gave up the streets on the strength of you, but my get down to make motherfuckers disappear hasn't change. Test me and find out." He was a heartless nigga with no soul, looking into his coal-black orbs.

My mouth hung open as my legs dangled to find the ground. The lack of oxygen caused my eyes to tear and I acknowledged my understanding with a whimper which was all I could muster in the moment. He kissed me on my nose and released his grip. I gulped in the maximum amount of air my lungs could hold.

"Now, I have to go out of town with Takiesha for a minute to handle business and I expect you to be at the airport when I get back. And don't waste energy calling the people. I got my people already on the last charges you filed." He allowed me a minute to gather myself before he walked in the opposite direction of the house.

Slowly regaining composure of my breathing, he had to be out his damn mind to think I would be waiting for his ass at the airport. Why the fuck I had left the damn stun gun in my purse was beyond me. I could have tested it right now to see if it would work on Deborah's ass, but then it would have made it too coincidental that Stone and Deborah were tasered days apart.

I could feel my neck had to have some bruising. Whatever the damage, it would be evident though with the low cut top that I had on. It was a good thing I had brought my car keys with me. Quickly changing into the polo style shirt, I proceed straight to the bathroom to assess Stone's damage back at the house.

My eyes widened as I pulled down my collar in front of the medicine cabinet mirror. Stone's thumb print was engraved into the center of my larynx. My caramel complexion was a bluish purple hue surrounded by the imprint of his hand onto my neck.

Buttoning the shirt to my neck, I relaxed on the couch to lay low the remaining few minutes.

"I'm about to head out to pick up the kids." Hollow snuck up on me, placing a kiss on the side of my neck that caused me to wince.

"What's wrong?" He gently stroked the side of my neckline.

"Nothing." I scooted over slightly to duck his touch. My injury was still sensitive and faintly throbbing.

His hand got caught in my collar, pulling the top button loose to reveal my war wound.

"What the fuck happened to your neck?" He snapped, jumping up off the sofa.

Cautioning him to keep his voice, I brushed the topic off.

"You about to have my baby and shit wasn't like that before that nigga called you outside. He is a straight ho. Whenever I catch him in the street, I promise on my children, including the one you carrying, he will get his."

No one but Mariah's nosey ass people would tell where I had went.

"I have told you already, I'm not having this baby."

He stormed out the house. I sat watching my momma and Craig doing an almost two-step move, while Na'Siah waved his handkerchief in the air to the brass band. I needed a way to get rid of Stone without getting my hands dirty when an idea came to mind.

I went through my cell phone and was happy to see that I had locked in Quincy's best friend, Jeremiah's number. Quincy had given it to me earlier in the week so that I could drop off some money to him. I needed to spread out and stop relying on my cousin to supply all my information for criminal activities. Jeremiah had better reach. Whereas Quincy dabbled in activities here, Jeremiah relied on it to feed his family.

6:55 p.m.: Hey Miah. This is Krissett. You busy?

7:05 p.m.: What's good? I'm headed to the D shop. What's good with you?

7:08 p.m.: I wanted to hook up with you next week and talk to you about a job at the restaurant.

I hope he picked up on my code for letting him know I had a job for him to do. Text messages could be used as evidence to a crime.

7:12 p.m.: No doubt. Tell me when and where. I'm there.

7:15 p.m.: Next Friday at 1pm. Armstrong Park so I can give you a tour after.

The tour would be to Stone's place. It appeared I would be at the airport picking up Stone after all. Little did Stone know he was about to fund his very own death by a contract killer. My heart skipped a beat with joy.

Chapter 32

Preparing for a night of absolutely nothing, I had a small glass of Merlot. Quameer had called on the way home to ask if Na'Siah could stay the night. Requiring these days just to recuperate from Mardi Gras and have the procedure, I packed his bag with no question.

Settling under the covers with the air conditioner on sixty degrees, an image appeared from Stone in the process of turning on my do not disturb feature.

8:39 p.m.: See you when WE get back!

Takiesha smiled with Stone in the background, eyes straight forward on his cell. I could tell he had no idea the picture was being taken. He must have stepped away to the bathroom for her to be in his phone.

I had no idea how that ho could maintain a smile with her fucked up ass face.

8:45 p.m.: Tell Stone me and the baby will have the key ready!

I attached a photo message of me and my belly from earlier today. Laughing, I was sure no one mentioned my pregnancy to her.

Have a good trip on that, bitch! If having the baby wouldn't have hurt me more than her, I would have gone through with it just to be spiteful.

Feeling rejuvenated, I wanted to get out the house and into something. The thought that Deborah was home alone popped into my head. Damn a couple of days, tonight was perfect for my plan.

Checking the time again, she would be at bingo a little while longer before arriving home. Hitting Jeremiah up for a last minute favor, he was still at the shop for several hours.

Quickly dressing, I searched the garage for something I could use in addition to the stun gun to subdue Deborah. I settled on soaking a rag in a Ziploc bag of ammonia. Retrieving the box of my friends, I was ready for the festivities.

Ducking on the far end of her porch, I cursed when Deborah was dropped off at the house. It would present a major setback in my attack mode.

"I'll be fine, girl. Go on and get home." Deborah called out to the driver at the base of her steps.

The lady obeyed and wished her a good night until next time. Little did she know her ass would never be the same.

Like a damn fool, she hadn't gotten her keys out in advance. I heard her acquire and fidget with the keys in the lock. Hearing the click, I moved like a thief in the night, placing the towel over her nose and jabbing her side with the stun gun. Her big ass almost pulled me down with her collapsing to the floor. For good measure I left the rag on her nose just in case she wasn't out as cold as I perceived. Scurrying to the car, I came back with the box of my friends.

Getting my supplies that consisted of a kitchen chair, bucket of water and large towel, I strenuously dragged her ass into the bathroom before gagging her mouth to silence her screams. Shaking the box to agitate the ants, I opened the box to release the six farms. She came awake as I doused her with water and dashed out the bathroom for dear life. I secured the towel along the door seal and lodged a chair under the lock to make sure she nor the ants could escape.

I knew they wouldn't kill her, but the pain she would feel would be excruciating. The species bites were compared to a bullet piercing the body that caused surges of throbbing and agonizing pain.

Glancing at my watch, it took less than five minutes for her shrieks to begin.

"Mmmhhh! Mmmhhh!" She frantically banged on the door.

Satisfied with my job, I blew a kiss at the door, wishing her well against the attack.

Although I had on gloves when handling the package or seeing the plan through, I went back over everything, making sure no evidence whatsoever could be found. Confident there wasn't, I left out closing the door behind me. Before I could start the car Deborah emerged from the house, naked and screaming for someone to help. I had forgotten to secure the fucking bathroom window.

The ants could be seen continuing their assault. Too bad her neighbors didn't care for her much long before the storm. I sat back through the tinted windows enjoying the view until she crashed face down on the ground.

To another successful mission. I patted myself on the back and pulled off.

196

Chapter 33

Turning on Thursday Night Football, my mom called for our nightly girl talk as I sat up watching the Dirty Birds get whipped. Shortly after we ended our conversation, Derrick rang to see what I was doing.

My intuition was right about him feeling me. Mardi Gras was over now. Filling him in on my activities, he was shocked to find out a woman knew about football. We chatted before he gave the main reason for his call, an invitation to dinner.

I asked him to suggest a place. Any place that had a two for anything was the wrong answer and would disqualify him from my time. Surprisingly, he tossed out Dickie Brennan's. I had heard about them, but never had the pleasure of dining in the establishment. Checking the time I noticed they would be closing shortly. He offered me a rain check for tomorrow and asked me what I had in mind. I really wanted Port-A-Call, however based on his selection that was too cheap. I confirmed a reservation for Dickie Brennan's with him tomorrow evening.

I sat on the sofa craving Port-A-Call until I could no longer fight the urge. Meishelle texted me as I was getting dressed to come by with the key for her garage. She and Quincy were leaving town this weekend to go house shopping in Tennessee.

"You can slide it under the door if I am not home." I informed her of my plans.

"No. Don't leave without me. I'm coming."

"What?" I couldn't believe my ears. "You willing to leave your husband alone this time of night?" I poked fun at her.

They had been on timed sex sessions in an attempt to conceive since her fertility test said she was close to ovulating.

"He's not home. He went to shoot pool at Shamrock with Chuck and them."

We walked in about twenty minutes later and were seated on the opposite side outside of the kitchen. I requested a table on that side to be as close to the cooks as possible. We discussed a marketing strategy for a new clothing line project she was working on. The client could solidify her promotion in the new office. With what she was throwing out, she had the shit in the bag.

Quincy texted Meishelle that he would be home within the next hour and my quality time was up the second she got it.

"Your dick-whipped ass make me sick." I giggled.

"Don't hate me because I'm getting the real thing." Her head fell back in laughter.

A fatal late night accident forced us to take the lake way home. I hated traffic and Franklin Avenue was much busier than normal. A full and sleepy pregnant woman was a combination for road rage. Meishelle turned on the radio and nudged me to sing along to *Catching Hell* by Natalie Cole. The bellowing that we called singing had cars in the next lanes staring to make sure we weren't hurt.

Caught in the moment, I lost total notion of where I was, my life in the same hell Natalie sung about. I paid no mind that Meishelle had stopped until the seat belt chime went off.

At cheetah speed, Meishelle raced over to Quincy's car that had pulled next to us at the light. Quincy immediately jumped out to block her from getting to the passenger side, but Meishelle hit him with a left hook that caused him to stumble. He stepped back and allowed the situation to transpire.

I struggled to unfasten the damn seatbelt while keeping my eyes on Meishelle. I couldn't get a clear view of what had her upset from my side. Reaching the passenger side, she demolished the window with her bare hand.

Coming around to the side of the car, the slaughtering screams of Janasia were music to my ears. Meishelle pulled her hair, ripping it from the scalp while administering sadistic blows to her face through the car window. I stood in intoxicating joy watching this ho get what she deserved. People hit their emergency lights and hopped out their cars ready to get a front row seat for the next World Star hip hop video.

Fragments of glass from the window became lodged in her neck, her head being dragged through the window. Frantically searching for the door handle to free herself from the car, the blood from Meishelle's battered hand mixing with the ones pouring from her busted nose and lips. Janasia found the handle and swung the door open, momentarily knocking the wind out of Meishelle enough to subdue her on the ground.

"Nah, bitch, it ain't even going down like that." I savagely side kicked her trick ass.

She collapsed to the ground and Quincy came over to stop Meishelle, who continued to brutally strike Janasia who lay lifeless and comatose. Even if she lost her memory she would remember this ass whipping.

Meishelle grabbed a shard of glass wedged in the window and charged at Quincy for attempting to intervene a second time. Now shit was about to get real, because I wasn't going to stand by for this one. Stepping between her and Quincy, she came down with the glass, slashing my left forearm open.

"Come on, Meishelle." I urged. The crowd began to disburse at the imminent sound of the police sirens. She stood eyeing Quincy with the utmost contempt. I tugged her arm to come on.

"Quincy, get your ass out of here." I commanded him. The last thing he needed was to even come close to the people.

Without hesitation, he left skid marks on the pavement with me on his heels.

I peered over at Meishelle's bloodshot red eyes. Her mother kept her so shielded from the world that Quincy had been her first real relationship. He was her first love, the most pure and powerful to encounter. Nothing I could say would console her broken soul. Squeezing with the small strength I had, the cries she suppressed exploded.

I pulled over onto the side of the Lakefront Arena, shortly before we descended onto the lake and got out. Pulling her out the passenger seat, I held her in my arms, silently praying for time to remove the pain inflicted on her tonight.

"Why would he do this to me?" Meishelle cried into my chest.

"I don't know, sweetie," I loathed lying to her, but no rationale would make it right. Although Quincy had done the shit out of love for her, his motives had also been tremendously selfish.

My insides were shredding from the truth that I held. I cursed Quincy for putting himself in this fucked up ass situation. Meishelle loved him broke, in jail and with no money.

"Can you bring me by my momma please?" She implored.

The last thing anyone needed was Ms. Williams nosey ass in this. She would fill Meishelle's head full of hatred toward Quincy, which wouldn't allow her to mend appropriately. Instead, it would harvest a breeding ground for bitterness and resentment. Rather than begin an unnecessary argument, I honored her request.

I envisioned the early morning hours of my procedure, snuggled in my bed and not waiting at New Orleans East Hospital. I took my seat, vexed at clearly the shortage of medical personnel in addition to the texts that Cionna kept sending.

1:43 a.m.: Your cousin pussy don't taste as good as yours.

1:45 a.m.: Fuck off!!!

1:46 a.m.: Only if I can bring you with me.

Finally called on by three a.m., the nurse had to wake me up after another five hours in the back to receive nine clear, dissolvable stiches. It would be a push to make my ten a.m. appointment at the clinic, but nothing was going to stop me.

Chapter 34

I sat up on the sofa, my nerves causing seizures of anxiety. Each passing day had brought worse nightmares of what I was about to do. I reassured myself that I was doing what was best for me. Hattie Mae infused powerful words into my spirit, even from the grave.

If it was meant to be it would come back.

My pulse accelerated questioning if this was my second chance with Ketoyia or if this wasn't the right decision, would I get pregnant again. With an hour left before my appointment, I settled on the latter and called for a cab while getting myself together.

Removing the bandage that the emergency room physician had placed onto my arm, I wanted no excuses from the clinic why they couldn't do the procedure today. It was bad enough that due to the wait it had turned into a two day procedure.

I checked in and paid the remaining five hundred fifty dollars for the procedure. The nurse ushered me into the small box-sized room, collecting my demographic information.

"The procedure today will only take five to fifteen minutes. We will insert cervical dilators then tomorrow we will do the evacuation. It will take maybe a little longer." She showed me the gown and directed me to position my feet in the stirrups like a gynecological exam.

In the cold empty room, I heard Hattie Mae and Ketoyia whispering in my ear, begging me to reconsider. The baby's first heartbeat in the emergency room resounded it my head. It had been so strong.

The nerves ravaging through my body caused tremors. I took deep breaths to calm my labored breathing to push them out my head. The nurse came in with a silver tray of instruments sitting on a blue protective sheet. The plastic tube looked more like a tampon. She handed me a single pain pill and prescription for more. I threw my head back, swallowing the pill and water.

"We are almost ready to begin." She left back out for a moment.

With every minute they waited, my mind juggled back and forth. I could understand a woman's plight battling to make the decision.

If this baby turned out to be Stone's, it would be a constant reminder of him raping me Thanksgiving night. After my revenge, I wanted to be able to move on with my life. I wasn't sure how I would be able to looking at a child conceived with him. Having a baby for Hollow would be reliving my entire Ketoyia pregnancy again. Her death still disturbed me.

"You ready?" The physician peeked his head into the door.

"Yes sir." I looked to the ceiling.

I drove home praying the decision I made had been correct. I couldn't bring myself to do it. Either way, it was final and the outcome had yet to be determined.

The pain pill that the nurse had given me had taken effect along with the sleep I had missed the night before. Derrick texted me after class to confirm our date for the evening and I was all too ready to see what he had to offer. I left early to pass by the house and check on Quincy. Worry had definitely taken over, because he had yet to return my call and wouldn't answer the door. My momma wanted to file a missing person's report, but I assured her that he was fine, claiming to have talked to him.

Derrick and I decided to park on N. Rampart Street, a few blocks away and take a nice stroll over to Dickie Brennan's. I paid a bit more attention than I had to his appearance at Mardi Gras. He was about 6'2", slim build and round brown eyes. He looked extremely handsome in the plaid button down shirt, jeans and tennis shoes. His pants resting on his waist was welcomed.

The walk gave me a chance to get to know him and if I would go through with this date or magically come up extremely nauseated and need a ride home. He had a little Cali sway remaining in his voice from Los Angeles, his original hometown. He had a three year old son that lived back home who he saw during the summer and holidays.

"So, how old are you?" I could no longer hold the question. The guessing game wasn't working well.

"You not supposed to ask a black man his age." He playfully grinned.

"It's that bad, huh?"

"Depends on what you consider twenty-four to be."

My guess was almost spot on in the age category. Throughout the evening I learned more about him and everything was positive. He had more going than men my age. Besides pursuing a career in the rap industry, he was a pre-law major at Tulane University. His dad sealed the family's financial stability by inventing a transportation app that he sold to cell phone companies. That was a sweet melody to my ears.

The music industry was no living according to his parents, so he appeased them by going back to school for law. He figured it would be a skill that would come in handy, reading contracts in the music industry. Schtanya had been referred in the meantime by one of his friends whose parents had used her before.

"Enough about me. I want some background on you. What's your age and how far along are you?" He inquired.

Before I could answer, my phone rang. Almost dismissing the unknown caller, my gut said to answer it. I pressed my finger across the screen to answer and hit the mute button to quiet the background. I wouldn't put it past Stone's borderline stalker ass to call me to hear where I was.

"Hello." Quincy's deep bass voice came through my phone. I nervously fidgeted to hit the unmute before he disconnected.

"What the hell is going on with you?" I immediately blew, excusing myself from Derrick for a minute. We had been too close for him to pull disappearing acts on me.

"I wasn't sure what was going to happen so I got the fuck out. What's the deal with old girl?" He referred to Janasia's condition. I filled him in on what I knew and he asked about Meishelle.

Mrs. Williams, unknowing that Meishelle had kicked Janasia's ass, said she was being kept in a medically induced coma for right now. Given she had heart and high blood pressure issues, the doctors were unsure how she would react to the pain. She had multiple bruises, broken ribs and a collapsed lung. I prayed her ass would just die right there.

"Man, you haven't called her either?" He owed her apologies until infinity and beyond.

"Nah. I don't know what to say right now. I'll call her soon and lay low for a few more days. If the bitch hasn't come to, I'm gonna come back home."

Meishelle and I had plans over the weekend for a wine and cheese tasting. Outside of work she had been solely going to work and returning home in the evening.

I cautioned him to make sure he did. My momma would get suspicious of me if I was the only one talking to him. She made sure to speak with both of us at least once a day.

"I got you." He hung up and I returned to Derrick. We strolled down Canal Street as I shared some of the historical buildings that had now been replaced by upscale hotels and other retailers. Surprisingly enjoying myself, we made a promise to hook up again.

On my way home, Stone emailed me his itinerary to come home Sunday. He said an emergency had come up with his grandma and it was the soonest flight he could get. Guess I would have to accompany him on Sunday with some flowers to see how she was. Me showing up would probably send up red flags everywhere, but I was dying to see my finished product and there seemed to be no crueler way to let her know me and Stone were back together than by showing up while she was already suffering.

Chapter 35

I sat on a bench watching the shooting fountain in the middle of Armstrong Park waiting for Jeremiah to arrive. He had texted me ten minutes ago that he was two minutes away. I was losing my patience quickly, but tried to keep focus on the task at hand.

He tapped me on my shoulder fifteen minutes later and took a seat next to him. I stared at him a minute for having me wait this damn long.

"My bad, Krissett. I almost got hacked up by them people." He read my facial expression.

"Yeah ok. You have always been untimely." I pointed out. There was no event I could remember him arriving on time.

"What you got for me?" He got down to business.

"I have a dispute with a contractor over the restaurant and need to find a mediator. This is our agreement and absolutely no one else can know." The business served as the perfect decoy for what I actually needed. I emphasized no one. That meant Quincy as well.

"You know I got you. Give me some time to get it together. Gotta make sure it's someone who understands the charge if anything happens."

"Take your time. In the meantime I'll be milking the nigga for the money to pay the mediator. Now let me show you the restaurant." We got up and took a quick ride past Stone's place and the actual restaurant for good measure.

Agreeing on his finder's fee being between ten to twenty five percent of the contract price, we shook hands and he promised to get back with me.

I pulled off with an overwhelming sense of satisfaction. Countdown to Stone's death was in full effect.

Quincy called Saturday night as Meishelle and I watched movies. I convinced her to come keep me company for the night, because being alone wasn't going to help anything. An idle mind is the devil's workshop.

He said he would be home the following week and was finally ready to speak with Meishelle. It went horribly. Meishelle burst the sound barrier going in on Quincy's refusal to provide an explanation for why he was with Janasia, which then turned into a crying fit questioning why she hadn't listened to her instinct.

I took Meishelle to church and lunch Sunday morning. Right now we both needed help from the Lord to push forward. The small family-oriented congregation had been recommended by Derrick. He came over after church to greet Meishelle and I, introducing us to his family. They were really down to earth people.

Stone texted that his plane was boarding and he would arrive shortly. The flight was approximately an hour which means he had gone to Georgia or Texas. Picking up Na'Siah, I headed to get Stone from the airport. Na'Siah talked my head off the entire way about the argument Quameer and his mother had. His mom was against him moving in with some woman. They hadn't learned yet about talking their business around a small child.

We sat patiently waiting in the pickup lane of the Louis Armstrong International Airport. I had gotten an arrangement of flowers from Rouses for Deborah. As I kind gesture, I made certain to get it mixed with tulips since she was allergic to them.

To play my good wife role, I put on my wedding ring that I had retrieved from my safe when Stone emerged from the airport. Takiesha came through shortly later with her rolling suitcase. She would want to have her own vehicle, because that bitch wasn't getting in my shit.

It's showtime, I told myself joyfully getting out the car to drive the bitch.

I got out and popped the trunk for his bags.

"Hey, I missed you." I greeted Stone with a generous tongue exchange.

"Hey, babe. I missed you, too." He came back for more, surprised by the display of affection.

Better enjoy this motherfucker, because this is the most you getting out of me.

Takiesha's eyes watered, obviously fighting back tears, complimenting the already fucked up appearance of her face. The saying a picture was worth a thousand words was a myth.

"You ready?" I glared into his no good ass eyes, smiling.

"Yeah, babe. I'll be right there." He smacked me on the ass as I went back around the car.

I positioned my arm to give Stone a flawless view of the dissolvable stitches. When he questioned me about what happened, I would blame Hollow for doing it in a jealous rage after telling him that we were working on our relationship. The nurse at the hospital received a similar story without including the name, though she persistently pushed for it.

Jumping into the car, I pulled off leaving Takiesha pouting in the taxi cab line. I damn near came on myself from sheer pleasure when Stone escorted her over and handed her money. She was one of a few women that I would never in my existence get tired of seeing be fucked over.

On the way, Stone wanted to stop at the new condo that he had purchased. We pulled up at the new luxury condos where the old Krauss had been years ago. I was relieved he hadn't been in town for my date with Derrick, because shit could have turned extra ugly. From his window he would have had the perfect view of us.

The four bedroom, high ceiling penthouse was fully furnished. Stone pointed Na'Siah to his room, decorated with Fat Heads of Drew Brees and Anthony Davis. He also had a nursery decked out for the baby. The master bedroom knocked me to the floor.

I snapped back to reality. Me, Na'Siah nor the new baby was staying up in here. The plan was for me string Hollow and Stone along, they kill each other, cash in the policies and live out the remainder of my life filthy rich with my babies. I'd be damned if I would lay my head somewhere that someone could put a bullet in me behind his bullshit. He had to be out his damn mind, I wasn't laying my damn head in this place.

"We'll wait in the car." I got Na'Siah and headed to the door. His face was crestfallen. I guess he'd been waiting on my approval of all he had done.

"You are so fucking ungrateful." He grabbed me by the back of my neck.

"Not in front of Na'Siah." I pulled away and returned to the garage.

At the hospital, Stone's family had gathered at Deborah's bedside. She was so damn dramatic. Stone's sister was holding the straw to her mouth as if her bumpy ass hands were broke. They glared at my entrance on Stone's arm. I'm sure my face was the last one they thought they would see.

"Good afternoon, everyone. How are you, Ms. Deborah?" I facetiously grinned, placing the flowers onto her tray.

Her entire body was covered with red miniature blisters. Hopefully, the flowers would agitate her situation even more.

"Why would you bring this bitch up in here?" Deborah sneered.

"Chill out." Stone interjected before I went in on her. I know fucking well she saw my baby standing at my side when she called me out my name.

Stone's sister and mother spoke as a formal pleasantry, but we hadn't got down since Takiesha's announcement at the party. I figured guilty conscious was a fool.

I took a seat in the corner and listened as they talked about Deborah's condition. One of her neighbor's heard the wails of her wounded ass and called an ambulance. Lucky for her they arrived in enough time to save her ass. She would be there a few days and then released. I sure would like to know what Good Samaritan decided to save Satan.

After an hour, I'd had enough of being in their presence. Stone stayed a few more minutes and said his good-byes as I rose without a word and left. I slammed the door on the way out, purposely hitting myself in the arm. Stone had yet to notice my arm.

"Ahhh! Shoot." The holler caught Stone's attention.

Stone reached out to rub my arm passing his hand over the stitches.

"What the fuck happened to your arm?" I smiled while he glanced down.

"Nothing and watch your mouth around my son." I shook my head.

"My bad, but you better tell me now."

I began the fictional narrative of my interaction with Hollow.

Chapter 36

I had lunch during the week with Hollow to inform him that I would be having the baby. My reminder of the abortion on Mardi Gras day had him distant again. I guess the realization that singing Charlie Wilson ballads in my ear could not initially convince me to keep the baby was a huge disappointment.

"Glad you could come." I greeted Hollow. He silently took his seat.

"What's the deal?" He childishly folded his arms on the table.

"Ok then. Let's do this. I've decided to keep the baby." I announced.

I noticed a tiny amount of his attitude shift, but he remained reserved. Declining to order food, he opted for water only.

"Are you going to act like an adult or child? I'm raising this one and not you?" It didn't matter to me one way or the other.

The comment struck a chord that triggered him to address everything on his chest. According to him, it was offensive for me to ever consider murdering his baby in the first place. Knowing that I needed him to go with the insurance policy idea, I feigned to care about his issues.

We still weren't on the best terms, but I knew something that would change his mind quick.

Back at work, Meishelle asked me to drive her home. Ms. Williams did just as I imagined, attempting to force hatred into her towards Quincy. Meishelle struggled to understand why she couldn't transform her love into animosity and it increased her confusion. I packed my laptop to work from home and left a few minutes early to beat the traffic picking up Na'Siah.

Dropping Meishelle off at home, we found Quincy already in the house with no notification. Shit went from zero to one thousand rapidly. Meishelle tossed glasses, lamps and anything else she could get into her hands. I begged her not to call the police, offering for Quincy to stay with me as an option.

"His ass has five minutes exactly," Meishelle barked.

Quincy went to protest her decision, but I asked him to at least honor her request for now, giving me a babysitter to get by Hollow's tonight.

Once Quincy and Na'Siah were knocked out, I jumped up from my nap to get ready. Hollow worked the late shift and didn't get off until two

209

a.m. I looked at the ensemble on the bed with an approving eye. It would guarantee to get Hollow to do whatever I wanted.

"We need to talk." He picked up before the second ring.

I pulled in the driveway of an abandoned house on Hollow's block. Hitting the emergency lights, I placed the changing equipment on the ground and got back into the car.

"Ok. What's up?" The TV was blasting for an early morning hour.

"No, in person. I'm down the street from your house. My tire went out on the way and the rim is scrapping." I set the remainder of the plan in motion.

"I'm coming out now." He hung up the phone.

I watched as he walked down the driveway in a pair of flannel pajama pants. His dick swung freely, revealing he wasn't wearing any drawers. Descending onto the sidewalk in a seven inch plaid school girl skirt, red leather thigh high boots, and the shoulder length wig made me unrecognizable.

He halted in the center of the sidewalk for a minute before continuing, biting his bottom lip.

I bent over by the tire, allowing a full view of the g-string resting in the crack of my ass. The tall oak tree shielded the street light just enough to keep me inconspicuous if his neighbors decided to get nosey.

"What are you doing out here in the middle of the night, woman?" He looked at the tire to assess the damage.

"I told you, to talk." I placed my hand on his chest to stop him from bending down to examine it closer. Unbuttoning the crotch part of his pajama pants, I wedged myself between him and the car. I drew him in using my mouth and then released him slowly. His head fell forward, placing his hands in an arrest stance on my car.

I used my tongue to circle the tip of his head, sucking it like a lollipop. I wanted to crack the mystery on how many licks it would take to reach his center.

After a few more seconds, I stopped and wiggled my way up. His eyes gleamed in the night, begging me to continue. Without waiting for his response, I strutted down the sidewalk to his house.

Chapter 37

Quincy's getting ready for work broke my rest. He needed to invest his money into a business where he could make his own damn hours. The three and four a.m. alarms on the weekday and weekend mornings were aggravating as shit. My sleep time was stretched thin creeping some nights with Hollow who was coming around, Stone coming over the other nights and mid-day lunch dates Derrick. Outside of my occasional church attendance, Derrick and I were seeing each other at least twice a week. I didn't know how women found the energy, but I guess the growing bank account should be my fuel.

Last night Stone had broken my rest trying to lay up under me. He had just left a few minutes before Quincy got up. He was pissed, feeling he had to tiptoe around because of Quincy, so I rotated a few nights at his condo. Takiesha was by Deborah's babysitting bump face. The blisters had healed, but she had scars that weren't going anywhere.

Na'Siah followed suit, rasping on my door at six a.m. for a bowl of cereal and Saturday morning cartoons. The minute I sat down on the sofa, the doorbell rang.

"Mommy, it's Stone!" Na'Siah flew to the window. The blinds clasped back together and he broke to the door.

"I heard you. I'm coming." I lethargically slid to my feet.

Stone stood with my favorite morning treat, donuts. The fried cake batter overlaid in the sugary goodness called glaze instantly made my mouth water over. Grabbing the box from his hand, we settled in the living room with food, occasionally laughing at Looney Toons.

"Na'Siah, I'm almost finished up working and then I can come home for good." Stone declared.

The only way he would permanently come back into my house would be in an urn if I decided not to flush his ashes down the toilet. I had been filling him and Hollow's head with fictitious stories during pillow talk.

"Can Mr. Hollow and Xavier come over sometime to play the game with us?" He questioned Stone.

I kept my eyes front and center. Na'Siah was unintentionally aiding my plan along.

211

"That's something me and your mom will have to discuss." Stone scanned me sinisterly.

Stone hung around for most of the day. I told Meishelle we would head to the mall about four p.m. and later she had agreed to have a civil dialogue with Quincy at my house. Hopefully, with Na'Siah in the house, she would refrain from making a scene.

"Yeah, I'm by Krissett's, but I'll meet you there." Deborah rung Stone's phone about two p.m. Her recent brush with death had her attending church. My flowers caused her a few extra days in the hospital. Stone didn't fall for her rave that I had done it purposely.

It was people like her that made me usually stay away from church. I figured I had a better chance praying and doing my own thing then allowing church folks to keep me in the faith. Derrick's church had turned out to be different. Meishelle and I were going back for our third Sunday tomorrow.

"Walk me to the door." Stone helped me up.

He went in about bringing Hollow and the kids around Na'Siah. I told him Na'Siah hadn't seen them in a while and that is why he asked. Truthfully, we had all went to dinner Wednesday night. Reassuring him there was no one else, I kissed him and let him out.

Getting Na'Siah cleaned up, we headed to Babies R Us to meet Meishelle. Five months into the pregnancy, pampers was the only gift for anyone to buy if there was a shower. I had already ordered a custom made, wooden convertible crib from rosenberrys.com with the last money Stone gave me.

I couldn't wait to find out the baby's gender. The first four-D ultrasound was scheduled at Peek-A-Womb next week and I had one the following a Bella Baby. Which man was attending what session had yet to be determined.

"Mommy, look. I want this one for my baby." Na'Siah struggled with a life size teddy bear that almost swallowed him.

"I like this one, sweetie. We can put this in the corner of her room, but we don't want this one to be lonely so we have to get some smaller ones, too." I reasoned with him.

"Ok. They have a lot of them." He ran back over.

Finalizing the purchases, I had worked up an appetite. Our next stop was Louisiana Kitchen. The small green building was a buffet style eatery that represented the hell out of the gulf coast. Stuffed crabs, chicken and sausage gumbo, crawfish etouffee, shrimp creole and other soul food delights sat under the inviting light. When it came to food, there was no place under the sun like home.

"Girl, look at that table over there." I motioned to a table that two women shared in the corner. I didn't want to say names, because Na'Siah would have hollered clean across the damn place.

"Is that?" Meishelle looked at me, sharing the name with me telepathically.

"Schtanya?" I called out before I fully approached the table, not wanting to embarrass myself too bad if I was wrong.

"Hey, cuz." Her roaming eyes couldn't have shown her shock more.

She had been M.I.A. for Mardi Gras day laying under Cionna all day. She texted me that shit as she was on a flight headed back to Atlanta. Now her ass was sneaking in town without telling anyone. I knew the shit was real when she asked me what I thought about this trick. Cionna's head game was magnificent, but not enough to risk everything over.

"Hey, Krissett." Cionna smiled brightly.

"What are you guys doing in town?" I ignored Cionna and continued interrogating Schtanya.

"Just hooked up for something to eat while I was in town for business with Derrick." She was telling a ball faced lie.

I had talked to Derrick last night and made plans with him for later today. He was the best man in his cousin's wedding this weekend. Last night had been the bachelor's party full of strippers at the hotel and today was the actual wedding. Business wasn't anywhere on his fucking agenda.

"Oh ok. Well, make sure you call me before you leave. We all need to have dinner together." I walked off.

I was going against Hattie Mae on this one. Schtanya had too much to lose dealing with Cionna. I would support her in any decision, but it was vital she had considered all the facts and repercussions prior to doing so.

Quincy called Meishelle to let her know that he was on the way to my house. I finished up my last plate, leaving Schtanya still ducked off in the corner with her boo. I waved to her as she glanced over when we rose from the table. My gut instinct said she wouldn't call, too ashamed at being caught.

Chapter 38

Me and Na'Siah settled into my room with *Despicable Me 2,* while the couple took the living room. Meishelle changed her mind on Saturday the moment she laid eyes on him and postponed it until further notice, which turned out to be Monday evening. It was rather quiet for about fifteen minutes when the tone in their voices started to rise. I left Na'Siah for a second to try to calm down the situation.

Quincy had settled on the full disclosure option. From what I could tell they hadn't got to the robbery portion yet.

"You knew he was sleeping with her and didn't say a fucking word to me. Heard me say I thought he was fucking someone else and didn't say shit!" She yelled venomously, rising from the couch.

There was no right time to tell her so I took my charge.

"I didn't know how to. You're my best friend, but he's my brother." I replied solemnly.

Ultimately, my reasons for not saying anything were almost more selfish than Quincy's. He didn't want to lose his wife and I didn't want to lose my best friend.

"Meishelle, that's my blood. Not some nigga on the street. Shit is all the way separate. He did it for you, to give you what he thought you wanted."

"Bullshit, Krissett! We have always called shit what it is. This nigga's wrong is no different than a nigga on the street." Meishelle had me dead right.

Conceding defeat, I returned to the room with Na'Siah. Turning up the TV to drown out their voices, I heard the front door slam and guest room close shortly after. It appeared Quincy would be staying with me a little longer, which was ok.

After dropping Na'Siah off Tuesday, Hollow came over to chill for the day. I had been working from home on days when no meetings were scheduled. Checking the call center stats, I placed my head in his lap while we watched *The Wood*. I never got tired of watching Omar Epps' bald-headed, chocolate self on my TV.

"I love you, ma." He whispered, holding me.

"Me too." Searching my inner soul, I beamed with pride. Deception was becoming one of my stronger qualities. A few nights of sex had Hollow's nose wide open. It was a slight turn off that he was so damn gullible for pussy.

"When we going to make this thing official? We good, spending most nights under each other, the kids like each other, so what's the deal?" The earnestness of Hollow's voice came through with each word.

"Maybe when the baby comes." It seemed to be the right time to bring up the insurance policy and coverage.

Hollow easily fell for the cookies and agreed to go through the physical. I excused myself momentarily, seeing Mrs. Populus' number on the phone. It served as a reminder to check the calendar for my upcoming court date. It would have been easier to just ask her, but I figured it might give off a wrong impression.

My nerves overpowered me as I tapped the accept button and closed the room door. After exchanging pleasantries, her tone hinted that it was something very serious. I could have been overreacting, but it was highly unlikely.

It had to do with Takiesha. That bitch made me sick. I should have slit that bitch's throat for Christmas and painted the walls with her blood.

Ms. Populus and I agreed to meet at Robin's on Canal Street at eight a.m., since it was close to the courthouse. She wanted to discuss the details over breakfast before we went to court that morning. I hoped she would have confirmed the date at some point, but she never did.

I was desperately in need of Meishelle, but she hadn't spoken to me since Monday. Needless to say, I was still waiting on that phone call or visit from Schtanya after catching her and Cionna snuggled in the corner. Cionna had managed to send a pussy shot, though, of herself, which I immediately discarded. Sasha was my next ace in line.

"What's up, boo?" Sasha came through for me.

"Girl, let me tell you about this old trashy ass bitch Stone using the shit out of." I took a seat on the bed.

The District Attorney had given my lawyer the bare minimum of information. Basically, she claimed that I had violated the protective order issued by the magistrate on several occasions.

"I saw her ugly ass a few days ago. Stone stomped that ho's face in outside ole boy's house. Any other woman I would have called the people, but for her, fuck no." Sasha brought some happiness with the news.

"When this trial is over, I am going old school and washing her ass." I knew Stone might throw a lick himself, since he had turned to whipping her ass.

"That's some low down shit, but you might not have to do shit. I'm telling you, the way Stone whipped her up the other night, I don't know how she is breathing. You be careful, though, because once men start beating on women, they ain't stopping."

"Don't you worry. I got this." I assured her, almost forgetting that Hollow was still in the living room. Making plans to attend the French Quarter festival the following weekend, we hung up. The Festival season was about to kick off. Me and the baby were ready.

Returning to the living room, the movie was cut short when Hollow received a call from the school that Xavier had been accused of starting a garbage can fire. He was being brought down to the juvenile detention center and faced possible charges of arson. Hollow leaped up off the coach with an expression that he would murder the child when he walked out the door.

Once I saw Hollow off, I relaxed on the sofa until Derrick texted me after class to confirm our date for the evening and I was all too ready to see what the young boy had to offer me.

Chapter 39

I chose Stone to attend the first ultrasound session by default. The argument Hollow and I had the previous night disqualified him. It was something small and petty, but Derrick's plans for us required no interruption. Following the ultrasound I would do the same with Stone.

By the time I arrived at the center, I was already pissed. Stone's untimely behind had shown up late to pick me up, knowing that he had to put money in my account to pay for the imaging.

The baby seemed so perfect. Ten fingers, ten toes that moved all over the screen. I swore at one point they waved at me.

"Alright, mommy. Here it is." The ultrasound technician handed me the envelope for the gender revealing party over the weekend after next.

Stone tried to snatch it from my grasp. My momma had insisted on the new fad of having a party to divulge the baby's sex. No men were allowed, which made it easy to sell to him and Hollow on why they couldn't come.

"So, what is Na'Siah asking me about Hollow and his son still coming by the house? When did they start?" Stone helped me start an argument.

"Stone, don't go there. You know me and him were chilling for a minute." I knew the nonchalant attitude would piss him off.

"Nah. Lil' man has seen him recently or he wouldn't have brought it up at all." He discredited my lie.

"Whatever. I'm not about to debate no shit with you. You know the deal."

"Man, that nigga better not be around none of y'all. I'm warning you."

"If you fucking act like you want us then he won't. Otherwise, what you don't want another man will."

The sting that crossed my face knocked me speechless. The force almost caused me to bash my head into the window as the taste of blood filled my palate. I knew damn well this negro had not put his hands on me again. He must have lost his damn mind. Arguing was one thing, but he had promised never to put his hands on me after Mardi Gras. I should have known better.

219

Within a few seconds, the shock wore off and I landed a fist in his jaw.

His reflexes sent another backhand. My face cracked against the glass. I swung wildly, not caring where the blows fell. More of his made impact than mine did.

"Motherfucker, have you lost your mind?" He maneuvered the truck out of traffic and pulled over.

I reached to the bottom of my purse searching for the razor blade I had placed in there to arch my eyebrows. I knew we wouldn't have time to stop with Stone being so late.

Securing it in my grasp, I flung it around like a mad woman. He jumped out of the truck to avoid my fury. Standing in the open door, he screamed obscenities that pissed me off even more, until I jumped out the truck to go around and dice his ass up. The second my feet hit the sidewalk, he hopped back in, pulling off with the passenger side door still open. About a block away he threw my purse and cell phone onto the ground.

Blood seeped from a small cut on my head and the swelling in my face could be felt. I cleaned myself up in a nearby Wendy's bathroom and caught the bus home.

An older lady who sat in the front stared at me. I kept my focus straight ahead, fearful for some strange reason of what she had to say to me.

"You know, whatever it is will never be worth the sacrifice. In these fights, the only one that loses is you." She called out to me. It seemed she could detect I was avoiding her so she began to talk, knowing that it would catch my attention.

"Yes, ma'am." I realize that as my eyes teared up.

One damn argument had turned into a fist fight. I could feel the baby flutters in my belly, knowing what happened had not been good. The idea of pitting Hollow and Stone against each other had been pretty good, but not at the expense of putting myself through all of this. I had never considered that before the plan worked, Stone could have beaten me to death.

"It's ok, sweetie." She hugged me tight as the tears fell.

Over a several day span, various gifts poured into my job and home from Stone. If he thought material trinkets could make up for abuse, he was sadly mistaken. I had some principles that I refuse to set aside for money. Each one was deposited into the nearest garbage receptacle with the exception of the expensive tennis charm bracelet. It seemed to be a sin to discard something worth so much, so I handed it to the gentlemen that panhandled on the corner by the job. It could buy him food or whatever he wanted for quite some time.

Dodging Quincy's suspicions was hell. Constantly wearing wakeup for twenty four hours a day there was skepticism written all over his face when I told him the doctor had put me on bed rest for high blood pressure. I swore he could see under the mounds of my Mac foundation, but he went into work late to drop Na'Siah off at school, picked him up and prepared meals. Waiting until late at night to try and bust me, he came into my room to hold random conversations, hoping to catch me off guard.

Hollow was allowed to attend the second ultrasound session. We settled our differences amicably once I had to cancel my date night with Derrick, thanks to Stone's stupid ass. Hollow decided to pay extra for the specialist to tell him privately the sex of the baby. He emerged from the room with a grin wider than the sun. I assumed it was another boy, because that's all he had been talking about. After lunch we stopped to drop the results off to my momma.

"We are still going to the French Quarter Festival tomorrow and then going to pick up last minute things for the party, right?" She stood in the door waving at Hollow in the car.

"Yes, ma'am." I reluctantly surrendered both envelopes, although I almost purposely left the first one at home.

"Ok. Meishelle will be there. I certainly wish you girls would fix this mess between y'all."

"I didn't stop speaking to her, momma. We have to run though." I kissed her on the cheek and left.

Hollow dropped me off at home for a work meeting, which was ok by me. I had money in my account and food in my belly. Picking out party favors, Derrick texted me to take a ride to the beach and Beau

Rivage for the buffet. It was Quameer's weekend with Na'Siah so I agreed.

Derrick and I headed into the open water on a jet ski. The sprinkles that popped up from the motor cooled the heat on my skin. He lost control at the warning pole, dumping us off. We shared a laugh as he shoved water into my face and we ran around in the sand. It was so much damn fun.

Cleaning ourselves off at a nearby motel, we proceeded to the buffet. The dinner menu consisted of all the Gulf South seafood one could eat. My first plate contained snow crabs, shrimp and crawfish.

Derrick was like the guy best friend every girl needed. He mentioned that he wanted Na'Siah and his son to meet when he came in town. His mom was arranging a trip for the two of them to Disney World and he invited us to tag along. Spring break was around the corner and Na'Siah would love it.

Quameer called that he was unable to get Na'Siah. He had an emergency doctor's appointment, due to complications with his transplant.

Quincy stepped up and by the time I arrived home, Na'Siah was passed out. The disarray of my living room told me that they had enjoyed hours of fun time. Derrick and I watched a movie until we passed out together on the couch.

Chapter 40

My momma was at the house at the crest of sunrise Saturday morning. Startling Derrick and I out of slumber, she wanted us in the cake store by eight a.m. so we would be knocking down the gates of Jackson Square by ten for her spot. Quincy left to head to his house and pick up Meishelle.

The weather was gorgeous, causing thousands to walk the five mile radius. My momma and Craig had chosen to stay in Jackson Square for Irma Thomas' performance while the rest of us tested the eats. I invited Derrick along, but he wanted to freshen up first.

The floppy rim of my bright orange sunhat shielded the cheerful sunlight from my skin. Big, pregnant and heat was a bad combination. My mom encouraged me to drink plenty water, but the limited availability of bathrooms said that would not happen. We made our first selections from white tents decorating the banks of the Riverfront, all offering their individual taste of Louisiana.

Quincy took Na'Siah to get a snowball and dessert, while Meishelle and I sat silently in our chairs under the shade trees. We gawked at some of the attire these women had chosen to wear, exchanging an occasional glance for those that had gone to the extreme.

A woman passing on her cell phone with a multicolored pastel rayon material flowing flawlessly in the warm wind caught my attention. Her slim frame wore the hell out of the dress. She turned left and right, unintentionally walking the runway. I wanted to ask her where the dress had come from, but she appeared to be searching for the person on the other end of the line.

Hollow came up and greeted her with a kiss on the cheek, apparently introducing her to the kids who were with him. I peeked over to Meishelle whose head was down in her plate. Examining which way he should go he glanced in my direction. His eyes bulged like a deer in headlights.

"Hey, y'all!" I eagerly greeted, waving to him and the kids.

He tried to ignore me as if it wasn't him, but Xavier came over my way. I rose from my chair to meet them halfway. Hollow should have known I didn't give a shit. Baby or not, he was nothing to me. Now, I could ask about the dress, actually.

Hollow greeted me and the kids each gave me a hug. For the most part they were excited about the baby.

"Hi, I'm Krissett." I extended my hand to the lady. "You have to tell me where I can get that dress once I drop this baby."

"This is Holly." Hollow introduced the woman.

"Sure. It came from an online boutique." She smiled politely and gave me the information.

"Well, it was a pleasure to meet you, Holly. Hope you all have a great time." I made a memo of the website for Exclusively Fabulous in my phone.

"Same here." They all walked off.

Meishelle remained quiet when I took my chair. What just happened could in no form be equated to her and Quincy's deal. In a split second, I got a text from Hollow asking if we could talk. I knew what he wanted and no explanation was required. He was a single man and I was a heartless woman who wanted sporadic dick and dollar bills. I ignored his request, returning my phone to the cup holder.

Derrick showed up at about one p.m. and we went off on our own journey with Na'Siah. Walking down to the Riverwalk, we took in more of the numerous local artists that graced the multiple stages of music. The food had helped me last longer than expected. Finding my momma and Craig, we hung another hour, because they were enthralled in the artist on the stage before leaving at four p.m. Unfortunately, we didn't cross paths with Hollow again, so I could show him exactly why I could care less about him and Holly.

Monday morning I sat across from Ms. Populus going over this foolishness with Takiesha. She took the printed call logs and listened to the various voicemails they had been leaving to show the judge that their claims held little merit.

We settled in the hallway at court and waited for my case to be called. There was not a damn seat available on the wooden benches inside or outside of my section.

Takiesha and Deborah came sashaying the hallway in my direction, grins plastered on their faces. She must have had her makeup professionally done today, because it covered up more than usual. The dummy neglected to tell them not to draw attention to her busted lip by putting on shiny lip gloss.

Stone's slick ass was absent. He probably purposely missed court, just in case I had called the people on his ass. He was going to take that ride right around the corner on those warrants.

Takiesha maintained a distance, but Deborah came right over.

"Good morning, Sweetie! How's my great grandbaby?" She smiled, stretching to touch my belly.

"Deborah, don't come over here with that foolishness. I'm not about to play that way in this building." I knocked her hand away.

"Excuse us, please." Ms. Populus guided me past them to another area. Deborah had inadvertently just given her more to work with. The judge saw the majority of cases before calling a recess for lunch. We grabbed a bit to eat from the cafeteria and got upstairs as our case was being called.

"State vs. Robertson. Please step forward." The Baliff summoned us to the front.

Takiesha and Deborah followed behind us. I was so high-strung the swinging of the double doors that divided the gallery off made me unnoticeably jump. Gripping the podium tightly to steady myself, the judge went straight to the business at hand.

"How does the Defendant plea?" He addressed my attorney.

"Not guilty, Your Honor." Ms. Populus responded assertively.

I had elected the option of trial by jury, standing a greater chance of getting twelve individuals to agree that what I had done was wrong. Any woman in her right mind would understand my actions that night.

"Mrs. Robertson, the Court is willing to make you an offer of ten months, good time for one count of involuntary manslaughter, if you enter a guilty plea. The deal will become null and void if refused." The judge presented.

I shook my head to the lawyer to let her know my refusal. She advised the judge of my decision and requested that a date for the trial to begin.

"Your Honor, It has also been brought to our attention that the defendant is in violation of the protective order against one of the plantiffs, Ms. Takiesha Lee." The prosecutor spoke up.

According to Takiesha, I attacked her at the counter while her back was turned and then smashed the window of her car in a fit of rage. Neither could provide proof though. I assumed they would use this when Ms. Populus called me and had already contacted Walgreens. They only kept video footage for one month back.

"Your Honor, my client is not in violation of such an order. It was Ms. Lee who attacked my client. Furthermore, she and Mr. Robertson have been harassing my client with countless telephone calls and voicemails." She held up the print-outs of my cell phone logs.

Takiesha and Deborah stood astonished that I had been able to trap them up. The prosecutor interjected that it could not be proven to be his clients. He had ventured into the territory, so he couldn't close it out now. To refute his motion, I had also brought a copy of the paper bill from AT & T so that the Trap Call and iblacklist app information could be matched.

"Let me see what you have there, Counselor." The judge held out his hand for the telephone which my attorney graciously handed over.

Courtroom spectators in the gallery snickered and shook their heads. Takiesha and Deborah wore the dick look as the judge played the messages in front of the court, selecting the ones that seemed to be most childish. They mockingly chanted my name, singing their rendition of *What Do The Lonely Do* and created sex scenes. Deborah's voice was horrible at the male role.

"This is despicable and criminal behavior. Today is a warning, however, if I find out that it continues in any way I will charge both of you with Improper Use of Telecommunications. Mrs. Robertson you are also warned not to violate any orders of this court. Pregnant or not, I will have you remanded, as well. Do I make myself clear?"

"Yes." We all responded, simultaneously.

He concluded by advising us to see the court secretary. We proceeded to the front of the bench, where the court secretary had his computer set up busily typing away. He handed me a court date for July twentieth.

The dummies followed the flushed faced prosecutor out of the court room. I could tell he was giving them a nice piece of his mind for embarrassing him.

Fuck with me, bitches! I wanted to yell back at them. This would be the last time they tried me without a fool proof plan, so I didn't have to worry. Those hos were nowhere near on my level.

Chapter 41

The best part of my work day came with the news from the realtor that my condo would be ready to move in next month. She had an opening to give me a tour over the weekend for any last minute adjustments or upgrades that I wanted to make. An offer had yet to be made on the house, but between one of my generous contributors it would be taken care of. Quincy had the option to stay there or join me at the condo. Meishelle hadn't allowed him to move back in quite yet, but he was spending some nights there.

"Excuse me." My administrative assistant interrupted, stepping in my last boring ass meeting of the evening to hand me a folded note.

Normally, I would have had my cell phone, but the alarm had gone off in a prior meeting, causing my boss to give me the eyes of shame. Unfolding the paper, the message was a 911 from Meishelle to call her. I hurriedly pounded on the elevator button.

"Krissett! They burst through the door and took him," Meishelle shrilled.

Tears welled in my eyes. He had gotten away with it for too long. One of the dudes must have ratted him out.

Meishelle continually howled his name in the background, her cell phone fell to the floor. I had my secretary notify my boss of the emergency and burned rubber to Quincy's home. My first destination was to make sure Meishelle was ok.

The cracked door barely hung on the last hinge. I found Meishelle sprawled out on the floor in the fetal position. While I had experienced the jailhouse and grave life, she had done neither. With the exception of this, Quincy had been walking the straight and narrow since they became serious.

"Come on, chick." I helped Meishelle up onto the sofa.

I rubbed the hair stuck to her face, assuring her everything would be ok. Contacting my attorney, she referred me to a male associate in the practice to avoid any conflict of interest. He took down my contact numbers and said once he had more information he would call us back.

My mom came a short time later to debrief and I stepped out to find a company with an emergency service to repair the door. Meishelle, still ignorant to the situation, told my momma that Quincy had come over to check on her and get some more clothes. As usual an argument ensued and carried into the room where he was gathering some of his stuff. The police burst through the door and cuffed him up. Hysterical, she hadn't heard them say the charges and they wouldn't tell her anything.

Meishelle got up to pack her bags, while my mother and I continued talking. I felt at this time it would be better to cancel the party on Saturday, but she wanted to continue it. She said it would help keep her mind off everything going on. I went in the room to check on her and found her staring at their high school prom picture. To help her, I retrieved her overnight bag from under the bed and found Quincy's cell phone in the process. I would hold it for safe keeping.

We finished up and headed out to the cars, our conversation continuing well into the night. I wanted to interject an apology in somewhere, but things were almost back to normal. The lawyer, Mr. Maurice, returned our call to inform us Quincy was being held on armed robbery charges, surprising my mom and Meishelle. It could be up to three days for a bond to be set and up to fourteen days before Quincy made an initial appearance in Federal Court. Mr. Maurice arranged to meet tomorrow for the retainer fee and ask questions about the arrest. He said any discrepancy, although unlikely, could be used to our advantage.

After going to the bank the following morning, I found out the Feds had frozen any accounts that had Quincy's name on it. I damn sure wasn't going over to Hattie Mae's house into the stash. Quincy had hidden it in one of the bedroom walls after her funeral. The remaining money was enough to finish up the business. Once we had paid all the contractors and fees, I had plans to lease it to one of my cousins.

Mr. Maurice advised us there was a slight possibility he could have the funds released, if he could prove it to be earned from a legitimate source. That could take a couple of business days though. I took the money from my other bank account and would handle the rest later.

I received the first call from Quincy on the way to the attorney's office. Quincy had done some shit in his time, but he didn't deserve this.

"Hey, bro. You hanging in there for us, huh?" I couldn't disguise my sadness.

"Off top. I'm not about to let this shit break who I am." He replied confidently.

"What are they saying?"

"Trying to play good cop and bad cop, but I ain't worried, because I didn't do shit. Claiming they have both of us in custody, but no nigga can tell something that I didn't do." Quincy explained.

"Oh ok." That was unimaginable to me.

There had been at least four niggas involved and Quincy said they had been brought in together. Through process of elimination we both knew who it had to be. To my knowledge her condition hadn't changed.

"I have to go, but let me holla at my wife for a quick minute. You let her know the real deal. Love you, Krissett."

"Love you too, Quincy." Letting him know that we all had money on our account, I handed the phone to Meishelle. By the end of the call, she was in another crying spell.

The meeting went well and ended in enough time to pick up Na'Siah from school. It was a must that I create an excuse on Quincy's whereabouts. He had been asking since last night.

He jumped up and down with a slip in his hand as his teacher opened the car door, announcing his role in the spring play. His excitement was heartwarming, although spring programs were normally held before Easter.

"Can I call and see if my daddy can come?" Na'Siah rambled in the back of the car about everyone he wanted to come.

Quameer had called earlier for a face-to-face conversation. He was becoming distant lately, not calling or answering his phone for Na'Siah. We had not heard from him since the last flake out for the doctor's appointment. His mother was the reason he was seeing him at all. Why he couldn't talk about it on the phone mystified me. He acted as if the phone was bugged or tapped.

"You sure can. First tell nana and then let Tee Meishelle call him, ok?" I got on the interstate. Hopefully, Quameer would answer for my baby to at least stay on my good side until the heart-to-heart we just had to have.

My mother had agreed to keep him so Meishelle and I could have a talk. We were going to have dinner at Dish. During the middle of the week it would be empty, providing the perfect environment to eat and talk.

Quameer promised Na'Siah he would come and scheduled breakfast with me for Sunday morning.

Dropping Na'Siah off, I began the task of telling Meishelle the whole truth and nothing but the truth from beginning to end.

"I didn't need no damn ring, just him." She shook her head.

"Quincy has a tremendous amount of pride and love for you. He probably would have sold his soul to the devil if he could have." I had seen him give up more than a little for their relationship.

5:35 p.m.: You out yet? Janasia messaged Quincy.

"What's wrong?" Meishelle read the frown on my face as I checked the phone, walking into the place. She paid no attention that it was Quincy's phone, because we had the same case.

"Girl, nothing. Quameer ass trying to have breakfast in the morning." I dropped the phone into my purse.

We walked into the restaurant/bar playing Bell Biv DeVoe's *Poison*. Meishelle's mood had gone into the dumps again. Fighting to keep upbeat, I nudged her to check me out doing the snake. She lightly smiled as we took our seats at the table.

"I knew she woke up, but I said nothing." Meishelle took shots of patron.

"It wouldn't have made a difference." It would have had no bearing on the outcome, unless we had killed her before she could say anything.

Chapter 42

Due to the circumstances with Quincy, I brought my phone to each meeting, but found myself texting Derrick instead. He made the time go by, causing sore stomach muscles from laughing at him all day. During our standing lunch date on Wednesday, we finalized plans to Disney World in two weeks.

Quincy called to tell us the federal judge ordered him held without a bond. The murder charge for the armored car employee had been added onto all four of them leaving us all disappointed.

He had displayed some sympathy, relinquishing the money in our accounts for availability within the seven business days. The legitimate income counted for almost every penny in the bank minus maybe three thousand. I had broken my silence with Hollow for his check stubs to argue it was money given to me for the baby. We would see if the Judge had gone for it.

Janasia's daily texts to check if he was out, had me wanting to beat down her door. In code, Quincy talked me out of the idea. She intentionally waited until the news broke before sending the first message. I was on to her dumb ass trick.

Hollow being the single, possible baby daddy, that my mom knew of, was invited to the gender reveal party. He and the kids came extra early to help set up the up. Hollow arranged the table and chairs in the yard with Craig, while the kids placed food on the trays. The men showed up a short time later with the huge tent that would keep the sun out, but allow all the spring time breeze in.

The guests arrived shortly after four p.m., bringing cases of pampers in hand. I had included a message in every invitation as a special request. To my amazement out of the pink and blue boiled eggs, the slip appeared in the pink. I was having a girl, Anjali Janiya. Her last name had yet to be determined.

"Two girls and two boys." Hollow hugged me.

"I thought the smile meant it was another boy." I lightheartedly laughed.

Na'Siah's chest poked out at the idea of becoming a big brother.

233

I had to cancel the breakfast with Quameer Sunday morning to finalize the plans at the restaurant and the condo in Slidell. Quincy being indisposed made it another primary project on my plate. Meishelle and I had a meeting after the trip to discuss the candidate pool and pay rates for the restaurant. The condo had been set back slightly due to all the April showers and was slated for June.

The chat Quameer wanted to have waited to Thursday. We were flying down I-10 to Na'Siah's program, late as I usually was for everything. He sat quietly in the passenger seat, instead of using the time to his advantage and talk.

"You wanted to talk, right?" I initiated dialogue. He wasn't getting another dinner to say what could be said now.

"So, despite the matching and meds, my body is rejecting the new kidney. As it stands, I only have a few more months to live. I'm on the list, but since I had a transplant they might not be so willing to give me another one." He paused.

Quameer had given up fighting for his life the day he became paralyzed.

"I'm sorry to hear that." I lied.

Life was finally on my side. First, his inability to walk and now death. It couldn't get much better than this.

"Yeah, it's life though. From cradle to the grave. While I'm around, I want to be able to spend as much time as possible with Na'Siah, which is why I called you."

"Uh huh." I was hoping his ass wasn't about to try and come back for my baby. Filing formal paperwork in court to establish custody became high priority.

"Here's the deal. I get a check every month and for the most part I am self-sufficient, so I can take care of my own. I'm asking if I could stay with you, until whenever, to be able to spend my last times with my son. If I live longer than six months, I'll go back by my mom's."

It had to be the argument Na'Siah attempted to tell me about months ago. Quameer had to be fucking joking to think he could come stay in my damn house. The chump change he got was nothing to warrant further consideration. Had it not been for Na'Siah, his ass would have been through years ago. His face remained serious.

234

"Wow, Quameer. I'll give it consideration. Knowing this information though, what provisions have you made for him to be taken care of once you are gone?" He had long been worth more dead than alive.

"Man, you have become a cold-blooded motherfucker. A man tells you that he is dying and you worried about a dollar bill. My momma has a policy set up that she took out on me as a kid. It pays her and she will make sure my son gets what is his." He shook his head.

I know fucking well Quameer wasn't talking. The definition of a gigolo, Quameer had been using women all his life for financial gain. For the few months he was with Janasia, the child support checks came drawn on her account every other week. Finally we both opened up Chase checking accounts so we could go automatic transfers from her account to mine. She rubbed it in my face that she knew how to have a man's back until he could get back on his feet. Nothing was wrong with his feet, he just didn't want to work, never lasting on a job a full year. Mariah did the same, but she took his ability to ever get back on them again away and *I* was cold blooded?

Quameer is a joke.

"Let's be honest about this. You've treated me like shit for most of this relationship. The only thing that humbled you is the shit Mariah did to you. Otherwise, you would still be shitting on me. So am I sorry to look out for me and mine? *Fuck no,* because at the end of the day my babies are what I have." I replied, brashly shaking my head in disbelief. It was in his best interest to leave it alone.

We pulled into the handicapped parking spot at the school and waited for his mom to come over with the wheelchair.

Na'Siah's eyes lit up seeing me wheel Quameer's chair onto the front row. He stumbled minimally through the lines, but to me it was perfect. He leaped off the stage into Quameer's lap at the end of the performance.

"Don't forget to get at me about the other issue." We had checked Na'Siah out of school and ate at Ryan's before dropping Quameer off.

"I won't." My heart wouldn't allow me to sympathize with his plight, although Quameer had done a 180 degree turnaround in the father area.

Even for money I could only pretend to care for a short period of time and that was an added concern. While it would be good for Quameer to spend the max amount of time he could with NaSiah in his last days, a hostile environment would be worse.

An unexpected visitor was waiting for me and Na'Siah when I got home.

"What's up with you?" Stone hopped out of his truck and took a sleeping Na'Siah out of my arms.

"I ain't got shit for you." I reached for my baby back.

I swore to myself when I moved, none of these niggas would know where I lived. These pop-ups were really getting out of hand. Until I could convince Hollow to kill Stone of my own merit or hire a contractor to at least kidnap his ass to torture him, I had nothing more to say to him.

"Man, I been texting you for days." Stone had been on a lunatic rant in an attempt to get me back. He came with an anger management certificate to show me he was getting help. He needed it to stop beating on Takiesha, because his times with me were done.

"Don't do this in front of Na'Siah. Put him down first." I put my hand up to stop him from going further in front of Na'Siah. He might be playing sleep while taking everything in.

He nodded his head in agreement, taking a seat on the sofa inside after placing him on the bed. I would have to rush this conversation along, because my baby needed a bath. Due to an in service for the teachers, they were out that Friday and Monday. We had to be at the airport early to leave for a four day package at Disney World with Derrick tomorrow. Our rouse was to play friends who coincidentally met at the airport going to the same place. Derrick had already paid for our airline tickets and separate hotel rooms.

"Stone, there really is nothing more to discuss. We are in divorce court, because I no longer wish to be married to you. You have Takiesha and whomever else. I'm ok with that. When Anjali is born we can take the DNA test. Other than that, we are done." I replied calmly.

"Anjali, huh? So I'm having a daughter. On that other stuff, a nigga done running behind you and acting all crazy. I'll accept your wishes. Remember every action has a consequences behind it." He rose from the sofa and placed a box on the table before leaving.

Stone had become like the weather. You could never one hundred percent know what would happen on a daily basis. Some days he was sunny, others rainy with tornados. I hoped that the classes are what had him so cool about the situation at hand. Maybe he had finally accepted things for what they were or maybe I had accepted his offer to make my life a living hell. Either way, it couldn't be any worse than he had been putting me though. I locked the door behind me and set the alarm for the night.

Chapter 43

"Where are we, mommy?" Na'Siah sleepily wiped his eyes on the short term parking shuttle.

"It's a surprise." I rubbed his legs. He had been extra cranky this morning, but was wide awake now.

The damn airport was far too crowded for 6 a.m., instantaneously annoying me. I cursed myself at the possibility of missing my flight, planning my time table on the airport being empty. Standing in the airline counter line, my foot impatiently tapped on the linoleum floor. One lady was holding up the entire line with foolishness about missing her flight. If it happened to me, she had an ass whipping coming her way. The counter attendant was visibly aggravated, consistently apologizing to those waiting in the line.

"How long have you been waiting, miss?" An older gentlemen behind me asked.

"Maybe about ten minutes. Looks like we will all be here a while though." I huffed in irritation, ready to take a seat at the gate.

"I sure hope not." I looked back at him, smiling. Derrick had arrived a few feet behind us in the line. His son stood next to him playing a handheld game. I breathed a sigh of relief that if the money went to waste it wasn't my doing.

The line erupted in applause when the woman finally decided to step to the side and allow us to make our flight. My eyes could have served as a machete when I cut them at her. I swore misery loved company.

Derrick caught up with us at the TSA checkpoint.

"Hey, Krissett?" Derrick called out.

"Hey, Derrick." I appeared surprised. "How are you?"

"I'm pretty good and you? It's been a minute."

"Yeah, it has. We doing. Heading on a mini vacation with my favorite person, Na'Siah." I raised my baby's hand that I was holding.

"Ditto. This is my lil' man, Navarro."

We headed through the machine and waited on them. Na'Siah whined for my phone to play games. He got his dislike from being awakened out of sleep honestly, but it was fifteen times worse. I prayed when we got on the gate he fell back to sleep. The kids came up from their respective devices, momentarily, to say hello.

After a few minutes at the gate, the boys began to hit it off. They chased each other around the row of chairs until the area became too crowded. I pulled out Na'Siah's fire truck that he insisted on bringing with him. Had it not been his favorite, I would have bashed it in. Most of the toys he had now was a constant reminder of Stone, since I held spring cleaning twice yearly. The kids crawled around the carpet while we went over the itinerary on my tablet.

"I thought I recognized you, Krissett." Deborah's lonely gold tooth ass smiled down on me. The huge roll of gut that was being pushed up by the low rise jeans, hung from underneath the shirt that was way too small. She had too much fucking money to be shopping in the kids section of the store. I pitied the man who wanted her funky ass. Every piece of her body had to be musty from the sweat the material caused rubbing against her skin.

"You should have kept walking then." I went back to checking my plans with Derrick.

"And so you could lie when I tell Stone I saw you here... Never." She had a stupid smirk on her face.

"I wouldn't give a fuck what you tell him, Deborah."

"I bet when he goes upside your head again you will." It wasn't surprising that she would gloat at another woman getting hit. Clearly someone needed to knock some sense into her old raggedy ass and it was about to be me.

Steady mouthing off, I was done talking to Deborah.

Derrick grabbed the tablet and threw it down, holding me back when Deborah screamed. She held her head back to stop the blood jetting from her nose.

"Let me go." I fought him off, the other airline customers were totally shocked. Good thing Na'Siah had been on the other side of the seats when it happened.

"Ma'am, I suggest you walk away." Derrick recommended. His ass was next, because his hold was hurting my stomach.

"*Help!*" She wailed like a wounded dog. "Where the hell is the police? Your ass is going to jail this time." Everyone stared at her like a damn maniac. The gate was peaceful until her messy ass came over. Her hand was doing nothing to stop the bleeding and it was beginning to stain her ratchet ass outfit. Without even trying, I had done her a favor by ruining it. Seeing that no one was paying her any mind, she stomped off in the direction of the bathroom.

Derrick got the kids together and moved us two gates down just in case Deborah came back. I highly doubted it, because with the warning the judge had issued, it wouldn't look good that she had approached me. In addition, she had minimal time to find an officer, explain and get back to the gate before we boarded the flight. Her fat ass would never make it. Derrick got the kids situated and carried on with our itinerary like nothing happened. The kids resumed playing and within fifteen minutes I stood at the boarding gate waiting to leave the drama and foolishness behind, even if it was for just four days.

He had definitely shown us a good time. The children went to the Zoo, Epcot Center, Magic Kingdom and the Disney parade. My poor baby almost passed out when he shook Mickey and Donald's hands.

"Na'Siah, no running in the house." I threw our packages onto the counter and started getting us together for tomorrow.

By the time we landed on Monday, the kids were inseparable. Na'Siah pleaded to for Navarro to spend the night and I obliged. He listened to me pretty well. Derrick had taken a ride to satisfy my craving for Olive Garden. He would probably stay over as well.

Quincy's cellmate called to inform me some dude had tried Quincy, leading to his first prison altercation and suspension of his phone privileges. I could have lit that bitch, Janasia, on fire without a match. My brother had lost his freedom, job and stood to lose much more because her trick ass couldn't get fucked on demand.

My mind ran rampant with ways to commit the next perfect murder. There was so much to be considered for this to be forensically untraceable. The time, place and funding were my first priorities. Already having tried injection, my interest peeked at inhalation or ingestion. I wondered what would happen to the human body when a mixture of bleach and ammonia was ingested. One thing was for certain, it had to be the most horrific way to perish under creation.

Chapter 44

I hastily walked into the office building on Tuesday. With no morning meetings, I returned home after dropping Na'Siah off to rest after clear case of jet lag. Searching the house for my laptop to log into the system, I realized I had left it at the office on last Wednesday. Halfway across the parking lot, the alarm on my car began going off. Hitting my panic button, it silenced for a brief moment before it began again.

"What the hell!" I screamed about facing to find out what was going on.

Approaching, there was a white sheet of paper on my car. I figured it to be one of many advertisements that I would find at the end of my day. My boss wanted to have a quick meeting about hiring more agents, due to the increased amount of calls that had been coming in. The switches on units were being turned from heat to air, causing a nice spike for those who set them at lower temperatures. Sharing my thoughts, I collected what I came for and headed back to the bed.

I grabbed the paper off my car, tossing it onto the seat. Giving it a second look, I realized that it was a folded sheet of copy paper. No one had better not have hit my damn car. Opening the note it was a typed message in bold: *Your day is coming bitch!*

Without a doubt the words were true, but fuck it. I would have those who had fucked over me to keep me company.

Meishelle and I had dinner where we selected the manager and employees to begin the business. The city had issued all the permits and the grand opening was scheduled for next month. In addition, we began our plans for the upcoming family reunion in August. It had been years since we had been able to come together and with Hattie Mae gone, the time was now.

The last issue on the agenda, I juggled with, but I couldn't think of anyone else. There was no one in the world I knew that hated Janasia enough and had more to lose if Quincy went to jail.

"Have you heard anything about Janasia? You know she's the one that turned Quincy in, huh?" I needed an inside scoop on her whereabouts.

"Yeah, I figured that's why the police hadn't knocked on my door for kicking her ass. The vindictive bitch found another way to punish me that would last longer. When I see her, though, I'm not finished." Meishelle vowed.

"I've been thinking about something a little more permanent than an old school ass whipping. It's time the bitch met a more everlasting fate."

Meishelle glared at me in silence for a moment before she replied.

"Are you out of your damn mind, Krissett?" Meishelle blared.

"Fuck no." My expression was harder than stone.

"You have to be. That shit is insane."

"What's inconceivable is a bitch who has fucked over me, you, and my brother, your husband, continues to live for the purpose of bringing misery to others. That, my dear, is fucking crazy."

"I can't believe you would even consider something like this. I want no part in it."

"No problem." I had killed a nigga once to silence my crime against a hoe, so for Quincy it was a no brainer. Rolling solo again might prove to be best. I wouldn't snitch on my damn self.

"Just remember karma is a two-way street, friend. The grave you dig for others might be your own." She warned.

"Yeah, I hear you."

***

Almost busting my ass on the mail, I cursed myself for not disposing of the junk when I walked through the door on Monday. Any important mail was sent to my post office box anyway. I gathered it off the floor, noticing a preapproved credit card advertisement for Stone. Was it a gift from above? I held the perfect way to order supplies for Janasia without it being traced to me.

I broke open the envelope which contained a code and telephone number to call. With the credit card in his name ordering supplies used in her murder would be hard to overcome. I could argue I dismissed the stolen mail, knowing that nothing for me was sent to my home address. Police looked for patterns when investigating crimes, so I wouldn't give them anything to connect.

244

Driving through Pontchartrain Oaks on my way home, three houses off the corner, I had already located the perfect house without an energy meter. The owners had blinds in the window, probably to make it not easily discernable to be abandoned by vagrants. I memorized the large print address before pulling off back to the house.

Quincy had a trial date and I couldn't allow that bitch to make it. I had settled on ammonia, bleach, ropes and a place where I could order rats from. Finding everything I needed, I shut my laptop down for the night and prepared to get Na'Siah from my momma. Today was her day to pick him up, since I normally stayed late.

"Hey, I'm on my way to pick him up." I went to the living room to get my keys.

"Krissett, I don't have him. The lady at school said you picked him up." I got immediately agitated. She must have been mistaken.

"Momma, tonight is my late night. I didn't pick him up. She has to be mistaken with Mrs. Williams or Meishelle. Let me call them."

"Ok. Call me back."

I called Meishelle, Quameer, Hollow and Stone none of who had my baby. I frantically called my momma back.

"Momma, my baby…" was the only words I could muster up before my phone fell to the floor with me crashing on to knees.

To Be Continued…
Don't Fu#k With My Heart 3
Coming Soon

Coming Soon From Lock Down Publications

GANGSTA CITY

By **Teddy Duke**

A DANGEROUS LOVE **VII**

By **J Peach**

LOVE KNOWS NO BOUNDARIES **III**

By **Coffee**

BURY ME A G **III**

By **Tranay Adams**

BLOOD OF A BOSS **III**

By **Askari**

DON'T FU#K WITH MY HEART **III**

By **Linnea**

THE KING CARTEL **II**

By **Frank Gresham**

SILVER PLATTER HOE **II**

By **Reds Johnson**

A HUSTLA'Z AMBITION **III**

By **Damion King**

THESE NIGGAS AIN'T LOYAL **II**

By **Nikki Tee**

DIRTY LICKS

By **Peter Mack**

BROOKLYN ON LOCK

By **Sonovia Alexander**

THESE STREETS BLEED MURDER

By **Jerry Jackson**

CONFESSIONS OF A DOPEMAN'S DAUGHTER

By **Rasstrina**

THE ULTIMATE BETRAYAL

By **Phoenix**

Available Now

LOVE KNOWS NO BOUNDARIES **I & II**

By **Coffee**

SLEEPING IN HEAVEN, WAKING IN HELL **I, II & III**

By **Forever Redd**

THE DEVIL WEARS TIMBS **I, II & III**

By **Tranay Adams**

DON'T FU#K WITH MY HEART

By **Linnea**

BOSS'N UP **I & II**

By **Royal Nicole**

A DANGEROUS LOVE **I, II, III, IV, V, VI**

By **J Peach**

CUM FOR ME

An **LDP Erotica Collaboration**

THE KING CARTEL

By **Frank Gresham**

BLOOD OF A BOSS **I & II**

By **Askari**

STREET JUSTICE

By **Chance**

BURY ME A G **I & II**

By **Tranay Adams**

BONDS OF DECEPTION

By **Lady Stiletto**

LOYALTY IS BLIND

By **Kenneth Chisholm**

A HUSTLA'Z AMBITION

By **Damion King**

THESE NIGGAS AIN'T LOYAL

By **Nikki Tee**

BOOKS BY LDP'S CEO, CA$H

TRUST NO MAN

TRUST NO MAN 2

TRUST NO MAN 3

BONDED BY BLOOD

SHORTY GOT A THUG

A DIRTY SOUTH LOVE

THUGS CRY

THUGS CRY 2

TRUST NO BITCH

TRUST NO BITCH 2

TRUST NO BITCH 3

TIL MY CASKET DROPS

Coming Soon

TRUST NO BITCH (EYEZ' STORY)

THUGS CRY 3

BONDED BY BLOOD 2